RISING FROM THE CURSE

THE CURSE OF SOTKARI TA: BOOK THREE

MARIA A. PEREZ

This is a work of fiction. Names, characters, places, and incidents either are the product of the author's imagination or are used fictitiously. Any resemblance to actual persons, living or dead, events, or locales is entirely coincidental.

Copyright © 2023 by Maria A. Perez

All rights reserved. No portion of this book may be reproduced in any form or used in any manner without written permission from the author, except for the use of brief quotations in a book review, and as permitted by U.S. copyright law.

Published by: Maria A. Perez

Editor: Stephanie Hoogstad

Cover Design: Christian Bentulan

ISBN: 978-1-7351133-7-1

Ebook ISBN: 978-1-7351133-6-4

Disclosure: Consensual Sexual Content, Violence

DEDICATION

The father figures in The Curse of Sotkari Ta series give it all for their families. Likewise, the fathers in my family are brave, dedicated, hard-working, and loving. I dedicate Book Three to Segundo, my father; Porfirio, my uncle; Gabriel, my brother; Oscar, my brother-in-law; and Carlos, my husband.

BOOKS BY THIS AUTHOR

The Curse of Sotkari Ta: Book One

Broken Bonds, The Curse of Sotkari Ta: Book Two

Rising From The Curse, The Curse of Sotkari Ta: Book Three

Song of the Caged Warrior, The Curse of Sotkari Ta: Prequel

Montor's Secret Stash of Poems (A companion book to The Curse of Sotkari Ta series)

HIDDEN

We don't remember
A time of peace...
We are hidden now

Our home was stolen
A floorboard ripped up
Leaving us falling and fallen

Our blood was not our blood
It burned us from within
Extinguished only by tears

We faced our fathers
We faced our mothers
Then turned away, in agony

Our future was forged in flight
We left it all, not in fear
But with courage of survival

We hid ourselves away
Beyond the revered past
In the wild jungle of dreams

This was our blacksmith shop
A place to forge our future
Molded from history, memory

But in that misty netherworld
A curse descended upon us
An energy dark of power

A fleeting touch, innocent
Set our minds ablaze
Aroused us in passion

Our plight crystalized
We were weaponized
Our very bodies violated

Life in swampy backwaters
On the galaxy's very edge
Could not save us

Shooting stars lit the sky
A virus of violence descended
This land withered to dust

So we returned, defiant
To our ancestors' sacred land
Not lost, not found, not Lostai

We are the Jomoloxti
Undaunted by this barren land
Unbending in the grey snow

Our life is below ground
We are part of the dirt
A beating heart in a dying beast

Tunnels reaching like veins
Giving life to the lifeless
Offering hope to the hopeless

A sandstorm rages above
Lava gathers molten heat below
We travel the corridors in between

Our world is one of quietude
Wrapping us like a tight glove
Our fingerprints concealed

For us, there is no past
Just promises of a future
Beyond our ready graves

We don't remember
A time of peace...
We are hidden now

1

___

Nothing could have prepared me for the call we received that morning. Montor and I had returned home the night before from a wonderful vacation. Commander Portars's call interrupted our breakfast. Thankfully, I hadn't started because it wouldn't have stayed down the minute Portars conveyed his message.

"There is an Earthian male among the people we rescued from the Lostai Coroxt prison camp who claims to be Mina's husband. Perhaps he is having trouble with the Lostai language, since we all know Mina is widowed from her previous Earthian spouse."

Montor's fists tightened ever so slightly, but he remained stone-faced. Portars's next words tore my heart in half.

"What most concerns me is that he says Zorla has Mina's Earthian daughter. I believe her name is pronounced *Aembuh*."

Zorla, an evil Lostai commander, had been my nemesis since the moment he orchestrated my abduction from Earth and held me hostage in a Lostai science station. I was forced through a grueling boot camp. Being utterly unprepared for that type of activity, I suffered many injuries while in captivity.

The scars on my back and wrist bore testimony to Zorla's cruel punishments. Had I not escaped, he intended to force me to do unspeakable things. In the years that followed, my marriage to Montor and the birth of our son, Josher, had brought me solace, but I knew Zorla would never abandon his obsession with capturing us. Now that he might have Amber, I could barely breathe imagining what she might be going through.

I let out a primal wail and buried my face in trembling hands.

Suddenly, a shot of adrenaline brought me to my feet.

"I demand to know exactly where is this Earthian male you rescued."

Montor turned to me and spoke gravely.

"Mina, sit."

Per Arandan culture, as a female, I was way out of line in addressing a military commander that way, but Montor knew I rarely conformed to his people's ideas of proper female behavior. Still, this situation could put Montor's honor in contention. We had lied about my previous marriage because, according to Arandan custom, it was deemed dishonorable to pursue a relationship with a married female without a duel between the two males involved. My first husband was galaxies away when I met Montor.

I summoned as much self-control as possible and, biting my lip, sat back down.

"We have taken the people we rescued, including this Earthian male, to Dit Lar to await transportation to their home worlds," said Portars to Montor.

"Fine, we have a charged *hanstoric,* so we will transport there this afternoon to have a talk with this Earthian."

"I will let Commander Larmont know to expect you."

Portars turned to me and softened his expression.

"Mina, the Arandan people and the United Rebel Front are

grateful for your help in getting many of our captured children reunited with their families. I hope your daughter is safe."

I nodded and whispered, "Thank you."

The transmission ended, and the shock of what we had just heard left me numb.

"It cannot be possible," I said, almost to myself. Then louder, "Oh, I forgot to ask Portars the name of the Earthian they rescued."

Montor rolled his eyes and stood abruptly.

"It obviously must be your previous husband."

"But how? If my daughter is the one with the Sotkari Ta genes, why was Joshua taken too?"

Montor walked away.

"You did not finish your meal," I called after him.

"I have lost my appetite. We will need to coordinate with Foxor and Lasarta to take care of Josher while we are away."

"Yes."

He continued towards the bedroom. Like an automaton, I cleared the table. Montor turned around again, a menacing look on his face.

My stomach flipped as he said, "I find I am looking forward to this meeting."

When we arrived at Dit Lar later that afternoon, Commander Larmont was waiting for us.

"I have the Earthian Portars spoke to you about waiting in the conference room down the hall, the final door on the left. There were several Earthians in this particular labor camp. It is unfortunate we did not find your daughter there."

My heartbeat accelerated the second Montor grabbed my hand and rushed me to the room. On our way there, we passed by the dining area. I saw several humans sitting at tables, hunched over their plates, focused on their food. One person vomited, apparently having scarfed down his food too fast. I overheard someone say in English, "Pace yourself or you'll feel even worse." It reminded me of the harsh conditions at the Lostai labor camps.

What horrors have Josh and Amber suffered through?

We arrived at the conference room. The door opened, and Josh stood.

"Mina! My God, it really is you," he said, his voice boisterous at first and then lower as he took in the image of Montor's arm tight around my waist, stroking and squeezing.

I prayed Montor would stop, but he continued, purposely displaying he had a right to touch me that way. My heart exploded in my chest. I couldn't meet Josh's eyes, and much less did I dare look up at Montor. When Josh took a few quick steps towards us, Montor placed his hands on my shoulders and moved me behind him.

I finally raised my eyes to see Josh had folded his arms across his chest and cocked his head as he asked in broken Lostai, "She prisoner?"

"No, she is my wife. It seems you intend to get too close."

"Wife? Mina, have they forced you—" Josh started to ask me in English, but Montor interrupted in a threatening tone.

"Do not speak to my wife in a language that I cannot understand."

"My wife," shouted Josh, clearly frustrated by his difficulty with the Lostai language. He gritted his teeth, pointed at Montor, and then jerked his arm toward the door, gesturing for Montor to leave. I couldn't help but empathize with Josh. Montor could be an ass sometimes.

Unimpressed, Montor looked down at Josh with a smirk.

"I think you and I should step outside so we can clear up your confusion."

I had heard enough.

"Stop it!" I shouted in Lostai, looking up at Montor. He raised his eyebrows as he usually did when I displayed the defiance that an Arandan female never would.

"*Joshwar*, it seems my wife and I need to speak in private."

Josh scowled. "I not from here move."

Montor side-glanced at Josh and spoke in a condescending tone.

"My wife and I can connect without speaking out loud. We do not need you to leave for us to communicate in private."

I looked up to meet Montor's eyes and said telepathically, "I want you to stop this behavior right now. Think how you would feel if you were in Joshua's place—your child kidnapped and the wife you assumed dead, with another male. He has no fault in this situation. I need time alone with him so he can tell me in our language what happened with our daughter, and I can explain to him about our relationship."

"Mina, there is absolutely no chance at all that I will allow you to be alone with him. All of Larmont's squadron must be already commenting behind my back about this male who claims to be your husband. Do you want to cause me further dishonor?"

I silently cursed the collective Arandan male psyche.

"OK, stay, but let me talk to him in our Earthian language. Montor, I will be equally stubborn as you on this point."

Montor sighed deeply, shaking his head. He took a minute before replying.

"Sometimes, I cannot believe the things I have put up with out of my love for you. Fine, talk to him."

"Thank you, Montor. Thank you so much," I said, ending our telepathic conversation, and then out loud in Lostai, "Let us sit and talk calmly, Josh. Montor has agreed that we can speak in our language."

Tension hung in the air for a few minutes as Montor and Josh glared at each other. Once I sat, they also took their seats.

As soon as I started speaking to Josh in English, Montor grasped my left hand in both of his. Josh took notice, and his tone became aggressive.

"Mina, are you really married to this creature?"

I finally had a chance to take a closer look at Josh. My breath caught in my throat. He seemed to have aged ten years in the four since I was kidnapped. Strands of gray streaked his dark, straight hair. Even after leaving the military, Josh had always kept up a fitness routine and muscular physique. Now, his gaunt frame was thinner than I had ever seen, and new wrinkles branched from the edges of his eyes. I took a moment to steady myself and try to mask my sadness at seeing him so deteriorated.

"Yes, I am. It's been two years now."

"But how? Why?"

"When the Lostai kidnapped me and forced me to train as one of their soldiers, I befriended the person who was helping me unleash some special abilities I have."

"Those bald-headed guys explained something to me about this," he said with a befuddled expression.

"The Lostai had a mission planned for me that I refused to accept. I begged my trainer to help me escape. She introduced me to Montor, who had also been kidnapped as a child and brought up to become a soldier in the Lostai army. He helped me to leave that place and go somewhere I could hide from the Lostai."

"And he forced you to be his wife in exchange?"

I kept trying to swallow the lump in my throat.

"No...no...I wasn't forced. I...I fell in love with him."

Josh's gray eyes turned angry, his lips pursed.

"Let me get this straight. While we were back home suffering your loss, you were having this celestial love story."

After seconds of awkward silence, I said, "What do you care? You have a new girlfriend. I guess you like blonds now."

He was incredulous.

"What? How would you know?"

I told him how I had traveled to Earth using the transportal on Dit Lar to return a little girl to her family. When I stopped by our house late that evening and peeked in, hoping to catch at least a glimpse of my children, I found him alone with a woman. By their gestures, it was clear the relationship was a romantic one.

"Wait. You mean to tell me you came home and then returned here? Didn't you think of our children? What's wrong with you?"

His eyes were cold slate.

"Be careful how you speak to her. I do not know what you said, but I dislike the tone you are using," said Montor, but I shot him a look that said, "Stay out of this."

"Josh, when I met Montor, it seemed very unlikely I would ever see Earth again. It was much later when we discovered the transportal here on Dit Lar. Montor and I were already married, and we had a son. My son, his name is Josher, looks just like his father. Even if I hadn't married Montor, I wouldn't have been able to bring my son to Earth."

Josh wiped his hand across his face.

"I guess it was easy for you to just forget all about us."

I could no longer control my emotions and started to cry. Montor stood, slamming his fists on the table.

"I will not allow you to upset her! She has been through enough heartache already."

Things could have escalated into physical violence if I hadn't pulled myself together.

"I am fine," I said in Lostai, brushing the tears away.

Montor paced around like a lion in a cage. I remembered Josh had sideswiped my question regarding his relationship with the woman I saw him with.

"Who is she...that woman? And why were the kids not at home?"

It was Josh's turn to feel the need to avert his eyes.

"She's a friend from my...Marine days. Your sister took the kids because I was a mess, drinking a lot and staying out late every night. I couldn't stand to sleep in our bed. I almost lost my job. Laura, umm, that's her name, started coming by to help me with dinner and cleaning up. After a year, the police still had no leads on your disappearance. I faced the fact that I'd never see you again."

"Josh, I understand. I reached the same conclusion," I answered, but his story reopened an old wound.

It reminded me how, when we were first married, he left our newborn son and me without warning to enlist in the Marines. We barely saw each other for the next six years, and I was basically a single mom during that time. After he returned, we never quite regained the intimacy and joy of our early relationship, although we did our best to maintain a happy family for our three children. I always suspected he had not been faithful during those six years, but now recalling his many subsequent business trips, I wondered since when he had become reacquainted with this "friend."

"So, have the kids been with my sister all this time?"

"Yes, well, except for Chris, who is in college now. I was unstable for a long time. Bobby and Amber got used to living with her family. I help your sister and her husband financially to cover their expenses. Plus, they don't agree with my relationship with Laura. They see it as some sort of betrayal."

What will they think when they find out I have remarried and have another child?

"Mina, I haven't always been the perfect husband, but believe me, I never stopped loving you."

The battle to hold back my tears became more difficult by the second.

"I never stopped loving you either, but it's a different love now. It's like the memory of someone who has passed."

"But we aren't dead, Mina. We are right here. I can touch you."

Josh reached across the table. I pulled my hands back, conscious that Montor could explode at any moment.

"Tell me what happened with Amber. How did you both come to be here?"

Josh slouched back in his chair and cracked his knuckles. I couldn't help but recognize that Montor did the exact same thing when he was distressed.

"It was spring break, and I told your sister I wanted to spend at least the holiday with the kids. I had seen them only a few times since they moved in with her. Laura went to visit her family in Connecticut to avoid any tension. The kids really wanted to please me and made a point to help me with little chores. One evening, Amber took out the garbage later than usual. At first, I thought nothing of it, but suddenly I had a memory of you so intense, I ran outside to check on her. She was slumped against a figure who was holding her up with one hand and a laptop-looking device in the other. I ran to grab her and whatever force transported them took me, too."

Tears flowed freely down my cheeks again, but I gestured to Montor to stay calm.

"Where...where did they take you?"

"We spent some time on a spaceship. Oh God, I still can't believe what I'm saying. They explained to me about your special...what is it called...Sot-Ka-Ri-Ta abilities. The guy in charge, Zorla, seemed very pissed at you. He said that Amber didn't have a complete set of those alien genes like you do, but they still could use her."

My chest tightened.

"When did you see Amber last?"

"We arrived at a planet where the Lostai only control a

certain area. They said that is where Amber would be trained. They took her off the spaceship, and I continued to the labor camp where I've been for, I think, six months."

I stood, doing my best to maintain control, while I explained to Montor what Josh had told me.

"Where do you think they might have her?"

"Well, in this sector, the Lostai still control Renna One and most of Tormix, parts of the Namson planet, and a continent on Sotkar. It could be any of those locations."

I looked up at Montor, my whole body shaking.

"Montor, I need to find her."

Forgetting about Josh or what he might be feeling, I rested my head against Montor's chest and wept. He held me close, stroking my hair and rubbing my back, trying to console me. In between sobs, I looked up at Montor again.

"Are you willing to help me?"

His voice took on a gentle tone he only used with those he cherished.

"Of course, sweetness. Your pain is my pain. We will search for her as if she were our own child."

We remained in that embrace for some time until Josh cleared his throat to remind us of his presence. I stepped away from Montor and turned to Josh.

"Montor is willing to help us find Amber," I said in Lostai.

Josh didn't reply. With anger, pain, and frustration plastered on his face, he looked away, running his hands through his hair. Montor sighed, almost as if he were questioning himself.

"*Joshwar*, we do not need to be friends to work together to rescue your daughter. You and I have unfinished business that we will find the right moment to resolve. In the meantime, out of love for my wife, and because I know what it feels like to lose a loved one, I will do everything in my power to find your daughter. Based on your description, a few places come to mind where she might be. Do you remember any other details?"

I wasn't sure if Josh understood everything Montor said. He paused before accepting the olive branch, then turned around to speak to me in English.

"They allowed me to say goodbye before they took her off the spaceship. Two males of another race accompanied her. They were much taller than the Lostai and gray-skinned, with blue eyes and hair."

I translated the information to Montor.

"Sotkari traitors," he said thoughtfully. "Then there is a good chance they took her to Sotkar. We need to gather intelligence related to the area of that planet that is still under Lostai control."

A glimmer of hope strengthened me.

"Montor, who are you thinking should join us?"

"The *Barinta* is stationed here on Dit Lar. I will ask Commander Larmont to lend us a few of his soldiers for this mission. We will head out to Sotkar immediately and talk to Kaonto to see what he advises. I will also ask Commander Portars to assign a security detail to Josher, Foxor and Lasarta on Fronidia while we are away."

My mind raced with thoughts of who else could help us.

"Should we reach out to Kindor, too?" I blurted out.

Montor made a deep guttural sound, an Arandan expression of disgust. Josh noted his reaction to Kindor's name.

"Who Kindor?" Josh asked.

Montor answered through gritted teeth, "Another rival who once tried to steal my wife from me."

Josh cocked an eyebrow and said to me in English, "Wow, Mina. I guess you've been busy these past few years."

Josh's sarcasm irked me and caused a lapse in judgment.

"Kindor was a loyal friend who saved my life more than once. Things just got complicated," I snapped in Lostai.

I should have kept that thought to myself. Kindor was a delicate topic between Montor and me. Montor's eyes narrowed, and his voice became a growl.

"Mina, you should know better than to make excuses for Kindor's behavior. My patience has been tested enough for one day." He bent over to get to my eye level and emphasized each syllable. "Let. Me. Be. Clear. We do not need Kindor's help."

Tension filled the room again. I could tell from the corner of my eye that Josh was trying to decide if he should somehow intervene.

Before things got hairy again, I waved my hand and said, "Fine."

2

———

Larmont had quarters set up for Montor and me. We would stay overnight on Dit Lar and head out to Sotkar early the next day. To appease any outstanding curiosity regarding Josh's relationship to me, I suggested we make up a story that Josh was a neighbor who happened to be outside when Amber was taken. We would say he was mistakenly using the Lostai word for husband when he spoke of me. Montor grumbled in agreement, and I made Josh swear he would go along with it.

As we lay in bed that night, Montor rested his head in his hand and stared at the ceiling like I wasn't even there, something he rarely did. Usually, there was cuddling and touching before falling asleep. I also was restless. Something he had mentioned when talking to Josh came back to me.

"Montor, I did not like what you said to Joshua about resolving unfinished business."

He turned to face me.

"The chance to erase my dishonor has finally come. Once we have rescued your daughter, I will challenge him to a duel and win you over in the proper manner."

"That is not happening! Everyone now believes he is just a neighbor. There is no need for violence."

He rolled on top of me, propping himself on his arms. His eyes flashed with fury.

"It is not only about what everyone else thinks. This shame burns in my chest. You denied me the right to defend my honor with Kindor. It will not happen again. I saw it in his eyes, Mina. *Joshwar* feels like he still has rights to you."

"Montor, I am not property to be haggled over."

Without warning, he kissed me hard, biting my lower lip and groping me in a rough way. I didn't like the aggressiveness, especially since this was so unlike Montor's normal behavior in bed. For all his swagger and arrogance, he usually asked me for formal permission before getting intimate. At the beginning of our relationship, I found this to be both a little odd and endearing.

"Stop it. You are hurting me, and I do not like it," I said while trying to push him off.

"You are MY wife. No one else's. Only I can touch you this way," he shouted, pinning me down with his body. He brought one hand to my neck. He could have choked me easily with only one of his large hands if he had wanted to. I couldn't help but recall the violence in my past and was overwhelmed with dread.

Is he going to force himself on me?

The idea of someone I loved taking me to that ugly place was too much for me to bear. I felt the color drain from my face. Tears rolled down my cheeks. It only took seconds for him to snap out of his rage. He wrapped his fingers gently now around my neck, his thumb pressing down on my bottom lip before wiping the tears away. Pain burned in his eyes, and then his mouth took over, this time with a tender kiss.

"Mina, I am so..." His voice cracked. "I am so sorry. I did not mean to scare you."

"You, of all people, know how that must have made me feel."

He rolled off me and onto his back again.

"Yes, I am an idiot." He clenched his fist and pressed it against his forehead. "It is just...this whole situation is making me crazy."

He looked childlike, dejected, and repentant. As usual, I was quick to forgive his bad behavior.

I turned over to bury my face against his chest.

"Montor, I am sorry too. I understand this must feel unbearable for you, but think about how I feel. My daughter—" The moment I said that word, the reality of everything sunk in.

Zorla. Has. My. Daughter.

"Montor, he has her. Do you understand what that means? Who knows what they have done to her?" I bawled like a baby. "I hate him. I hate him. Since the Lostai took me, I have been through so much. But this, this I am not sure I can handle. If something bad has happened to her..."

Unable to talk any more, my body shuddered with every breath. He wrapped his arms around me, rubbed my back, and ran one hand up my neck and into my hair. I ran my fingers across his chest and shoulder muscles. Our sexual connection was a powerful part of our bond. Raw emotion turned into full-on arousal.

He rolled on top of me again. His kisses were gentle this time. My body released its tension, and when his lips parted, so did mine. I accepted his tongue and knew soon I'd be accepting much more than that. One hand remained caressing my neck while the other traveled under my nightshirt until it reached my butt. He gave it a good squeeze before separating my legs with his thighs and touching me there. I pulled down his shorts.

Yeah, I'm ready.

His eyes met mine, asking for permission, as was his habit. I nodded ever so slightly, and with a groan, he pushed into me. Gasping with pleasure, it didn't take long for my hips to become impatient, thrusting my body up towards him in lusty gyrations until he moved so fast and vigorously that I came almost immediately. Our climax literally took my breath away. So much so, I felt I lacked oxygen. Seconds later, still over me, now flaccid and vulnerable, his lips brushed my ear.

"OK, sweetness, do not worry. I can carry any burden for you."

Early the next morning, Montor and I finalized the last details with Commander Larmont. He assigned five soldiers to come with us. Not much, but I couldn't expect an entire squadron to be assigned to rescue one person. While we waited by the cave entrance for the soldiers to arrive, Josh walked over, escorted by one of Larmont's lieutenants, who, after saluting Montor, went on about his business.

"Hello," Josh said in heavily accented Lostai, his eyes avoiding ours.

Montor, on the other hand, purposely made eye contact and failed at keeping his voice neutral.

"Good morning, *Joshwar*. Eager to start our trip, I presume?"

I heard the condescending tone. I'm sure Josh did as well.

Awkward silence followed.

The arrival of the soldiers we were waiting on provided a welcome distraction. After some cordial salutations, they led us to the transport pod that would take us to where the *Barinta* was docked. In the past year, the United Rebel Front had fortified their shields and increased the number of security ships orbiting Dit Lar. A space station had been constructed just outside the atmosphere.

Even though the pod was equipped with the environmental

settings to help with the gravitational change, Josh gritted his teeth as his skin took on a yellowish pale tinge. Montor chuckled under his breath until I elbowed him.

Boarding the *Barinta* was a surreal experience for me. It had been two years since I last walked off the ship. I remembered my first trip on the *Barinta* when we fled Fronidia with the Lostai hot on our trail. There had been both good and unpleasant times on the *Barinta*. In the end, I left in a bad way, written up for insubordination by the captain at the time, and ordered to remain on Dit Lar.

Montor must have noticed the memories were flooding my brain.

"It has been a while, sweetness, has it not?"

"Yes."

"Mina, is there a restroom around here?" Josh shouted out. Montor and I both turned at the same time to see Josh covering his mouth and still looking very sick.

I heard Montor's voice in my mind.

"I will be honest with you, Mina. Every time I hear him say your name, I feel like beating the crap out of him."

I pulled a face before pointing Josh in the right direction.

When Josh returned, Montor took us on a tour of all the important ship stations and quarters. After showing us around, he dismissed everyone, speaking first in Arandan, then in Lostai for Josh's benefit.

"Everyone, settle in, and we will have our first staff meeting in three hours."

Montor started the meeting by addressing the soldiers.

"My wife and I appreciate your help on what really is a personal matter."

The highest ranked soldier, named Noomar, replied, "I

know I speak for all of us when I say that we are honored to serve on this mission. The Chaperone returned many of our rescued Arandan children to their homes. It is only fitting that we help her rescue her daughter."

Many soldiers still called me The Chaperone, referring to my role in conducting the first transportal trips to return rescued children to their planets.

"Thank you," I said, touched by his solidarity.

"We believe they may have Mina's daughter on the Lostai-controlled southwestern continent of Sotkar. Kaonto is expecting us and is ready with the latest intelligence on that area," continued Montor. "The trip to Sotkar takes ten days, and although we have chased out most of the Lostai patrol ships in the area, it is not without challenges. We will assign a rotation of watches for everyone except the Earthian male, named *Joshwar*."

Josh, whose ears apparently were already fine-tuned to Montor's very particular way of pronouncing his name, turned to me and said in English, "He mentioned my name. What did he say? I barely can understand Lostai, and now he is speaking in another language."

I started to answer, but Montor waved me off as he looked down at Josh and said in Lostai, "Address. Questions. To. Me."

The marked rise and fall of Josh's chest made plain his frustration. He had learned some basic Lostai, but having just recently been rescued by the Arandans, had barely any knowledge of their language. Even I had trouble with the Arandan language sometimes. Lostai was the only alien language I was fluent in. My captors forced that upon me. Now I usually spoke in Arandan but was still in learning mode. I intervened, communicating to Montor telepathically.

"Montor, he does not understand Arandan. The practical thing is for me to translate. By the way, you should change your attitude. The soldiers will wonder why you are exhibiting this hostility towards Joshua."

It was Montor's turn to take deep breaths.

"Fine. Go ahead," he replied, his voice a grumble in my mind.

I turned my attention to Josh.

"Sorry, Josh. Montor can be a little difficult sometimes."

"He's an asshole. So now you are like what...rescuing me from him?"

"Don't make this situation even harder. Basically, what Montor said is he will establish a watch rotation with everyone except you."

"Tell him that in the time it takes to arrive at where we're going, I'd like to be trained to become an integral part of this crew and included in these rotations. Let him know I was a soldier once, too."

Montor's impatient voice entered my mind telepathically, interrupting my conversation with Josh.

"Mina, how long does it take to translate my simple introduction?"

I counted to ten in my mind and glared at Montor. He rolled his eyes but didn't say anything else.

I turned back to Josh and said, "Obviously, the language barrier will make training difficult unless I do it. I know his first reaction will be against us spending too much one-on-one time together. I'll speak to him about it later."

"Sounds like he's very controlling. I'm surprised you put up with that."

"Don't worry about me. Montor and I get along just fine."

That evening, back in our quarters as I was getting ready for bed, Montor walked up to me from behind and wrapped his arms around me, kissing the back of my neck.

"Sweetness, remember we spent the first nights of our marriage in this room."

My first instinct was to lean into him, my mind already recalling the sensual nights we had spent in that room. I forced myself to ignore the tingle between my legs and turned around.

"Montor, there is something important I would like to discuss with you."

He crossed his arms.

"I guess you are not in a reminiscing mood."

I sat on the bed and motioned for him to sit next to me.

"Joshua wants to be assigned responsibilities and integrated as a part of this crew."

Montor snickered.

"Perfect. I will train him. We will start with sparring."

"Not that kind of training. He knows self-defense already. I mean regarding the stations of the ship and our technology."

"I can train him on that, too."

"No. First of all, I know you would not have the best intentions."

"You offend me," he said in a mock-dramatic voice.

"Second, he barely understands you. My suggestion is that I train him."

"Oh, really?" His voice dripped with sarcasm. "Maybe I should let you spend time with him in his room, too."

"Montor, I am serious. I can take advantage of that time with him to find out about my children, my family, and my friends. There is so much I would like to ask him."

Montor stood from the bed, cracking his knuckles.

"Mina, I can barely stand when he says your name. Now you ask that I tolerate you spending long hours with him."

"What are you afraid of?"

His eyes narrowed.

"I am afraid of nothing. It is inappropriate," he barked.

"Why?" I stood, arms akimbo. "I will only be talking to him."

"Yes, but he will use that time to court you—" He punched into his open palm, by now extremely agitated. "To...to convince you to return to him."

Turmoil burned in his eyes.

"And you think I would just leave you?" I grabbed his hand. "After all we've been through. You're my husband."

He yanked his hand out of mine.

"And so is he!"

"He has a new partner back on Earth. They have been together now about the same amount of time that we have been married." I stared at my feet. "Actually, I suspect he may have had a relationship with her throughout our marriage."

"What an idiot," Montor muttered.

I embraced him, my face pressed against his chest.

"Montor, right or wrong, you are the one I love. You have nothing to worry about. Please let me talk with him about my children, my sisters, my father. I may never have this opportunity again."

I looked up, and our eyes met. His silence signaled he was mulling over what to say next, like rolling a new food in his mouth.

"Go ahead and train him. Spend the time you need talking with him to get updated on your family on Earth. Keep it out in the open, though. No quiet chats in a corner of the lounge late at night or that sort of thing. I will try my best to be patient, but Mina, warn him to keep his distance when he is with you. No touching or those Earthian embraces you use with your friends. I will not tolerate it."

I reached up to coax him to bend down so I could kiss his cheek.

"Thank you, Montor. Thank you so much."

He led me to bed, and in minutes we were both naked, our bodies pressed together, my legs wrapped around his hips. He cupped my chin, holding my face still, as if trying to find new ways to kiss me, tasting my lips from different angles. In an instant, we created fire.

When his mouth released mine to continue kissing my neck and breasts, I gasped, "Oh Montor, you have nothing to worry about."

3

During the next day's staff meeting, Montor announced Josh was an official member of the crew. As such, I'd be training him on our procedures and protocols during our trip to Sotkar. Promptly after the meeting was over, I had Josh convene with me in the dining area.

"Here," I said, handing him a tablet. "You get one of these."

I showed him how to activate the device and the basic communication and query functions. Instead of being pleased that his request had been granted, Josh's face scrunched up in a scowl, his voice laced with annoyance.

"So, I guess you convinced your alien squeeze to let you talk to me. I don't want to think about what you had to do for him to agree to that."

I controlled the urge to hurl my hot tea in his face. Instead, I stood.

"Josh, if you prefer, I can tell Montor you changed your mind. This is a tough situation for all of us. It's not my fault or Montor's. It's not your fault either, but I have no need to deal with your bad attitude."

He raised his arms in surrender.

"No, no. Please sit. Sorry. I'll behave."

After a deep breath, I sat again and took him through my proposed training schedule. Being in an unfamiliar environment, he had little to contribute, simply nodding and agreeing with everything I said.

"OK, do we start today?"

"Yes, of course. One more thing. Please avoid touching me in any way. It is considered very disrespectful in Arandan culture for a male to touch a married female."

"Really?" The acerbic tone was back. "Even if he's HER husband?"

"Whether or not you want to recognize it, Montor is my husband. And guess what? In one more year, I'll be considered legally dead in Florida. Then you'll be free to marry...ugh... what's her name? Oh yeah, Laura."

He lowered his eyes, and I continued.

"Our first stop is the environmental control station. Do you want tea or something before we begin?"

"Umm, is that what you're having? They gave me some bitter liquid once that made me gag."

"That's *yomoso*. It's kind of an Arandan coffee. I can't stomach it either. No, this is an herbal tea. It's pretty good."

I poured him a cup and took the chance to ask the questions that haunted me.

"Josh, talk to me about Bobby and Chris. How are they doing?"

His expression turned stone cold.

Will he be cruel with me about this?

He took a few sips of the tea before replying.

"Mina, I won't sugarcoat anything to make you feel better."

The tea felt like acid in my throat.

"Your disappearance was tough on all the kids. I'll admit, my behavior didn't help things any. Chris, being the oldest, I think fared the best. He threw himself into his studies, was accepted at Georgia Tech, and is in his junior year now. He's been dating a girl for the past year and barely comes home. It's like he doesn't want to be reminded of what happened."

He paused as I wept, my body shaking.

I somehow managed to ask, "What about Bobby?"

His lips became a fine line.

"Bobby was affected the most. He had some sort of psycho-somatic reaction that left him mute for a year. He lost that year in school. Your sister has done a good job with him, though. He's been in therapy and is doing better but has never regained his happy-go-lucky personality. Now he's starting his teen years, so we'll see what that brings."

I used a napkin to wipe my tears and blow my nose. There would be a million details I would ask for later, but now I could only handle a bit at a time.

"OK, let's get going."

As we walked, I asked him about Amber.

"You know how close you and Amber were. This hit her very hard, too. She tried to be a mother figure for Bobby and take care of the house while I was falling apart. It was too much on her shoulders. Her grades suffered, but she bounced back the last two years. UF accepted her in their astrophysics program. I was so proud of her. You know how you and her always went on and on about space travel and life outside our solar system..." His voice trailed off before it returned as a whisper. "I remember how much I made fun of you both."

I almost wanted to at least place my hand on his shoulder, but I remembered my promise to Montor. A somber shadow followed us as we walked through the ship's corridors.

"No one could ever have known what was in store for us," I replied.

I had never felt so inconsolable in my whole life, barely choking out my next words. "Josh, did you get to see her much while on the spaceship? How was she when you last saw her?"

He gulped and covered his mouth, taking a moment to compose himself. I avoided looking at him. We were both about to lose it.

"Umm, I don't remember much of the trip, but I was physically all right."

"Yes, it was the same for me."

"OK, so I assume Amber didn't recall much either. Once I woke up, we had already arrived to where they were taking her."

He covered his mouth again. A quick glance and I saw his eyes tear up. Several minutes went by before he went on to say, "Lostai soldiers brought Amber to my room. I was in restraints. At least she looked physically fine. The female Lostai who spoke English said Amber was being dropped off at a military station for training and I'd be taken to a labor camp on another planet. Of course, Amber was upset, calling out to me, screaming and resisting them. They put something on her wrist that must have been very painful because she collapsed."

"Oh my God, no!"

Memories of having that same wristband put on me was too much. The Lostai used the wristband to track a prisoner and punish them with excruciating burns. My sobbing was so violent I couldn't continue walking. Josh made a motion as if he was about to hug me. I waved him off.

"No. Just let me be."

I suppose to combat falling apart, he finished his story.

"When she stopped struggling, the same female Lostai told Amber that soon enough she'd see her mother. I guess Amber believed it and calmed down a bit. I told her to be strong, that I'd find a way back to her. And that was it." He turned away from me. "They took her away. I ended up, I guess about a month later, at some prison camp doing hard labor in caves."

I don't recall how long it took us to walk again, and we didn't speak until we reached the environmental control station. Once there, I became a robot spewing out facts, procedures, instructions, schedules—anything black-and-white to numb my brain from what Josh had just shared with me. He was in the same mode, taking copious notes and asking pertinent questions.

We worked until hunger pangs distracted me and I realized it was way past our normal lunchtime.

"I'm hungry, Josh. You want to head back to the dining room and get something to eat?"

"I'll catch up with you in a bit. I want to go over my notes."

No one else was in the dining room when I arrived. Relieved, I hastily warmed up a small bowl of *teronix*, dough pockets filled with savory vegetables swimming in a tasty broth. The image of Amber suffering similar punishments as I had at the hands of the Lostai returned. Hot tears flowed down my cheeks as I ate. Someone walked in, and I looked up to see Montor's concerned expression.

"Sweetness, what is wrong?"

I wiped my tears and shook my head without replying. He rushed to sit next to me, pulling me into an embrace.

"Has *Joshwar* upset you?" he said in a stern voice.

After a long exhale, I answered, "No, no. It is not his fault. I am upset because he told me the Lostai put the wristband on Amber when she resisted them. Also, my disappearance has deeply affected my younger son, Bobby. I am so heartbroken, Montor. None of them deserved to suffer. It is all because of what I am, because of the Sotkari Ta genes I was born with."

I leaned into Montor's body as he soothed me, running his fingers through my hair and massaging my scalp.

"Mina, it is not your fault. You have suffered too. The only guilty party here is Zorla and the Lostai military in general."

When I pulled back, I saw Josh sitting alone at the other end of the dining room. Our eyes met before he stared back at his plate of food.

What would our lives have been had I not been abducted in the first place? We might have separated eventually.

We had been a good team, but I sometimes had sensed that once the kids were all grown and gone, there probably would be little left to hold us together.

My mind shifted. A thought caught me by surprise.

"Montor, I want to be in the best physical and mental condition possible to rescue my daughter. I will work out harder than ever before, and I want you to teach me mind manipulation."

"Hmm, you have always expressed disapproval of that."

"Zorla and the Lostai military do not deserve my morals. I need to have all weapons at my disposal to defeat him. Once my daughter is safe, if I get a chance to kill him, I will."

His brow furrowed.

"Mina, of course I will try to teach you, if that is what you want. It just concerns me you would allow Zorla to change who you are. You have always stood by your values."

I huffed and turned away. He guessed I was done discussing issues of morality and changed the subject.

"So, how is the training going?"

"I think as well as one could hope, given the circumstances." I glanced at my tablet. "It is time to get back to work."

"OK, sweetness. I know how difficult this is for you. Tonight, these hands will provide you a relaxing massage." He kissed my forehead and stood. "But now I will leave you to your student. If he bothers you in any way, let me know."

Montor left the room, and I walked over to where Josh was sitting.

"Are you ready to get back to the station? Any questions from what we discussed this morning?"

Josh only nodded.

Halfway back to the environmental control station, he stopped in his tracks.

"Mina, I still can't believe you sleep with that...creature."

I turned around, shaking my head.

"What are you talking about? Why wouldn't I? We're married. He's the father of my son."

"He's not human. It's weird. I can't believe you forgot about me for him."

"I didn't forget about you. I fell in love with him. I can't explain how or why. The embedded Sotkari Ta genes we both have are a part of it, drawing me to him even when I still didn't like him much. It was the same for him. He didn't want a commitment, and yet he risked so much for me." Pausing, I recalled everything Montor and I had been through. "He has changed so much as a person for me. Our bond is a powerful thing."

Josh rolled his eyes.

"How sweet. I just can't wait till you explain it to Amber."

I thought I might cry again.

"Why are you being so combative? I thought we were over this already. I could be questioning you, too."

"Me?"

"What about Laura?" I got up close and spoke through gritted teeth. "Look me in the eye and tell me you were not having an affair with her long before I disappeared."

"Huh? Where is this coming from?" He tried to look innocent, but I had hit a nerve. "You never accused me of this before."

He was right. I never did.

Shit. Maybe I didn't even care.

"Well, I never had any concrete evidence, but I suspected it. I dare you to deny it."

He couldn't hold my stare. I barely heard his next words.

"You became so independent. It was crystal clear you didn't need me."

"I had no choice," I said under my breath. "You left me when I needed you the most."

"But I came back," he shouted.

I scanned the area, making sure Montor was not around to hear Josh raise his voice at me.

"Shh! Keep your voice down."

"I took care of our family!"

"Yeah, you took care of our family, but you didn't take care of our relationship," I snapped, turning away from him. "Josh, I don't want to discuss this anymore. Finding our daughter and getting her out of Zorla's clutches will be no simple task. We need to be laser-focused. I don't want to be distracted by arguing over the past."

I resumed walking towards the station, hearing his exhale and heavy steps as he followed me down the corridor without another word.

4

———————

Over the ten-day trip to Sotkar, I spent the equivalent of ten Earth hours daily training Josh. During the early morning before working with Josh and after dinner, I put in another four hours of physical and mental workouts, one hour of meditation, and one hour poring over military intelligence reports.

On the fourth evening of walking into our quarters long after Montor had gone to bed, I tried once again to slip under the covers without disturbing him, but this time he was wide awake and checked his tablet before pulling me close.

"Mina, it is very late. You are working too hard and not allowing yourself enough rest time," he whispered in my ear.

"I appreciate your concern, but I am fine."

"I miss you," he said in a lusty tone.

His hand slid under my night shirt and caressed my breast. He shifted one of his legs between mine. The warmth of his skin was inviting, but I was so tired. I cleared my throat.

"I need to rest now, Montor."

"That is a first." He was right. Our chemistry and libido

were always in tune. We never rejected each other's overtures. "You see what I mean? Instead of getting stronger, you will overwork yourself. The body needs time to regenerate and re-energize. I think you should cut down your schedule by at least two hours, and—"

My muscles ached. I could barely keep my eyes open.

"Do not tell me what I need to do. You are right. I need rest. Can you not understand me? *Shermont!* I am tired, so let me sleep!"

I was never one to use curse words, much less not in my native tongue. A moment of silence went by, and then Montor turned away from me. I let out a guilty exhale.

Damn it!

I turned, pressed my face against his back, and put my arms around him.

"Oh Montor, I did not mean to be rude, but understand me. So many things in the last four revolutions since I was taken from Earth have been out of my control. My mental and physical readiness for this challenge is something I CAN control. Otherwise, I will drive myself crazy thinking about what my daughter might be going through while I am here lying comfortably in your arms. Imagine if it were Josher, instead. What would you do?"

He turned towards me.

"OK, Mina. I understand. Tell me, how can I help?"

"One of your great neck and shoulder massages would be awesome right now."

"Of course, sweetness. I will be right back."

He went to the reproducer and requested a special blend of massage oil. I turned face-down and inhaled, listening to the sound of him rubbing his hands together. He started by placing both hands on my upper back and refocusing his Sotkari Ta energy from lust to healing. My tension melted away as he moved his hands to my neck and shoulder area, his fingers kneading away each kink.

"Montor, that feels awesome. Thank you."

"I am glad, Mina. I want to help you be as prepared as possible for this mission. And you know what else? I would like to know more about *Aembuh*. Tell me, what is she like?"

His voice was tender and sincere. Moments like these made me love him even more.

"Oh Montor, she is a beautiful and smart girl. She was fourteen when the Lostai kidnapped me. She is eighteen now."

"So, if I remember correctly what you explained about Earthian development, she is on the cusp of adulthood."

"Yes, but she has always seemed mature for her age. I do not mean only in intelligence but in how she deals with people. You know adolescents can be self-absorbed and sometimes cruel with each other. She is generous and brave...and charms everyone she meets. More than once, I heard stories from her friends about how she stood up to bullies who were harassing them."

"Sounds like she takes after her mother."

"That is nice of you to say. I am so saddened that I missed these formative years of her life. We were very close. Many of my friends with daughters her age said I should expect her to detach from me once she entered adolescence and her teen-aged years. That was not the case with us. We enjoyed the same things. For example, we both were fascinated with what might exist in the star systems outside of ours."

"Hmm, I am sorry for how you both ended up being exposed to another galaxy."

His hand had shifted down to my lower back and pelvic area.

"Ouch!"

"Should I stop? You are holding a lot of stress in this area, Mina."

It's crazy how you don't realize how sore you are until someone presses on a tender spot.

"No, it is good. I need this."

"Sweetness, I know how horrible it must feel worrying about what she is going through, but I bet she is a survivor, like her mother. I am sure we will find her and bring her back to safety."

"Thank you, Montor."

He moved on to my arms and legs and finished with a wonderful foot massage. We cuddled. He kissed me on the head, and I finally got the rest that had eluded me in previous nights.

In the following days, Montor shifted some of his routine so that, besides training me on mental manipulation, he could coach me through my physical workouts. Some of the crew joined us during our exercises and sparring sessions. Josh stumbled upon us one day when he came to the fitness room, not expecting to find anyone there. Montor and I were exchanging blows, kicks, jumps, feints, chokeholds, and blocks. I smiled to myself as an expression of utter disbelief swept across Josh's face.

"Mina, who are you? You truthfully are a different person."

Montor's eyes narrowed, always on guard when Josh spoke to me in English outside of our assigned training sessions and lunchtime, especially in front of others. He tried to repeat the last of what he heard in English. "What does *'ore a theferend parxen'* mean?"

I covered my mouth so Montor couldn't tell that I found his mangled English funny, but there was no fooling him. He crossed his arms over his chest and grimaced, frustrated at what he knew was poor pronunciation.

Montor is never going to have the patience to learn English.

I explained to him what the sentence meant and turned to

answer Josh. "Well, I went through a year of Lostai boot camp, and ever since I escaped them, I've been involved with the United Rebel Front. I practice my skills every day."

The other crew members swapped sparring partners and even called Josh to join them. His ex-Marine psyche switched on, and he didn't hesitate. The others were impressed with his ability to hold his own against them despite the months he had spent in a Lostai labor camp. The soldiers knew better than to suggest Montor and I swap partners with them. That would require them to touch me.

Josh sparred a couple of brief bouts with the other soldiers. Intoxicated by the adrenaline and testosterone rush, he forgot my earlier warnings about Arandan culture and gestured with his hands for me to come have at him.

"Come on, Mina. This may be a good way for us to air out our issues."

The others understood the gesture and froze. Montor's eyes blazed, his pupils enlarged. I rushed to grab him by the arm.

"Disregard it, Montor. He did not mean any disrespect. He was only joking."

Too late. He shook my arm off and in one long stride faced Josh.

"You want to spar, *Joshwar*. Why not pick a fight with me instead of my wife?" he growled.

The palpitations made my chest ache.

"Montor!" I shouted, but no one listened to me.

The soldiers, knowing what would follow, lined up against a wall, opening space in the center of the room for Josh and Montor. Josh also had a crazed look on his face. I prayed, on top of everything, he wouldn't slip and say I was his wife, too. Instead, moving into a guarding stance, he raised his fists and glared up at Montor.

"You right. You better choice," Josh said in Lostai.

"I will enjoy this, *Joshwar*," replied Montor, cracking his knuckles.

I feared this would not be an even match. Montor towered over everyone in the room, including Josh. Josh was still regaining his strength after being a Lostai prisoner for six months. The soldiers were eerily quiet. They knew Josh had crossed a boundary. This sparring session had morphed into a very personal fight. I heard Montor's voice telepathically in my mind.

"Stay out of our way, sweetness. If you get hurt, it will only serve to anger me more."

Exasperated, I blew air out of puffed cheeks, walking to the edge of the room with the others.

They moved around at first, sizing each other up. Montor let Josh score the first blow. That was always his style because he had a devastating counter punch and kick combo that never failed. I winced as Josh landed on the floor with a thud, his brow swelling in an instant. Montor chuckled.

"Get up, *Joshwar*."

Josh scrambled up and lunged at Montor, grabbing him by the torso and pushing him hard against the wall. The force of Josh's movement and the strength behind it caught Montor by surprise. Josh's advantage lasted only seconds as Montor launched an attack of vicious strikes and kicks.

Josh was on the floor again. He got to his feet and found a way to land a few punches to Montor's midsection, but at a painful cost. Montor grabbed him by the base of the skull, pulled him down and delivered a series of knee strikes to the face and ribs. Blood spewed out of Josh's nose. He doubled over and was no longer defending himself. Montor followed with another pulverizing punch.

Oh my God. Oh my God. Make them stop!

Josh went limp. I watched, horrified, as Montor picked him up and body slammed him against the mat.

"You want to fight, *Joshwar*. Get up." Montor wiped his brow, his chest heaving, and eyed Josh with a predatory glare. "We are just getting started."

"Stop it!" I shouted at the top of my lungs.

I wanted to run over to Josh, who, sprawled on the floor, seemed to be in awful shape. That would only have ignited Montor's anger. I ran to Montor instead and pushed him away from Josh.

"Enough! We are supposed to be training to fight our enemies, not each other."

To my surprise, Josh stumbled to his feet once again. He looked terrible but stood fearlessly. I should have known. Josh was a stubborn man. The typical Rocky. He'd be dead before he backed off.

"You should have stayed down, Earthian," Montor taunted.

"Get out of the way, Mina," Josh sputtered.

I ignored Josh and shoved Montor again, as hard as I could, and spoke to him telepathically.

"Montor, if you do not stop this right now, you will sleep alone for a long time. I will not tolerate this stupidity!"

He rolled his eyes but stepped back and nodded in agreement. I turned to our acting medical officer.

"Take Joshua to the infirmary and tend to his injuries. This session is over."

I shot Josh and the rest of the soldiers a stern look. They knew by then I was not the typical submissive Arandan wife.

"Josh, this is over. Go to the infirmary. Now."

The soldiers and Josh shuffled out of the room, except for Noomar, the highest-ranking Arandan soldier. He looked back at me and at Montor, consternation and confusion in his eyes. Montor and I did not fit his Arandan understanding of husband-and-wife roles. It seemed he was about to ask Montor something, but before he had a chance, I said, "Noomar, leave us alone."

Montor pursed his lips, his eyes fluttering like those of a scolded child. He waved Noomar off. Once alone, I stepped closer to Montor and poked him in the chest.

"What is wrong with you?"

"Why are you angry with me? It was his fault." His voice deepened. "How dare he attempt to spar with you."

"It was so easy for you to take advantage of the moment and act as a bully. That was not a sparring match for you. It was the stupid duel you are fixated on, and an unfair one, at that. You know how conditions are at those Lostai labor camps." The more I spoke, the more my breath shuddered in anger. "He was in no shape to face you. As leader of this mission, I expect you to behave like an adult, not an adolescent."

He cracked his knuckles again and again but didn't reply.

"Well, how are we going to move forward, Montor? There is no way we are going to launch a successful rescue mission if I must constantly worry about you and Josh killing each other. Maybe you both can stay behind and beat each other up while I try to find my daughter!"

Montor took a moment to turn away before staring down at me.

"What about him? He is aggressive towards you. I will not stand for it, much less when he does it openly in front of others."

He does have a point.

I rubbed my forehead, pressing hard as if that could release the stress concentrated there.

"Yes, Montor, I know. I will speak to him, too. You said you wanted to help me be as well prepared as possible for this mission. We all need to be in top shape and put our bickering aside—"

He huffed.

"This is not just bickering for me, Mina."

"OK, OK. Can we at least agree to put these issues aside until we find Amber?"

My voice was suddenly at a higher pitch. Saying her name out loud caused my chest to tighten. I found myself leaning against him. He embraced me, his arms both strong and comforting.

"Mina, you are right. I am being a terrible captain. Our focus should be only on rescuing *Aembuh.* I give you my word of honor, going forward, I will do my best to avoid distracting confrontations with *Joshwar* while on this mission."

I would have preferred he simply agree to drop the issue altogether. At least the commitment to set aside his dispute with Josh for the time being relieved my stress a bit.

"Thank you, Montor. I will have a similar chat with him and make sure he agrees to do the same."

Even after what he had just committed to, I saw the irritation in his eyes.

"Fine. I think I need to go do some extra meditation."

I waited a few hours to give the acting medic time to complete the healing process before going to see Josh. I found him sitting on a cot in the infirmary, getting ready to leave. The medic had just declared him fit to return to duty. Advanced medical technology healed even broken bones and muscle tears in less than an hour.

"How are you doing?"

Josh pulled a face, avoided meeting my eyes, and didn't answer. I cocked my head to force him to look at me.

"Well?" I insisted.

"I'm good to go."

"Josh, I had a serious talk with Montor about what happened, and I'm about to have the same one with you."

"I don't need you to fight my battles, Mina. I'll be ready for him next time."

"Listen, that's exactly what we need to talk about. I don't

want anyone on this rescue mission who's not one hundred percent focused on finding and rescuing Amber."

Again, hot tears filled my eyes at the mention of her name. He jumped to his feet and raised his voice.

"And you don't think that is my top priority, too?"

The medic turned around and cocked an eyebrow. He couldn't understand what Josh and I were saying in English, but Josh's tone caught his attention. I gestured to Josh to lower his voice.

"I don't know. You seem more interested in picking fights with Montor and me," I whispered.

He lowered his tone, too.

"Me? It's not my fault you married some insanely jealous creature."

"I'm not going to debate my choices with you. If we all can't work together as a team, I'll have the soldiers drop you off somewhere. I'm too stressed out to deal with anything that distracts me from rescuing my daughter."

"Our daughter," he said.

The words hung in a moment of silence. Josh ran his hands through his hair. Our eyes met.

"Montor has promised me he will avoid confrontations with you. Can you do the same and stop all this hostility towards me? Please. We need Montor's help to rescue Amber."

He rolled his neck.

"You're right, Mina. I'll be on my best behavior."

For the remainder of our trip to Sotkar, Josh made good on his promise. The only time we even engaged in casual conversation was during lunchtime. We sat together to eat, and that was my short time to ask about my family on Earth, to cry or laugh as he described things like my dad's bout with cancer or my younger sister's wedding. Although I grieved over the fact I had missed all these important events, I couldn't get enough of these stories.

Montor also behaved himself, and the rest of our trip to Sotkar went smoothly. We landed in the evening on the island of Tremoxtar Mor, booked a hotel for the night, and traveled to the Sotkari insurgency base on Marimbo Tu the next morning. Kaonto, the leader of the Sotkari rebellion, and now the interim Chancellor, welcomed us by grasping our forearms in the typical Sotkari salutation. Because Kaonto wasn't Sotkari Ta or Pasi, he had no evolved abilities, but his son was telepathic, one of the reasons Kaonto had made it his mission to unite the different factions within the Sotkari community and drive the Lostai out of Sotkar.

"Although pleased to see you, I wish it were under different circumstances. I am so sorry about your daughter, Mina. You have been through so much, and now, this," he said thoughtfully.

With a heavy heart, I replied, "Thank you, Kaonto."

Montor cleared his throat after too long of a silence.

"Umm, these are the soldiers Commander Larmont so kindly assigned to help us on this mission."

After introducing the soldiers, he turned to Josh. As much as he tried to keep his expression indifferent, I detected the clench in his jaw before he continued.

"And this is *Joshwar,* the neighbor from Earth who tried to intervene when Mina's daughter was captured. He was inadvertently transported as well. He only speaks a bit of Lostai and is now trying to learn some Arandan."

After some additional small talk, Kaonto invited Montor and me to his office while the soldiers and Josh waited outside. I avoided Josh's eyes, imagining how frustrated he must have felt being treated as an outsider instead of the father of the kidnapped girl we were planning to rescue.

"So..." Kaonto started. "You said you believe they have her here on Sotkar, in Losarex."

Losarex was the name of the territory on the southwestern continent of Sotkar still under Lostai control.

"It is just a guess, based on what Joshua told us. They told him they would take her to a planet where the Lostai only control a certain area. Two Sotkari males escorted her off the ship. Afterward, they took Joshua to the Coroxt labor camp in this same sector. We know the Lostai have a top security military base in Losarex," I said.

"I see. Then it seems a good guess. Their atmospheric shields have proven impenetrable. Do you have any new technology?"

"I am afraid not. Even if we did, it would be of no use. The *Barinta* landing in that area on its own would have no chance of success. Their forces would overcome us before we even had a chance to find the military camp. Our idea is to enter by land," Montor said.

Kaonto's brows furrowed in confusion.

"By land?"

The Lostai had only installed protection from a space-launched attack. They purposely omitted a land barrier, looking for opportunities to enter what was now known as Liberated Sotkar to retake territory. In response, the Sotkari government put in place surface-to-air shields to keep Lostai military from breaching the land border.

Montor went on to explain that we needed those surface-to-air shields to be deactivated for a brief amount of time to allow us to slip into Losarex. Kaonto looked at us like we had our heads chopped off.

"Perhaps I have misunderstood you. You know they are constantly monitoring for breaches in our surface shields. They will send their border troops to take advantage of the opening, try to enter our territory, and, in the process, surely find you. How is this any better than you landing from the air?"

"Yes, you are correct," said Montor. "That is why we will

need you to bring down the entire surface shield system around Norimar Yu. While you are defending the border, we will slip into their territory."

Norimar Yu was the Sotkari province bordering Losarex.

We let the request sink in. Kaonto stood, both palms pressed to the desk. He bent over, looking down at his hands for a while. This was no simple matter.

Kaonto looked back at us, his expression grave.

"Montor, Mina, you know I want to help, but you are talking about inviting a Lostai invasion into Liberated Sotkari territory."

"Yes, but you would be ready. To them, it would look like a breach in the system. They would not know you purposely brought it down or that you have combat pods at the ready to face them."

Pangs of guilt took over. I grasped Montor's hand.

"Montor, maybe we are asking for too much."

Kaonto met my eyes.

"Mina, I truly want to help, but this is not even a decision I can make on my own. I am an interim Chancellor, not a dictator. I would need to consult, at a minimum, with the Norimar Yu province governor and the senate leadership."

Montor stood from his seat and approached Kaonto's desk, a determined look on his face.

"Kaonto, at the risk of being rude, the Sotkari government owes Mina and me some consideration. I helped you when this planet was overrun by a pandemic. I fought with your troops against the previous Lostai land invasion. Mina brought back many of your rescued children through the transportal. Please call a meeting with the Norimar Yu province governor. Is it someone I know?"

Kaonto steepled his hands.

"To complicate matters further, the Norimar Yu province

governor suddenly passed away last week. I recently assigned an interim replacement until we organize elections."

"OK, fine. I can speak to whoever is in charge now."

"Well, now that I think about it, this turn of events might be to your advantage. You do know the interim governor of Norimar Yu."

"Great. Who is he?"

"Kindor Grahmon."

5

———

Montor's face turned to stone, and I heard him cursing loud and clear in my mind. Luckily, Kaonto was not telepathic, although not blind to Montor's expression.

"Montor, is there a problem with Kindor?"

Montor paced the room, annoyance plastered on his face.

"No, no problem at all."

"Do you want to discuss on a video call or in person?"

"A video call is fine."

"I will contact him and set a time for tomorrow. In the meantime, I hope you decide to stay awhile and share a meal and some drinks with my lieutenants and me. Also, did you know some of your friends have been working here with me during the last lunar cycle? I can invite them as well."

Montor said nothing, perhaps still digesting the uncomfortable idea that we would soon be asking Kindor for help. I jumped in before Kaonto could notice.

"Who, Kaonto?"

"Damari, Komar, and Kristom."

This was pleasant news. Montor and I both smiled. He had

spent time in battle with the three of them, and Damari's wonderful personality always cheered me up.

"Oh, yes. That would be excellent," I said.

"Perfect. Excuse me while I take care of the arrangements. Make yourselves comfortable in our resting area, and I will let you know when everything is ready."

That was our cue to leave his office. Montor and I had been here before and were familiar with the facilities. We joined the others and led them to the resting area, a large room with comfortable seating, viewers and reproduction devices.

"Would you like something to drink?" I asked Josh.

Ignoring my question, he replied impatiently, "What happened in there? What's the plan?"

Montor, who always paid close attention to Josh's tone of voice, especially when he talked to me, turned around. Our eyes met, and he understood not to intervene.

"I'll explain in a minute," I said to Josh. "I'm going to get some tea. Do you want some? They also have beers and other alcoholic-like beverages, if you like. Arandan brandy is actually very good. I think that's what they all are having."

"Yeah, I'll try it."

Montor and the other soldiers were already at the reproduction devices putting in their drink requests. Josh followed me as I walked over. The three of us had not been in such close proximity to each other since the fight.

"Joshua would like a glass of brandy."

Many Arandans took pride in the potency of their aged brandy and felt other people weren't worthy to partake of it. I saw the flicker of arrogance in Montor's eyes and nipped it by sending a telepathic message.

"Remember. Behave. Also, know that I will need to translate to Joshua what our next steps are. He is anxious to know what is going on."

Montor experienced a moment of empathy for Josh.

"As a father, I can understand how he feels. Go ahead. Sit aside and explain to him while I brief the rest of the soldiers."

"Thank you. I appreciate that."

Montor and the soldiers took their drinks and sat around a dining table.

"Josh, let's sit over here so I can update you on what we discussed with Kaonto."

I led Josh to a separate tall cocktail table with barstools.

"Are you sure your..." He could not bring himself to say the word. "Umm, is he going to get all bent out of shape with you sitting here with me?"

"It's OK. Believe it or not, underneath all the obnoxious behavior, he can be a softy. As a father, he understands how you must feel."

Josh was not impressed, so I jumped right into bringing him up to speed on what we had discussed with Kaonto.

"That name, Kindor, sounds familiar. Isn't that the guy Montor said was his rival?"

"Umm, yes, but that is an old story. Kindor is with someone now. I haven't seen him in months."

Josh shook his head.

"So, let me get this straight. We have to ask this old flame of yours—"

"He's not an old flame. He was a good friend, but he developed feelings for me, and things got complicated."

I didn't think it necessary to tell Josh that Kindor and I had been lovers during a brief time when Montor and I were separated, and I was suffering memory loss.

"Whatever. So, we have to get this guy's permission to start a war on the border of his province so we can sneak into the territory where we think the Lostai may be holding Amber. What are the chances that is going to happen?"

"We'll see," I replied.

I was fairly confident Kindor would be willing to help me

but didn't want to make it sound like he might still be carrying a torch for me. Josh took a good gulp of the brandy. His eyes watered a bit, but he pursed his lips in approval. He finished his glass in a second gulp and asked for another.

"It's strong but good."

I could almost feel Montor's eyes follow me to the reproduction area, where I requested Josh's second glass.

I turned and smiled at Montor while I said telepathically, "He likes it."

Montor smirked and returned his attention to the soldiers.

A half hour later, Kaonto came to the resting room with four other Sotkari, two males and two females.

"These are my lieutenants." After introductions, he continued, "Let us all go to my home. We will have our meal there."

We followed him outside, where we got into a transport pod that took us further into the forest. It landed in a clearing surrounded by six homes. Worried that the Lostai might want to kidnap his telepathic son, Kaonto had moved his family to the rebel base a long time ago. His lieutenants had done the same. The shields that protected the base somewhat assured their safety.

Although I had been to the island before, this was my first visit to Kaonto's home.

"What beautiful architecture," I said, observing its unique, circular structure and open-air courtyard in the center.

The lush landscaping popped with magenta, gold, and indigo flowers. A long table with booth-style, cushioned seating on either side was positioned at one end of the courtyard. A buffet-style table sat at the other end, covered with an assortment of food and beverages.

"Welcome to my home. Feel free to serve yourself and get comfortable."

A boy the size of a human twelve-year-old came running from inside the house to meet us.

"Son, meet some friends," said Kaonto.

Kaonto introduced Montor and me, and then Montor introduced the soldiers and Josh.

"How did I do, Father?" asked the boy.

"Everything looks excellent, Son."

Kaonto's wife had died a year earlier from a disease spread by a Lostai biological attack that resulted in a planet-wide pandemic. The boy's eyes looked old for his age. Clearly, his father leaned on him for help around the house.

"Montor, your distaste for reproduced food is legendary, but hopefully, this is not too bad."

"Oh, no worries. I am sure it is fine."

We formed a line to serve ourselves food and return to the table. No sooner than we had all sat down, three figures entered the courtyard. Damari, Kristom, and Komar had arrived. Damari wasted no time rushing to my side.

"Mina, whaa gwaan? It good fi see yuh. Yuh look good."

I loved the rhythm of his Jamaican accent. He gave me a bearhug and smacked a loud kiss on my cheek. Montor would have admonished anyone else severely for these public displays of affection, but he, Damari, and I had been through a lot together. He was like family by now. Josh observed silently. I'd have to find a moment later to bring him up to date on Damari.

"I'm fine, Damari. You look good, too."

Komar, Kristom, and Montor exchanged Sotkari salutations, and soon we were all seated and eating. Before long, the conversation turned towards the mission at hand. Damari hardly ever scowled. He was upset now.

"Mi cyaw believe de Lostai still a fuck wid yuh, Mina. One day when we hol de one Zorla, we a guh mek him pay."

"I know. Right now, I just need to find Amber and get her away from them."

Damari switched to Lostai, which had improved a bit since last I saw him.

"Kaonto, I want join Mina and Montor on this mission. Is acceptable?"

"Yes, of course."

Kristom and Komar requested the same. These were people Montor and I could trust our lives with. They knew this could be a matter of life and death. A safe return wasn't guaranteed for anyone.

"I could never have asked you to take this risk for me and my daughter, but since you have offered..." I lowered my eyes, hand on chest. "I cannot express what this means to me."

In chorus, they all replied that there was no need to thank them.

"We are a team," said Kristom, using sign language. As all Sotkari Ta, he was mute.

"Montor, Kindor is available to talk with us in the morning," Kaonto interjected.

"OK, we will be back here early tomorrow."

We changed the subject to lighter matters. Someone asked about Josher. I passed my tablet around so everyone could see recent images of him. Those who knew him commented on how much he had grown and how much he looked like his father. Montor told stories about how well Josher was doing with his studies, sports, and Sotkari Ta abilities.

"He already moves small objects with his mind and communicates telepathically quite smoothly," Montor boasted. "And mind you, only two and a half revolutions of age."

At two and a half years old, Josher was the equivalent mentally and physically of a six-year-old human, tall even for an Arandan child. The soldier sitting next to Josh passed the tablet to him. After a quick glance, he passed it on to the next person, but his jaw clenched, and his face flushed with color. As if it were contagious, my cheeks burned, too. I wished I could say something to him to make things better, but even if we had been alone, I probably wouldn't have found the right words.

Oh Josh, I keep forgetting how this must feel for you. I'm so sorry.

It was late afternoon by the time we were done with dessert and several glasses of Sotkari wine. We said our goodbyes and piled back into the transport pod, arriving at our hotel in Tremoxtar Mor by early evening.

I used the communication system and viewer in the room to contact Lasarta and Foxor so we could chat with Josher before going to bed.

"*Ta Ri! Ro Ma!*"

"How are you doing, Son?" said Montor.

"Great! *Lo Ro* made my favorite dinner today. She said it was a prize for completing my lessons early." He held up a tablet to the screen. "Look, a perfect score."

"Oh, *honey*," I said. By now, both Josher and Montor understood it was a term of endearment in English. "We are so proud of you."

"When are you coming home?"

Montor and I exchanged looks. We had already explained before we left that we would be away for a while, but it was clear that beneath all the exuberance, Josher was troubled by our absence. The three of us had not been separated from each other for an entire year now, except for when he visited Kindor, who he adored. Prior to that, our time as a family had been marred with separation and instability.

Is he somehow sensing we are about to embark on a risky undertaking?

That was probably a stretch. He just missed us, plain and simple. Still, I had been so heartbroken over Amber and preoccupied with dealing with the Josh and Montor situation. Now, it hit me. Anything could happen on this rescue mission. One or both of us might not make it back.

Will Josher have to suffer the loss of his mother, like my older children once did?

My heart tore apart yet again.

"Son, we will be away for at least one lunar cycle. Maybe more. When we get back, we can do something fun together," said Montor, as I remained speechless. Tears were coming. I looked down and wiped them away with a quick movement so Josher wouldn't notice. "The job we are doing is going to take some time, so we need you to be a big, patient boy until we return."

"There are soldiers following us everywhere we go, *Ta Ri.*"

We had been through so much as a family. Montor did not spare any expense to make sure Josher wasn't at risk.

"Yes, Son. So, you see? You can be sure you and your grandparents will be perfectly safe until we get back," answered Montor.

I found my voice and said, "*Honey*, I miss you a lot, but hopefully it will not be so long before we are back home. Tell me, what are your plans for tomorrow?"

The change in subject was successful. Josher launched into a detailed discussion about his martial arts training and a visit to his favorite recreational holographic center.

We ended our conversation with Josher, and Lasarta took him to bed.

"Foxor, I appreciate your and Lasarta's help with Josher. I know he can be persistent about the things he is passionate about. It seems he misses his mother," said Montor.

"Mina is not the only one he misses. He often talks of the warrior and sports games you two play together, but do not worry. We love having all this extra time with him and will keep him occupied," replied Foxor.

"Thank you," said Montor, looking down. I placed my hand over his. Although better than me at hiding his feelings, he was equally affected by our separation from Josher. Lasarta returned and asked about our next steps.

"Our best guess is that Mina's daughter is being held in Losarex. We intend to create a diversion at the border to try to slip in undetected," explained Montor.

Lasarta and Foxor looked at each other but said nothing.

They must think we're crazy to go into enemy territory. Lasarta and Foxor have grown to love me, but maybe they think I am forcing their foster son to take too much of a risk.

Montor probably sensed my thoughts because he added, "Commander Larmont assigned five of his soldiers to assist us, and Damari, Kristom, and Komar will be coming, also. We have a well thought-out plan."

"Sounds like a good team," said Lasarta. "We will pray for a successful rescue. I look forward to meeting your daughter, Mina."

"Thank you," I said.

After closing the call, I plopped into bed, turning away from Montor and covering my face to hide that I was, yet again, crying. There was no fooling him. He said nothing at first, inching closer to me and rubbing my hair.

"Mina, although you know I do not believe in such things, you have always talked to me about your faith in a higher power—I think it is pronounced *Gohd*. Trust that everything will be fine. We will rescue your daughter and be back with Josher soon."

I turned around and pressed my face against his chest.

"Thank you, Montor, for being my rock."

"Rock?"

"I mean, for being my strength. I can always rely on you for support."

"Yes, well, I will need some support too," he said in a mock-worried voice. I looked up to find irritation in his expression.

"...In order to get through this conversation with Kindor tomorrow without breaking the viewer."

6

———

Similar to the previous day, Montor and I entered Kaonto's office while Josh and the others waited outside. I said a silent prayer as Kindor's image appeared on the viewer. Kaonto kicked off the conversation with pleasantries.

"Good morning, Kindor. I hope things are going well with you. Thank you for accepting this meeting on such short notice."

The passage of time didn't make interfacing with Kindor less awkward. He had been a special friend, saving my life more than once, but he also had broken a bond of trust between us, the reason for our current estrangement.

As Josher's *Ta Masa*, Kindor was something similar to a godfather in Arandan culture. Because of his close relationship with Josher, Montor and I had agreed he was the best person to occupy that role. That didn't make the situation between Kindor and us any easier. Even at our last encounter six months earlier at Josher's *Bendorai*, we had kept our exchanges with Kindor to a minimum.

As a mute Sotkari Ta, Kindor required the use of his tablet to communicate when telepathy wasn't possible. He punched in the words, and the tablet emitted audio.

"Montor, Mina, it is good to see you again."

Montor took my hand in his.

"Yes, thank you."

"Kaonto has explained you have a problem you believe I can help with."

As much as Montor might have tried to avoid it, he couldn't keep the displeasure out of his voice.

"Yes. Kindor, here is the situation. We have learned Zorla sent one of his minions back to Earth to kidnap Mina's daughter."

"*Kantarext!*" Kindor exclaimed a Sotkari swear word. He stood and approached the screen. "Mina, I am so sorry."

Before I could reply, Montor stood from his seat as well.

"Well, I am glad to hear that because we have a plan to rescue the girl that requires some extreme tactics."

Kaonto's eyes widened, I'm sure shocked at Montor's less than amicable tone, considering what we were about to request. Kindor wasn't fazed at all. He knew what to expect from Montor and returned to his seat.

"OK. Explain it to me."

Montor had Kindor's full attention as he went through the details of our plan. When he was done, Kindor wasted no time typing into his tablet.

"So, this is simple. You want to start a war a few miles from where I live."

He had tried to inject some levity, but the furrowed brow revealed the seriousness of the proposition.

"Not start a war," replied Montor. "You will be ready when the shields come down. We will only need you to engage the Lostai for half a day to give us enough time to slip deep enough into Losarex territory undetected. I know for a fact you have enough combat pods to face the Lostai down."

"It is not only the combat pods we need to think about. We would need to evacuate the Sporia region."

"That area is sparsely populated."

"Why do you even think this is a viable plan?" challenged Kindor.

"I also know the Sotkari government took advantage of the last border skirmish to do the exact same thing as I am proposing. That is how you slipped some Sotkari spies into Losarex to pose as Lostai sympathizers."

"OK, although I admit that is true, we would be burning a lot of resources. To squash their attempt to come into our territory, in addition to the combat pods, we would need to mobilize additional surface-to-air missiles. It is not a minor undertaking. Kaonto, what do you think?"

"We also need to consider the soldiers that could be injured or lost in a half-day's worth of battle," answered Kaonto, shaking his head.

I hated that they were discussing the situation like a business transaction. Amber's name had not even been mentioned, yet her life hung in the balance. I stared at my hands as the discussion halted, then raised my eyes at the sound of Kindor's feet shuffling. He had approached the screen again, staring as if searching for something.

Time to advocate for my daughter.

"I know we are asking for a lot, and you are bringing up important considerations, but my daughter." I fought back tears. "My daughter, Amber...Her name is Amber...is in the hands of that monster. I intend to do whatever it takes to rescue her."

My trembling hand rushed to wipe away the tears. Montor's patience ran out. He got to his feet abruptly.

"OK, we are done supplicating. Are we doing this or not? Otherwise, Mina and I need to look for other options."

Kindor crossed his arms over his chest, walked around a bit, and stared at the screen long and hard one more time. I stared back. The equivalent of eyes locking, and then I saw it. He'd made up his mind.

"Kaonto, I think Mina deserves our help. Hardly any civilians are in that area. If you agree to it, so do I. If in the aftermath the public learns we purposely brought down the shields, we can say it was part of a counter-intelligence mission."

At that point, Kaonto had no choice. I jumped up from my seat, got closer to the screen, and hugged myself. Montor's eyes narrowed. The message was obvious. I was giving Kindor a hug of gratitude.

"Kindor, I do not know how to repay this. Thank you so much."

Kindor now looked everywhere except at the screen. Montor's voice sounded gruff as he moved on to wrap up the meeting.

"OK, I will acquire an amphibious vehicle. We will reconvene tomorrow to nail down the final details. Kaonto, we will also need at least twelve fully charged *hanstorics*."

Hanstorics were laptop-sized devices that stored and harnessed a transportal's geomagnetic energy. We used them to travel long distances in space in mere seconds.

"I will travel there this evening and meet you in person," Kindor said. "Lorret will come with me. I am sure she will be happy to see you both."

"Hmm...Fine," grumbled Montor.

The next day when we arrived at Kaonto's office, Lorret and Kindor were already there. Montor and Kindor greeted each other with the Sotkari wrist grasp. Kindor only nodded to me, as he knew that was the respectful thing to do based on Arandan custom. Lorret placed her hands on my shoulders.

"Mina, you look so good. I wish we were meeting under other circumstances."

"You look great, too. Thank you for coming."

Kindor, Montor and I could have communicated using telepathy, but Lorret and Kaonto could not. As soon as Lorret and I finished our greetings, Kindor typed words in his tablet.

"Lorret and I have something we want to discuss before we get into the details of this mission. We have a request before I agree to move forward."

This prompted one of Montor's signature impatient looks.

"OK, what is it?"

"Lorret and I will join you on this rescue mission. I can pose as a Lostai sympathizer and walk around more freely in Losarex than you could. The rest of you will need to remain hidden."

Montor's reply was quick.

"Umm, that is very kind of you, but unnecessary. Kristom and Komar are coming with us."

"Still, one more Sotkari Ta would be even more beneficial, and I understand you do not have a medic among your crew. Lorret can fill that role. In solidarity with Mina, we would like to do our part to help rescue her daughter."

Kindor glanced at Lorret. As if on cue, she added, "Mina, you made a brave sacrifice for me, the *Barinta* crew, and our cause when we were captured at Dit Lar. You could have spilled secrets to avoid all the pain they put you through, but you were steadfast. As if that were not enough, you agreed to go with that evil person to save us from torture. I will never forget it. Please allow me to stand with you against Zorla."

Montor cracked his knuckles.

"What we are attempting is very dangerous. We cannot

discount the possibility that we may lose our lives. Kindor, we have designated you as Josher's *Ta Masa*. Who will fulfill that role if you, too, are lost?"

The words coming out of Montor's mouth were fake. He usually charged into things, feeling omnipotent and confident he'd be victorious. He just didn't want Kindor around. The only one he was fooling was Kaonto. Kindor's eyes reflected a bit of unusual sarcasm.

"I thank you, Montor, for worrying about my welfare, but I think Josher would prefer to see his parents again. So instead of planning for failure, let us ensure that we work together to rescue Amber and bring everyone back safe and sound. The more resources you have at your disposal, the more likely you will be successful."

If looks could kill, Kindor would have dropped dead at that point.

"Kaonto, Lorret, please excuse us. Kindor, Mina, and I need to discuss this in private."

"Do you want us to leave?" Kaonto asked.

"No need. I am advising you out of courtesy before we go telepathic."

"Feel free," answered Kaonto, as he occupied himself scrolling through his tablet.

"Wait," I interjected. "Montor, why are we excluding Lorret from this conversation? She has expressed her desire to join us as well. Let us go into another room to discuss this."

He's being an asshole again.

Lorret's brow furrowed as if she were thinking through a hard decision.

"Mina, I appreciate what you are trying to do, but I actually would prefer to sit this one out," she said.

Lorret hadn't quite finished speaking when Montor's annoyed voice was in my mind, transmitting his thoughts to Kindor and me in conference mode. Lorret stood and looked out the window. She knew the conversation would not be a pleasant one.

"OK, Kindor, let us stop with the pretenses and get to the point. I appreciate you agreeing with our plan. I really do because I cannot stand to see my wife suffer. That does not mean I have forgotten what you did. You disrespected me. You took advantage of my absence and Mina's memory loss to fulfill your obsession with her, an obsession that you still indulge in."

As I feared, it didn't take long for Montor's temper to take over. Apparently forgetting that we weren't alone, he took one long step and glared down at Kindor, who, unintimidated, stared back.

"And the worst thing you did..." Montor poked Kindor in the chest. "The worst was betraying Mina's trust. She trusted you as a close friend. You lied to her and used her for your own selfish pleasure. I do not want you anywhere near us."

Kindor flinched at those last words and looked away. Heat rose from my neck to my face. After a few seconds, Kindor looked back, a pained look on his face.

"Montor, you are right. I understand you cannot forgive me for what happened. I have not even been able to forgive myself, but I am with Lorret now. I do not have romantic feelings for Mina anymore."

Montor laughed out loud.

"Sure, Kindor, sure. Even now, everyone can see how you look at her. I do not know what Lorret is thinking."

Kindor's eyes froze into blue ice as he stepped closer to Montor. I worried about where this was going.

"I will not allow you to offend Lorret with your words and insinuations," said Kindor in a menacing tone.

Time for me to jump in.

"Montor, I want Kindor and Lorret to join us. We can use all the help we can get. You do not have to be best friends with Kindor to work with him. Look how you have been able to overcome your issues with Joshua. And frankly, I would like not to be the only female on this mission."

"*Jochuar?*" Everyone seemed to have trouble pronouncing his name. "Who is that?"

"Mina, my patience has limits," Montor said, exasperated.

Kindor repeated his question. "Who is that?"

"Her daughter's father," muttered Montor.

Kindor took a moment to digest that piece of information. The grimace on his face said it all.

"You mean her Earthian husband?"

Kindor's eyes widened. Montor's were like balls of fire.

"Yes," I whispered.

Kindor shook his head and, understanding all the implications, shifted the conversation back to his request.

"Well, anyway, Montor. Like Mina says, I do not expect you to like me. You never did. But we want to help. Also, to be honest, I have another vested interest. While in Losarex, we can gather intelligence and perhaps connect with the spies we have implanted there."

I searched Montor's eyes and communicated my next words only to him.

"I know this is a lot for you to deal with, my king. I just want to rescue my daughter as soon as possible. Why would we reject anyone's help?"

He let out a long, exaggerated exhale.

"Is there anything I will not do for you, sweetness?" he said, running his hand through his hair. "I suppose I will need to get a second vehicle to accommodate all of us. For sure *Joshwar* and Kindor will not be traveling in ours."

I leaned into him, pressing my cheek to his chest. He tilted my chin up and kissed my forehead before turning and saying out loud, "OK, Kindor, you and Lorret are in."

Lorret heard her name and turned from the window, pretending to be distracted. She and Montor made eye contact.

Her relationship with Montor dated from a time many years before he and I met. She was a fellow Arandan and knew his personality well. He nodded to her, and she smiled, a relieved look on her face. Kaonto looked up from his tablet, his eyes revealing nothing.

"I am glad you reached an agreement," said Kaonto. "I will make the arrangements this afternoon."

7

———

We moved to a larger conference room and invited Kristom, Komar, Damari, Josh, Noomar, and the remaining four Arandan soldiers that had accompanied us to join our strategy session. After a long day hammering out the details of our plan, Kaonto handed Montor and Kindor six *hanstorics* each and sent us off with a Sotkari Ta blessing.

"May the Farthest Light guide you to where Amber is and illuminate your path back to safety."

My eyes watered. "Kaonto, I owe her life to you. I do not know how to repay you."

Kaonto smiled and waved me off.

"Mina, it will suffice that when you come back, you prepare for us that stew you are so famous for."

Everyone except the five Arandan soldiers had tasted my stew before, and all nodded in agreement.

"Deal," I said.

We arrived at the hotel and ate a light meal. As soon as we were back in our room, I activated the viewer and called Josher.

"*Honey,* how are you doing?"

"*Ro Ma!* I miss you."

"I miss you, too."

"*Ta Ri*, are you coming back tomorrow?"

"Not tomorrow, Son. Remember, I told you we may be away for a full lunar cycle or two."

Josher crossed his arms and pouted. I looked down, covering my eyes. The sting of hot tears was back.

No, not tomorrow.

Tomorrow, we would sneak into enemy territory amid a border battle. We only had an approximate location of the military base. The possibility of being captured or killed was quite real.

I can't breathe.

"I need to go to the restroom," I blurted out.

Montor wondered, I'm sure, why I had unfairly left him to deal with Josher's disappointment alone. In the restroom, I inhaled and exhaled slowly, trying to control my anxiety.

I may never see Josher again.

After allowing myself to cry, really bawl, for a few minutes, I closed my eyes and elevated a prayer.

"Lord, please watch over our rescue mission. Help me be strong and remain faithful. I know if I believe you are with us, there is nothing that can stand in our way."

More centered, I washed my face and returned to find Josher asking his father for help with a problem from his arithmetic lessons. They finished the calculations, and I praised them both for being so smart.

"*Ro Ma*, can you tell me a story before I go to bed?"

"Of course, *honey*."

He liked Arandan folk tales about heroic soldiers fighting fantastical creatures. I had a bunch of them loaded on my tablet and was proficient enough in Arandan to read to him. He paid close attention till the end, but once it was done, he rubbed his eyes and yawned.

Foxor was nearby and picked him up.

"Looks like it is your bedtime."

Josher protested, but a stern look from his father quieted him down. I stretched my arms and pretended to yawn.

"I am ready to sleep too, *honey*. Have sweet dreams. I love you very much."

I blew him a kiss, and he did the same—human gestures I had taught him that were foreign to Arandans.

Before Foxor carried him away, Montor said, "Josher, do not forget what I told you earlier. Your mother and I are about to go somewhere without communication systems, so we may not call you in a while. But we are thinking of you always."

"OK, *Ta Ri*. Love you."

"I love you too, Son."

As soon as Foxor took Josher to bed, Lasarta came into the screen view.

"Mina, I can only imagine how stressful this is for you. Foxor and I will pray three times each day until you return with your daughter."

"Thank you, Lasarta."

I could almost taste blood as I bit my lips. Lasarta cocked her head, her brow furrowed in concern. She was the closest thing to a mother I had right now.

"I wish I could be there to give you one of your *hugs*." Arandans only embraced romantic partners, but by now she was used to my friendship hugs. She approached the screen. "I know you will find her and come back safe and sound. I am confident of it."

"Your words give me strength and faith. I am not sure how often we will be in touch, but we will try to update you when it is safe. I appreciate you so much, Lasarta. Good night and rest well."

Montor spoke with Lasarta a bit more while I got changed

into my pajamas, a button-down blouse made of a cotton-like material.

I came to bed. Montor was already lying down. He put the tablet he was reading on the side table and observed as I clasped my hands to pray. Knowing that "Amen" signaled I was done, he waited before saying anything.

"Mina, we will be successful."

I leaned into him. He usually slept only wearing loose shorts.

"Montor, thank you again for supporting me in this."

"How could I not?"

"You have been so patient. This whole situation with Joshua has been difficult for you. Now, we are leaving Josher behind to embark on this dangerous trip. We once agreed we would never separate from him or from each other. Ever again. Yet now, you do not seem to even have second thoughts to help me rescue Amber."

He pulled me even closer.

"Shhh, Mina. We are bonded, like one person. What you feel, I feel. You would have done the same for me."

My heart swelled with emotion. He had a bad temper, was cocky and insanely jealous of anyone who looked at me twice. Then there was this side of him. So caring. So selfless. I ran my thumb over the hard ripples of his abdominal muscles.

So sexy!

My hand moved further down under his shorts and between his legs. I let it rest there.

He cleared his throat.

"Mina? You have been...ummm...tired since we left Dit Lar."

"Yes, but who knows how long it will be before we sleep in a comfortable bed again?"

Amazing how it comes to life in my hand.

I remembered something important. During our vacation,

we had decided to try to conceive another child, so I reversed the tubal ligation that avoided pregnancy. The advanced medical technology available to me here made this a simple process. Now, I couldn't risk getting pregnant while on this mission. Since arriving at Dit Lar, we had already made love once unprotected.

"We need the contraceptive."

He bounced out of bed, almost taking my hand with him, and returned within a couple minutes with a vial. The vial contained a clear, odorless liquid that, once applied to the male's member, evaporated while creating an invisible spermicide barrier that lasted for hours.

"Let me," I said.

I moved down, pulled off his shorts, and applied the liquid using my fingers and gentle strokes. In seconds, he was fully erect again, impressive in size and girth. He shuddered and pulled me back up, flipping me on my back.

"Let me taste you first before I lose control," he said, gliding down my body and tugging my blouse out of his way.

His breath warmed the inside of my thighs. I bent my knees and let my legs fall to either side. He was so good at this because he genuinely enjoyed it. This was no chore for him.

Holding me down, he used his fingers to further expose me, making a point to be thorough. His tongue and lips tantalized me. My heels dug into the mattress as my hips fought to be released from his grip. There would be bruises on my thighs and butt tomorrow, but it was sweet agony, and I cried out in ecstasy. Rapid-fire orgasms shook me, but his goal was the big one, the one that rocked me from head to toe.

"Please, please...Montor."

He lifted his head and, shifting his body up to tower over me, unbuttoned my blouse. I raised my arms to help him dispose of it in one quick movement. His feline eyes glowed in the dark, wild with frenzy. My back arched, and we connected in midair for a second, where he pushed into me, pinning me to the mattress. From there, our bodies moved in perfect rhythm. I held on to the sheets, his arms, anything I could grab because the mind-blowing pleasure made me feel like I was falling. The sounds of his panting and my moans exploded in my ears until finally my body melted in orgasmic waves, and then, the big one. He knew it and let himself go.

Our bodies, slick with sweat, remained connected for a few last seconds before he pulled out and rolled to my side.

"Wow, my king. That was just...wonderful."

"Yes...amazing. I love you, sweetness."

"I love you, too."

It was a while before our breathing returned to normal. Routine mandated I turn on my side, my back towards his torso so he could pull me close and cuddle. I don't remember who fell asleep first.

8

———

Montor was up earlier than me and had stepped out to check on the others while I finished getting ready. Our clothing and gear reflected the mission at hand. I stepped into the legs of a baggy garment and pulled on the long sleeves. Tapping on the collar area caused the blue-and-black material to contract and cling to my skin, creating a waterproof and radioactive-resistant seal that also shielded the body from some types of weapons. Footwear also molded to my skin from the ankles to the toes, with extra protection for the soles.

Montor arrived back at the room as I was finishing up. He wore a similar flight suit. The clingy material highlighted his muscular build and everything else. He sported a similar unitard when we first met. I remembered feeling embarrassed at how little it left to the imagination.

He looked me up and down. A sly smile flashed across his face.

"You look good."

He helped me strap on the utility belt that was part of our gear, squeezing my butt as part of the process.

"We'll never leave if you keep doing that," I joked.

The utility belt allowed us to carry several important gadgets, including adaptive eye goggles, a beam pistol called a *vimor,* explosive shatter pellets, a vaporizing rifle and a knife/scissor/tool combo. We each would carry a backpack containing a protective face mask, a manual compass, thirst pods, nutritional bars, a force field generator, heating crystals, our personal tablet, an earpiece communication device, some toiletries, a change of clothes, a small towel and a medical device called a healing pad. Montor, Damari, Kindor, Komar, Kristom, and I carried two *hanstorics* each. The others didn't know how to use them. Kindor and Montor each also carried a portable reproducer and extra earpiece communication devices.

We met with the others at the docking station where the *Barinta* was parked. It took us an hour to travel to the Norimar Yu / Losarex border, where two amphibious vehicles awaited us by the ocean. Kindor and Montor would command and pilot each one. I explained to Josh that Montor preferred he travel with Kindor's group, which also included Lorret, Kristom, Komar, Noomar and one other Arandan soldier. Josh's reaction was the same as anytime I talked to him about Montor.

"Whatever."

Damari and the three other Arandan soldiers joined Montor and me.

The vehicles were the size of large buses and could navigate on rugged terrain and under water. We synchronized our chronometers and waited.

At precisely three hours after sunset, Kaonto took down the surface-to-air shields at the border. The Sotkari border defenders remained hidden and appeared at ease to give the illusion that they were caught off guard by the shield failure.

It took the Lostai military about ten minutes to detect the shields were down. In another ten minutes, Lostai combat pods started flying across the border into Norimar Yu. The sky lit up with battle fire. Each bombardment felt like an earthquake. With the fighting at its worst, we sealed the vehicles and plunged into the water, not knowing what the outcome of the battle would be.

My stomach knotted up as we submerged deeper into the ocean. The battle sounds became more distant, but that only served to increase my anxiety. Emotions got the best of me, and tears streamed down my cheeks. I unbuckled my seat belt, ran to Montor's seat, and hugged him.

"Mina, give me a minute. I need to stabilize our descent. What's wrong?"

"I am having second thoughts now whether we did the right thing. It seems like so many Lostai combat pods are crossing the border. I feel guilty about what might happen."

He glanced at the control panel and then back at me.

"Mina, please buckle in. The strong currents can make things bumpy down here." His voice started out with an impatient tone, but he stopped and took a deep breath. "I understand your concern, sweetness, but it is too late now. Kaonto has this under control."

I wiped my eyes and sat back down. Looking out the window distracted me. Bioluminescent sea creatures of all shapes, species and colors swam around us. We descended amid the cranking and creaking of the hull, the glub-glub sound of water, and the equipment's pings and beeps. No one said a word. Even Damari, who usually enjoyed chatting with me in English, silently studied his tablet. Montor broke the silence.

"It will take us all night to reach the location where we will disembark, so we should take turns resting."

Montor, one of the Arandans, and I took the first watch. When it was our time to rest, instead of reclining our seats like the others, Montor led me to the back where we somehow both fit on the small berth. He covered us with a blanket and pulled me close.

"Mina, I understand your earlier misgivings," he said telepathically, "but trust me, if the Lostai would have captured Kaonto's son, he would have done no less to recover him."

"I suppose you are right. I pray they stopped the Lostai incursion and brought up the shields again with no losses."

"There will be some, but that is what we signed up for the moment we rebelled against the Lostai. It is the price we pay for freedom and dignity. Hopefully, they will be minimal."

I closed my eyes and did my best to rest but didn't get much sleep. Before I knew it, we were back in our seats and Montor was bringing the craft to the surface. When the water was shallow enough, he let down the treads. A thump signaled we were no longer floating but driving on the ocean floor. As we surfaced, I looked out the window to take in the view. There was not much to see other than a thick purplish fog. The murky environment worked to our advantage. Video surveillance was virtually impossible here. Once on the shore, we exited the vehicle, and after we were at a certain distance, Montor activated a self-destruct sequence that vaporized the craft. A bluish haze enveloped the entire vehicle for a second before it disappeared all at once.

"Everyone, make sure your tablets are in ghost mode," said Montor.

This meant the tablets would only have basic functionality and nothing that required connectivity with other devices or communication systems.

A few yards away from us, the other craft with Kindor and his group appeared on the shore. They did the same. Our only way back now would be via the *hanstorics*. These were necessary precautions to avoid being tracked by Lostai digital surveillance.

Kindor's group joined us. Montor scanned the area.

"I am surprised this place is so desolate. Is it always this foggy?"

Kindor replied, using his tablet for the benefit of those who were not telepathic, and in Lostai, I suppose so Josh could understand.

"Yes, and the high tide here is very unpredictable. The area can flood at a moment's notice. We must hurry and get as far as possible from the shoreline." He pointed to the hills behind us. "Based on the intelligence we have received from our embedded spies, the military camp is on the other side."

"OK, it looks like those hills are a good half day's hike from here," said Montor. "When we get there, we will rest until nightfall and then launch our attack."

Montor took the lead while the rest of us fell into little groups behind him: the five Arandan soldiers; Kristom, Komar and Damari, who had served together on several missions; Lorret and me; and to my uneasiness, Kindor and Josh. Lorret must have read something in my expression.

"*Joshwar* and Kindor are getting along very well," she said in Arandan, a bit of mischief in her eyes.

"I see that. I suppose it is good, but it is somewhat unexpected."

"Not really, if you consider the one big thing they have in common."

"Really? And what would that be?"

"Their dislike for Montor."

I pulled a face. She laughed.

"They secretly mimicked him and made jokes about him throughout the trip, but do not worry. When it started to get out of hand, I reined Kindor in. He knows I have a lot of respect and affection for Montor. Not to mention, Montor is our leader on this mission. The Arandan soldiers that are with us would not tolerate too much of that either."

Of course, she would have Montor's back. He was her first

love, but that was long before he and I met. This caused some friction between Lorret and me when she first joined the *Barinta*, but by now, a strong friendship had grown between us.

I blew air out of my cheeks, wondering about Kindor and Josh's conversations.

"I hope they all behave. Montor can be overbearing and jealous."

"It must be a strange situation for you, Mina. Your ex and current partners, all together."

She knows!

"You know about Joshua?"

"Do not be mad, Mina. Kindor shares everything with me."

"You must not tell anyone."

"Of course, Mina. I care about both you and Montor. I would never do that to you."

"Thank you, Lorret. And yes, strange does not even begin to describe my current situation, but my focus is on rescuing my daughter."

I switched the conversation away from me.

"How are things going with you and Kindor?"

She paused before replying.

"Things are going very well. Let us be honest, Mina. There is a piece of Kindor's heart that will always belong to you. I know it. I also know he has come to care for me deeply, and I have grown to love him, too. He is strong and kind and a person of integrity. Not a day goes by that he does not regret what happened between you and him. It was his one downfall, and yet you have not forgiven him. The distance between you hurts him."

I looked away.

"I miss our friendship, too. It was something special he ruined with deceit, taking advantage of me when I was suffering memory loss and at my most vulnerable. He allowed us to become lovers, knowing I was married to Montor. That will always feel like a betrayal of trust."

"I understand, Mina. He let his love for you cloud his judgment. The whole situation was unfortunate. You and he alone for so long while Montor was away. I mean, he is not made of stone."

"I am surprised you would be so understanding."

"I have no right to be jealous about something that happened when Kindor and I were only friends."

"Lorret, I admit that, in my heart, I have forgiven Kindor. Montor, however, will never let this go, and out of respect to Montor, I must keep my distance."

As if on cue, Montor turned around.

"Mina, Lorret, do not lag behind. Stay close to the rest of us."

We reached the hills by early afternoon and hiked up halfway, a distance that Kindor deemed would keep us safe when the high tide rolled in but conceal us from any Lostai patrol on the other side. Montor and Kindor hiked to the top of the hill and confirmed the military camp was located a mile away. They also saw some soldiers patrolling the area. When they returned, Montor reproduced a sheer material the same color as the vegetation. He strung it across the trees to create a canopy for cover. After the long walk, we welcomed a chance to sit and rest.

"Kindor, it would be preferable if we did not have to put up a force field. Do you think we are in danger of any wild animals?" asked Montor.

"No, there are only birds and small reptiles in the area. We should be fine."

Montor ordered the Arandan soldiers to take turns keeping

watch. He suggested those of us with Sotkari Ta abilities get rest or meditate. We needed our abilities to be at top strength.

Montor took my hand and led me to a separate covered area he set up just for us two. He sat with his back leaning against a tree trunk and pulled me down with him.

"You look so tired, Mina. Did you get any rest last night?"

"Honestly, I did not sleep at all."

"Come here, sweetness. Lie down and get comfortable. Place your head on my lap."

There would be nothing to do for the several hours till nightfall, and it wouldn't serve me well to be exhausted when we attempted our rescue. I did as he said.

"Close your eyes and relax, Mina. If you listen carefully, you can hear the waves."

I looked across from me where the others sat. Josh was watching us. I tried to read his expression, but Montor began to massage my scalp. My eyelids became heavier and heavier until I drifted off.

Night had fallen by the time I opened my eyes. I turned my head up to face Montor.

"Good that you are awake, sweetness. It is time to make our move."

"I hope you were able to nap a bit too," I said.

"I did. Let us go and round up the others."

With everyone awake and ready to go, Montor used his vaporizing rifle to disintegrate the canopy. He was intent on not leaving any evidence of our stay there.

We climbed to the hilltop, and I studied the military camp layout. A solitary one-story building stood in the center. All the better for us. Several buildings or multiple floors would have complicated things even more. At least ten shuttles and three mid-sized interstellar-grade spacecraft were parked on the east side of the campus.

"I am surprised at the minimal number of spacecraft,"

Montor said, stroking his chin, "considering these smaller crafts are the only means of transport in and out of here for the Lostai."

He was referring to the fact that the Lostai could not use large spaceships to access the small territory of planet Sotkar they still controlled. Those large spacecraft could neither land directly in that area nor dock on Sotkar's space station that was now under United Rebel Front control.

Our plan was to use the *hanstorics* to transport ourselves inside the Lostai military building. We had experience transporting up to five people at a time, so the thirteen of us would divide into three groups, each group huddling together around the person operating the *hanstoric.* Anyone within a certain circumference from the *hanstoric* would be transported. As the most experienced with the device, I operated the one in our group. Kristom and Komar operated the other two.

"Everyone ready?" I asked.

They all nodded. I set up the target location, said a quick prayer, and touched the display.

9

Traveling via the transportal didn't hurt but was a jarring experience, like being forcefully awakened from anesthesia. I had traveled through the transportal many times before but never quite got over that initial jolt. For some reason, traveling across short distances caused an even more intense sensation. Once I got over the few seconds of disorientation, an adrenaline rush took control, my pulse speeding up and my senses becoming hyper aware of my surroundings.

Considering we didn't know exactly where in the building we would "land," we were lucky. We ended up in one of the prisoner cell blocks, the most logical place to start searching for Amber. To our surprise, the area appeared empty, with no Lostai soldiers in sight.

Perhaps this block is vacant.

The second we arrived, Montor switched to military mode, his facial expression focused and emotionless. Scanning the area, we identified five corridors leading to other sections of the building.

Montor assigned one Arandan to guard each entrance, and

the rest of us split up to check every single prison cell. Rooms with locked doors lined the wall across from the cells. My Sotkari Ta telepathy allowed me to sense all living creatures in the immediate area as lights in my mind, even those not in plain sight. I could also tell whether those lights corresponded to people with enhanced abilities or not. The lights of Sotkari Ta people appeared brighter and farther away in my mind compared to lesser evolved beings. All the Sotkari Ta in our group performed similar telepathic scans to confirm there were no living beings in the rooms.

"OK, there is nothing here. Let us move to the next cell block—"

I grabbed Montor's arm and met his eyes.

"Montor, I need to be sure."

"OK, sweetness."

He approached each room and vaporized the doors with his rifle so we could check inside for anyone, dead or alive. The rooms included an infirmary, a laboratory, several offices, and a conference room. We found no one.

Montor gestured to the first hallway to the right. We followed him down the corridor, which led to a similar prison cell block. This one was empty as well. We returned and sped down the second corridor. When we faced the same situation, my heart sank.

Oh no! What if we aren't in the right place?

As we made our way down the third corridor, we sensed life forms and heard hushed voices. Montor gestured for those of us with Sotkari Ta abilities to come up front. We focused on all the dim lights in our minds, excluding Lorret, Josh and the Arandan soldiers, and used our telepathy to render them unconscious. I counted fifteen of these dim lights in my mind. We did not sense any Sotkari Ta individuals in the immediate area other than ourselves.

Montor and Kindor entered the area first and then gestured

for us to follow. This block was a dormitory area. We found five soldiers unconscious on the floor. These were surely some of the dim-lighted minds we had sensed and rendered unconscious. Montor vaporized each door, and we found the other ten Lostai also passed out on the floor or in their beds. We carried each of them back to the prison cell block and locked them up. All other rooms were vacant.

"Clearly, this military camp is not at full capacity," observed Montor. "That probably explains why there are so few space-crafts outside."

An uneasy feeling crept from my stomach to my chest. Focused on the task at hand, I hadn't made eye contact with Josh until now. He looked at me. We shared the same anxiety.

When we walked down the fourth corridor, I sensed a lot more lights in my mind and louder conversation. A few were farther away and bright, alerting us that we would be facing Sotkari Ta Lostai sympathizers this time. This section was another dormitory block. We tried to use the same strategy as before, rendering some of the Lostai unconscious.

"We do not have enough mental capacity to manipulate all their minds and deal with the Sotkari Ta helping them. Get ready to use your weapons," Montor instructed. "Our goal is to strike them all down before they have a chance to call for help or notify Lostai command that we are here."

Of course, the minute the Lostai saw several of their fellow soldiers pass out, they knew something was up. Included among the soldiers were about six Sotkari Ta. They were our biggest threat, so we jumped into position and fired on them first. One got away and bolted down the remaining corridor.

While half of our team confronted the remaining Lostai soldiers, the rest of us needed to check the dormitories before reinforcements arrived. We raced to the doors, vaporizing them and checking inside, finding only Lostai soldiers. By now, things were hectic. No time for finesse. We killed them on the spot. I rushed to Montor, my voice frantic.

"Montor, where are the prisoners? We keep finding only Lostai soldiers."

"Calm down, Mina. There are areas we have not checked yet."

After rendering unconscious or killing all the remaining Lostai soldiers in that section, we moved to the last corridor that led to the Operations Center. A squadron of Lostai soldiers armed to the teeth welcomed us.

I used my telekinetic abilities to disarm many of them, but it was a daunting task, as we were so outnumbered. The buzzing and burning sounds of weapon fire filled the room. I rolled across the floor and crouched behind desks to take cover. Amid the noise and flashes of light, I heard someone cry out. One of the Arandans had been wounded. Lorret and Noomar pulled him out of the line of fire, and Lorret began first aid.

"We cannot sustain this. I need to find the Lostai commanders, so we can interrogate them," said Montor telepathically. "Kindor and Mina, follow me."

As the rest of our team continued to engage the Lostai soldiers, Kindor and I slinked behind Montor, making our way farther into the Operations Center. Montor scanned the room and spotted two Lostai wearing commanders' uniforms. He gestured for us to follow him.

"Kindor, you take one, and I take the other. We need to find out where the prisoners are and specifically ask about Mina's daughter. Mina, cover us."

The Lostai commanding officers realized we were coming for them and made a run for it. Montor was quicker and got each one with a minor flesh shot to the leg. He and Kindor grabbed them and pulled them aside, I assumed using mind control, to get information from them.

I turned my attention to the oncoming soldiers. As they

approached, something weird clicked in my brain. Every Lostai soldier reminded me of Zorla. A murderous rage took over.

This is what I've been training for.

It wasn't enough anymore for me to render them unconscious and move on. I wanted each and every one of them dead. Closing my eyes, I disarmed those closest to me and shot them point-blank. When they went down, I moved towards those behind them, *vimor* in one hand and the vaporizing rifle in the other. Although efficient, I couldn't get them all. Dozens of soldiers surrounded me. I put my weapons away, took a deep breath to summon my mental power and hurled a bunch of them across the room. Having spent a lot of mental power on telekinesis already, I went on a reckless hand-to-hand combat rampage to deal with those remaining. Damari and one of the Arandans were forced to come to my aid. Between the three of us, we covered Montor and Kindor and gave them enough time for their interrogation.

I had just broken the arms of a couple of Lostai soldiers when I heard Montor's voice in my mind.

"We are leaving. There are no prisoners here. They have transported them to another location. Everyone, get in groups and use your *hanstorics* to transport outside where the spacecrafts are stationed. We will meet you there. Make sure no one is left behind."

I froze. The air was sucked out of me.

Did someone punch me?

No, yet I found it harder and harder to breathe.

Kristom and Komar confirmed telepathically that all our team members were accounted for. I was in charge of the *hanstoric* that would transport Kindor, Montor, Damari, one Arandan and myself.

We can't leave. We haven't looked hard enough. We can't leave.

"Mina, you transport everyone except me. I will use mine to

bring these Lostai commanders with us. I have a plan," said Montor.

The thought that we were leaving without Amber was too much for me.

"I will not...I...I...am not going anywhere without my daughter."

My voice sounded shrill and incoherent.

"Mina, we must leave now!"

I ignored the urgency in Montor's voice and the sound of more Lostai soldiers storming the room.

"Kindor, here. You take care of these guys. Mina is out of control."

Montor grabbed me by the shoulders. I stepped away from him.

"Let go of me! You leave if you want. I am staying here and searching for my daughter."

"Mina, she is not here. We must go. Now."

He gestured to Damari and the Arandan that they should get closer as he pulled a *hanstoric* out of his bag. Instead of following suit and huddling up with the rest of them, I bolted without even thinking about where I was going.

"Mina!"

Montor's voice sounded angry now. He ran after me.

"I said, let me go, you idiot. Since she is not your daughter, you do not care, and..."

I opened my eyes and found myself in a strange bed and cabin.

Footsteps.

Montor walked in and got into bed. I rubbed my forehead.

"What happened? Last thing I remember, we were inside the Lostai Operations Center."

"You were out of control. I made you lose consciousness."

"What!"

"You were putting our lives at risk," he said, annoyed. "I had no choice."

Confusion and regret boiled up inside of me. The last thing I would have wanted was to risk the lives of our crew members. I pressed my lips into a hard line to avoid becoming a blubbering mess.

I waited until the tremor cleared from my voice before asking, "So, what is this place? Where are we?"

"We are on one of the Lostai spaceships."

"What? How is that possible?"

"I mind-manipulated the Lostai commanders into giving me the access codes to this craft."

All the pain and anguish I had survived since the Lostai abducted me bombarded my brain. Knowing that Amber was in Zorla's clutches with slim chances of a rescue plunged me to a new, unimaginable low. My soul went dark.

After a long pause, I said, "Montor, I am so heartbroken. I do not even care if I live or die at this point."

Montor bolted up to a sitting position, his eyes widened.

"Mina, do not say that! What about Josher?"

Another long period of silence.

"You are right, of course. What am I saying?" I buried my face in my hands. "But I assure you, Montor, I will never smile again. A piece of me has died here."

"Mina, listen to me. I have a plan. We are not giving up."

"What do you mean?" I said without much enthusiasm.

"The Lostai commanders told me Zorla became suspicious when the Sotkari easily squashed the Lostai border invasion. He ordered Amber and the other prisoners to be transported to the Lostai home world. They do not know the exact location but are confident it must be in the remote region of the planet known as Morzaki."

I was glad to hear that the Sotkari closed the border shield back down without losing any territory to the Lostai, but despite Montor's words, finding Amber seemed even more hopeless.

"Oh no. If she is on Losta, we will never be able to rescue her."

"Listen to me. Losta is a densely populated planet. The Lostai government cannot afford for the public to learn of the military's nefarious activities. Morzaki is the one region where they could get away with hiding a bunch of prisoners no one is supposed to know about. That is where we are heading."

Incredulous at what I had just heard, I turned to look at him.

What have I done? Has trying to please me caused Montor to lose perspective?

"Montor, by now Zorla might suspect we were coming to rescue Amber. He might be baiting us...bringing us onto his turf. He will be waiting for us."

"I know you think I am an idiot who does not care about your daughter's fate, but you are wrong."

He sounds resentful. Did I call him an idiot?

"Montor, I am so sorry if I said anything offensive to you. The idea that Zorla is treating my daughter the way he treated me is driving me insane."

I couldn't stop my lips from trembling until I lost it and started to cry.

"No, Mina. Do not cry."

"I do not want to keep falling apart in front of you, but you are right. I have lost control."

Oh yeah. Now I remember. I did call him an idiot.

He leaned over and stroked my hair as he spoke.

"I understand, Mina, that what has happened with your daughter is devastating for you. You are right. Zorla might be expecting us to make a move on Losta, but things will not be so easy for him. First of all, I sent off all the shuttles and the two other spacecrafts that were parked by the military camp on autopilot to Losta using different flight plans. Kindor helped to change the scanning system so that Lostai sensors cannot detect that there is no one on those crafts. They will have to figure out if we are on those ships or whether they are filled with Lostai soldiers escaping our attack."

He paused, considering his next words.

"Secondly, we used this ship's photon beams to destroy the Lostai military camp. Unless they sent transmissions before we left, there are no survivors to give Lostai military headquarters any information about what happened. Well, except the commanders I am holding here under my influence. That also will gain us some time."

I propped my head up on my hand to look him in the eyes.

"What, Mina? Was I too cold-hearted?"

Instead of being scandalized, his determination filled me with renewed energy.

Shit, they got what they deserved.

"No. I am actually feeling more hopeful. Maybe we still have a chance."

He tilted his head and gave me a curious look. I was not the same woman he first met four years earlier as a Lostai hostage.

"Yes, I think we do. It is definitely not an easy mission, but I have not given up."

"What do the others think of this plan? We are taking them into enemy territory. I feel guilty about pulling them into such a dangerous situation."

"Mina, I explained to them the plan and offered each one of them the option of returning to Sotkar. Given the risks involved, I said I would not think less of them for it. They all remained committed. Plus, now it is not only about your daughter. The Lostai commanders confessed there were other young prisoners on that base—Arandan, Namson, Sotkari, Tormixian children."

I returned my head to the pillow, staring at the ceiling, digesting the implications of what Montor was explaining. He lay back down next to me.

"This brings me to my third point. Up until now, the focus for the United Rebel Front has been to liberate planets invaded by the Lostai and rescue prisoners. We did not want to give credence to Lostai military propaganda that we are a menace to their society. Now that we have evidence of children and young adults being held captive on the Lostai home world, an attack on their planet would be justified. The United Rebel Front is convening an emergency meeting to decide whether to begin strikes on Losta. The Lostai military will have their hands full dealing with that threat. Hopefully, all of this will give us a chance to land in the Morzaki region undetected and search for that military base."

My mind went into overdrive, thinking through everything Montor had explained.

"Montor, if Zorla sees the United Rebel Front threatening the Lostai home world, he could just transfer the prisoners somewhere else to avoid the confrontation."

Montor shook his head, his lips pursed.

"I do not think so. I know how Zorla's mind works. He is really not so patriotic and more concerned with his own personal agenda. Getting back to what you first said, at this point, it is likely he is baiting us. He is angry I stopped working with him and that we upset his pet project of breeding Sotkari Ta children. He wants to make us squirm and bow down to him. What better way to manipulate us than to use your daughter as leverage? That is what the Lostai military does best."

I stretched my neck to ease the painful tension. No amount of optimism could erase the fact that we were about to embark on an even more dangerous mission than before. Leaning against Montor's bare chest, I listened to his steady heartbeat.

"Montor, I wish I could be like you. As much as I try to be strong and fearless, I am afraid. What if Zorla captures us and we cannot rescue Amber? That might even put Josher at risk."

"Mina, do you think I am not worried about all of this? Of course I am, but I use those feelings as fuel to prepare as best as possible."

"Yes, I know. I will continue to work out as hard as possible while we travel to Losta."

He kissed the top of my head gently.

"Mina, I must say I am very proud of you. After all the hard practice you put in since we left Dit Lar, your abilities have grown exponentially. I could not believe my eyes when I saw how you hurled so many Lostai soldiers across the room at one time. Your telekinetic abilities are impressive. I am not exaggerating when I say they now rival mine. Your fighting skills are on point, and you are in the best physical shape ever. We can do this."

I wrapped my arms around him and kissed his chest.

"Thank you, Montor. I love you."

"I love you more."

His words calmed me. Closing my eyes, I allowed my body to relax and dozed off.

10

Before we got out of bed the next morning, the first words out of my mouth were, "Is it safe to contact Foxor and Lasarta? I would like to talk to Josher."

"Yes, we can have encrypted communication. As an extra precaution, I would like to keep it to a minimum."

Using the viewer in our room, we contacted Foxor and Lasarta. After salutations and assuring them we were OK, Montor explained what we were planning to do.

"This sounds like a perilous endeavor, but I would do it for my child, too," said Foxor.

"I will continue to pray for the success of your mission," stated Lasarta.

Their solidarity filled my soul with gratitude.

"Thank you. It means a lot to me that you support the quest to rescue my daughter."

Foxor frowned and crossed his arms over his chest.

"Mina, we are family. She is part of our clan."

I didn't say thank you again because I sensed I was offending them. Instead, I asked for Josher, and Lasarta went to get him.

"*Ro Ma! Ta Ri!* Look, *Lo Ro* made my favorite tiny pies today!"

Thrusting his little fists towards the screen, he opened them to show us the miniature tarts he held in each hand. They were tiny enough to fit in his palms. Montor chuckled.

"How many of those have you eaten already, Son?"

"Not so many." Josher tried to look as innocent as possible. Then, almost with the wisdom of an adult, he diverted attention away from himself. "Are you on your way home?"

"No, *honey,* not yet," I answered. "Tell me, how was your day today?"

With that, Josher launched into a detailed recounting of everything he did, starting from what he ate for breakfast, lunch and dinner to the games he played, the lessons he practiced and a visit to the park with Foxor. I savored each word he said and recorded his angelic smile in my memory. When it was time to say goodbye, I wished I could reach through the screen and touch his cheek. Hiding my anxiety, I blew him a kiss instead.

We signed off, changed into our flight suits, and headed to the dining area for breakfast.

"You have been silent since our call with Josher," observed Montor.

After a deep breath, I admitted, "Yes, I cannot shake off all these emotions. I feel depressed and angry and worried—" I looked up from my food. He met my eyes. "Montor, I want to speak with the Lostai commanders."

A deep line creased between Montor's brows.

"For what possible reason?"

"I want to understand their thoughts about the terrible things they do."

"What difference does it make?"

"I do not know. I just want to talk to them."

Montor rolled his eyes.

"I suppose I will have to accompany you in case you lose control again."

"No, I want to go alone."

"Mina, I need to keep them alive to use them as a diversion if we are confronted by a Lostai ship."

"You think I am going to kill them? That is ridiculous."

"Well, back at the base, you were pretty vicious, even by my standards."

I ignored his remark and walked away, shouting over my shoulder.

"I just want to talk to them. I do not need to be supervised."

I heard Montor grumble what sounded like a curse word, but he didn't stop me.

Like any typical Lostai military spaceship, this one was equipped with prisoner holding cells. The walk over there gave me time to think about what I wanted to say. The two Lostai commanders were finishing up a meal when I arrived. Although the cells were secured by a force field, Montor ordered one of the Arandan soldiers to stand guard over them.

"Please leave us alone," I instructed.

The Arandan knew by now not to question my requests. The two Lostai looked at me with disdain.

"What are your names?"

No answer.

"I suggest you pay attention to me, or I can make things very difficult for you. I can use my abilities to force you to answer me, but I prefer to have a normal conversation with you."

They fidgeted in their seats and made me wait a few more minutes before the younger of the two replied, "My name is Roxar and his is Temdax."

"Thank you. So, Roxar and Temdax, I am curious. Do you have family, spouses, children, relatives?"

Roxar answered for both of them.

"I have two siblings. My parents are dead. Temdax has a spouse and three offspring."

"How would you feel if an alien race invaded your planet and enslaved your family members?"

Silence.

"It is not a rhetorical question. This is exactly what you Lostai are doing. Do you feel no remorse?" Their blank faces angered me. "Tell me!"

"We are following orders. Our leaders have explained to us that tough decisions are required for the greater good of Losta and the rest of the sector."

I thought I could stay calm and collected.

"You make me sick! Your leaders are evil people."

I turned to walk away.

"My parents were soldiers. They died fighting this stupid war."

I turned around. His eyes were filled with bitterness.

To my surprise, Temdax, the older one, spoke up.

"Listen here. We are taught that it is our duty to help primitive races improve themselves. This makes sense to me. Our leaders are not evil. They only require fifteen revolutions of service. After that, we are offered opportunities to pursue whatever other goals we have for ourselves and our families. It seems a fair request, and we are doing our part to better the world around us. Your rebellion's only accomplishment has been to sentence both of our children to live in war. You are the evil ones here."

"No. You are totally brainwashed."

Whatever I had hoped to accomplish with this conversation was clearly lost. Not only the rescue of my daughter, but the battle for freedom would be a bloody one. Both sides were convinced they were in the right.

❆

The United Rebel Front determined they would coordinate their attack on Losta with our approach to help us have a better chance of landing safely and undetected. The twenty days of travel to Losta could not have gone by fast enough. All of us were on edge. We focused our energy on planning and preparing for our mission. I barely spoke to anyone other than Montor during that time, as I continued my strict physical and mental workout routines. Montor allowed us one evening of relaxation a few days prior to reaching Losta. He hosted a Captain's party in the lounge where everyone indulged in drinks, music, and informal conversation.

Montor was joking with the Arandan soldiers, Kristom, Komar and Damari when Josh approached me as I was making myself a cocktail.

"What are you drinking?"

His strength and health appeared much improved since being rescued from the Lostai labor camp, and he was recovering muscle definition in his pecs, biceps, and legs.

"It's something the Arandans call *stampu*. They take it in shots, like tequila, but I mix it with a fruit juice because it's very strong."

"I'll have a shot."

I knew he'd say that.

"To kicking some Lostai ass," Josh said as we clinked our glasses, a gesture foreign to the Arandans and Sotkari. Of course, it happened just when Montor glanced our way. His brow furrowed, and I heard his voice in my mind.

"What is that, sweetness...what you did with your glasses?"

"Umm, it's like raising a toast."

He walked over to us. The Arandans, Kristom, Komar, and Damari followed him. Kindor and Lorret, tucked in a corner of the room, swayed to the music. When Kindor noticed the group converging around Josh and me, his voice entered separately in my mind.

"Is everything OK, Mina?"

Unbelievable, but he still behaved as if he were my guardian.

"Yes. No problem."

He took Lorret by the hand and led her over to us anyway.

Once everyone was around, Montor said out loud, "What were you toasting to?"

"Kick butt Lostai," answered Josh in broken Lostai.

Everyone waited for Montor's reaction. He chuckled, grabbed the bottle, and served shots to everyone. When everyone had theirs, he raised his glass.

"To kicking filthy Lostai butt."

"Yes!" everyone shouted as they fist-pumped and drank their shots in one gulp. He served another and asked me to guide us in the glass clinking. We were all joking and conversing as part of one group with a pleasant buzz by the time Montor called it a night.

As we walked to our room, I commented to him, "I liked how you behaved this evening with Kindor and Joshua."

"Ahh, Mina." He twirled one of my loose curls around his fingers, a thoughtful expression on his face. "As a captain about to lead my crew into a dangerous situation..." He tilted his head to look down into my eyes. "I need to push my personal feelings aside and seize those team-building moments."

I was already turned on when we tumbled into bed, pulling at each other's clothing.

11

When we were one day away from Losta, the United Rebel Front began bombarding major Lostai cities. Some of the spacecrafts Montor had launched from the military station on Sotkar also arrived at the Lostai space border. We observed on our scanners how, one by one, they were destroyed by Lostai security patrol ships. This was to be expected. Being on autopilot, they were not even making the required security stop, serving their purpose by keeping border patrol busy.

By the time we made our approach to Losta, the area around the planet had become a battle zone, lit up with photon blasts and littered with debris. Montor manipulated the minds of the Lostai prisoners and brought them to the bridge. Under Montor's influence, Temdax, the older one, contacted Losta border security. Montor and the rest of us stood in a corner outside of the viewer range, *hanstorics* in hand in case things went downhill. Our plan was to avoid depleting the *hanstorics* until the time came to rescue Amber and other hostages, but if we were not allowed to land, we'd have to use them.

"We have escaped the attack on Losarex and request permission to land," said Temdax.

"Yes, we have been informed of that attack. Several of the ships that were stationed there have arrived at our borders on autopilot with no passengers and shields that obstruct our scans. This has caused a lot of confusion here. Who did this?"

"The leader of the group that attacked us."

"And you two were the only survivors?"

"No, there are others coming via alternate flight plans."

Montor snickered under his breath as he thought about how border patrol would be kept busy with the other ships on the way.

"How did the attackers escape your base? Were they not impossibly outnumbered?"

"They used transportal devices."

"Lieutenant Temdax, did any of the attackers appear to have Sotkari Ta abilities? There have been cases where our officers have been victims of mind control."

"Yes sir, we believe so, but they did not come anywhere near Roxar or me."

"Hmmm, stay in posi—" The video was interrupted. "Umm, Temdax, we would have preferred to board your craft and do a physical inspection, but we are under heavy attack and cannot afford to divert any of our officers. Since we cannot inspect your ship, you are not allowed anywhere near our populated areas. Our docking stations are also compromised. You will need to land in the Morzaki region and call for ground transport. We also expect a full report of what happened at Losarex once you are picked up."

Montor fist pumped in silence. This was going even better than we had expected. We were being asked to land exactly on target.

"Yes, sir."

Once the communication was cut, Montor instructed Temdax and Roxar be returned to the cells.

"Everyone, prepare for landing and next steps."

We all dispersed except the Arandan in charge of navigation. Our intention was to use one of the vehicles in the shuttle bay as transportation once we landed, but we needed to be prepared for any eventuality. I suited up in combat gear and grabbed my backpack.

Our Arandan pilot expertly dodged debris and crossfire, landing without any issue. Before we boarded the land shuttle, Montor moved the prisoners back to the bridge, strapped them into their seats, and put them into a deep coma.

"They will wake up two days from now with temporary memory loss of what happened. That will keep them and the authorities off our trail for a while."

We departed the ship in the land shuttle and took a moment to take in our surroundings. Gray snow and ice covered the ground and hills. Only patches of brown grass and moss interrupted the frozen landscape. Winds howled outside, and I was grateful the shuttle shielded us from the harsh elements with space to carry supplies.

Montor turned off all digital navigation devices on the shuttle to lower the chance of being detected, but it meant we were navigating blindly. As in Losarex, we put our tablets in ghost mode.

"Before putting those pieces of crap to sleep, they revealed to me where they believe the Lostai are holding the children. However, an old-fashioned compass, map, and long-range ocular device are all we have to guide us."

Stiff after twelve hours of travel, we got out of the vehicle to stretch our legs. Montor scoped out the area as best he could. The wind was getting worse, and gray snow fell from the sky in clumps.

"We are still a few days away from our target, and the

weather is degrading. Nightfall will be upon us in about three hours." He pointed to his right toward a mountainous area. "I think we might find caves in those mountains that can serve as shelter."

Night fell by the time we reached the mountains. As Montor expected, there were some cavernous areas where we could spend the night. Montor and Kindor ventured into the largest cavern and walked deep into its main tunnel to be sure there were no wild animals or other types of danger. Once they signaled everything was clear, we rushed in, eager to get some reprieve from the cold.

"I think it might be risky setting up a force field. Technology might trigger sensors. We will need to establish a watch rotation."

"I will take the first watch," volunteered Komar. "You have been navigating the whole time, Montor."

"Next, me." Josh followed, with others subsequently calling out their turns.

Overnight temperatures would drop well below freezing. We had loaded the shuttle with sleeping bags made of a special material that would keep us warm. Montor and I utilized one that accommodated both of us. Kindor and Lorret did the same. Everyone else used individual ones. We gathered stones to create a small pit in the center of the cave and added heating crystals. These crystals lit up and provided heat and glowing illumination without emitting any smoke. Montor led me to the deepest part of the cave where he set up our sleeping bag. We removed our utility belts and combat gear but kept our flight suits on. Inside the sleeping bag, Montor snuggled up to me and slid his hand from my waist to my butt. Caressing me, his voice lowered to a purr.

"Mina, I like this."

"Montor, get some rest. We should not start what we cannot finish."

He flashed his signature sly smile.

"Who says we cannot finish?"

He tapped the collar area of my suit. It inflated in what was already a tight space and slit open from neck to crotch. Slipping his hand under the material, his fingers found their way between my legs, expertly rubbing me just how I liked it.

Well, if you put it that way.

There was something about our bodies being confined in that tight space, the howling wind, the crackling light from the crystals, and the musty smell of the cave that made me forget for a moment the sad reason we were there. I reciprocated by tapping his collar and giggled at the thought that the ballooning effect might cause us to roll across the cave floor, right smack in the middle where the others were sleeping. Luckily, both suits were now loose, baggy material. He covered my mouth with his other hand to muffle my laughter. I tugged his hand away.

"Wait, Montor. Did you bring the birth control vial with you?"

"Yes, it is in my bag."

I reached out and grabbed his bag, groping inside till I found the vial. With some maneuvering, we pulled our arms out of our suits and rolled the material to just below our pelvic areas. Hot desire took care of the rest.

"Oh, Montor," I whispered as he pushed into me.

"Shhh."

He covered my mouth again. The limited space forced our bodies to connect in a slow, satisfying grind. I couldn't stop myself from biting down hard on the palm of his hand as my body climaxed. Our addictive Sotkari Ta connection made it almost painful when it was time for him to pull out, but soon we relaxed into a peaceful slumber.

❄

The next two days were uneventful. We traveled in the shuttle until just before nightfall, keeping close to the mountain range, so we could shelter in the caves at night. The third day, photon blasts awakened us. We piled into the shuttle and sped off. Although traveling at maximum speed, the blasts got closer and closer. Montor's expression grew graver with each explosion.

"I fear they may have locked onto the shuttle somehow. By now, it is probable the Lostai prisoners we left on the ship have regained consciousness and contacted local military forces. Grab your backpacks and combat gear and get out! We will need to continue on foot and temporarily change our direction."

We rushed out and headed perpendicular to our previous trajectory. In the time it took us to cover a mile, a blast made a direct hit on the shuttle. We looked at each other, shared a collective gasp, and ran even faster. The blasts continued but no longer seemed to be gaining on us. We escaped the attack but at the cost of completely deviating from our target and losing our transportation and most of our supplies.

Trudging through blizzard conditions and massive drifts of snow was no walk in the park, but no one complained, adrenaline fueling our pace. We maintained a zig-zag pattern, to not stray too far from the mountain range, with brief stops every few hours to drink a warm nutritional beverage produced using the portable replicator.

As nightfall approached, Noomar asked, "Sir, should we head back to the caves?"

Montor eyed the mountain range, deep in thought. "No. We will spend the night out here."

"But I thought you kept us close to that area with the idea of sheltering there again."

"You heard me. I have changed my mind. They would expect us to head back there, considering the harsh overnight conditions. We will walk for three more hours away from the mountains. Then use your *vimors* and vaporizing rifles to dig out a trench. Not too large and make it a fast process. I do not want to do anything conspicuous. We will set the crystals on a heat only setting, no illumination."

We barely looked at each other as we digested the idea of walking for three more hours in the bitter cold. Once Montor indicated it was time to stop, the Arandans dug out a trench only large enough for the thirteen of us to sit side by side in a row. Montor replicated a tarp that matched the gray snow and stretched it over our heads across the upper limit of the trench. It served as camouflage and to protect us from the elements. Montor and I sat on one end, Lorret and Kindor on the other, with the rest of the crew in between.

Montor cleared his throat before instructing us to try to get some sleep. Barely able to see each other's faces, we mumbled goodnights to each other as the crystals crackled in the dark, emitting heat. Montor pulled me close and announced he would take the first watch. Everyone shifted and stretched, trying to get as comfortable as one could while sitting in what felt like a frozen tomb.

I rested my cheek against Montor's chest and exhaustion was about to take over when a flash of light lit up the sky. An explosion followed. Montor jerked up to a standing position and pulled back the tarp so we could observe what was happening. Photon blasts rained on the mountainous area. We had traveled far enough from the caves to avoid danger but could still feel the tremors.

"Should we leave, Montor?" asked Komar.

"I think we are safe here." The deepness of Montor's voice and the slight increase in the rise and fall of his chest were the only signal of how heavy each decision he made for us weighed on his soul.

There was no resting that night. I closed my eyes, but my

heart jumped with each blast, which continued until the early morning hours. At sunrise, the Arandan soldiers were the first to get up, assuming we would have an early start. Montor had other ideas.

"Stretch your legs if you like, but now that the attack has quieted down, we should take a nap. It is not wise to try to make our way through these conditions without proper rest."

We established the next watch rotation and finally got some sleep.

12

We woke up in a puddle of gray slush. The temperature skyrocketed during the morning hours. No wonder this area was so inhospitable. We broke off into pairs for bio breaks, taking turns holding up the tarp to create some privacy. Damari, being the kind soul he was, immediately offered to go with Josh. While we snacked on nutritional bars, Montor studied his compass and manual map and surveyed the area.

"We have a two-day hike before we get to where I believe they are holding the prisoners. We should take advantage of the warmer weather to cover as much ground as possible. Tonight's temperature will be well below the freezing point again."

I was amazed at his sense of direction.

Or is he faking it to give us a sense of security?

All I saw ahead of me was a vast gray tundra. Snow-covered hilly areas were the only variation in the landscape. Before starting off on our trek, Kindor, Montor, Damari, Kristom, Komar, and I separated from the rest of the group to do our Sotkari Ta workouts and meditation. This was like religion for

Montor, Kindor, and the other Sotkari Ta. Damari and I followed suit. While I practiced levitating different sized snowballs and stones, I couldn't help but feel I was being watched. Josh seemed hypnotized as I went through my routine. We returned to the group, and without fanfare, Montor pointed out the direction where we were headed and took the lead position. Kindor took the rearguard. After a few minutes into our walk, Josh caught up with me.

"Hey," I said to him, while shooting a furtive glance Montor's way.

Things had been very copacetic since we left Sotkar on this mission, but I was still wary of how easily Montor's jealousy could be triggered.

"I've been watching you every time you do your practice. It's pretty amazing. I also saw what you did to those Lostai soldiers back at that military camp."

So, he's been observing me as I go through my Sotkari Ta workout.

"Yeah, it used to weird me out, but I embrace that part of me now."

"I wonder if someone has already trained Amber how to do that, too."

"She might not have that ability." The rest of my words came with a shudder. "Honestly, I try not to imagine her in that situation at all. It was all so scary for me at first...and then what I went through. I just can't."

I stopped in my tracks, burying my face in my hands.

"I'm sorry, Mina." He quickly changed the subject. "I wonder who you got it from."

Montor turned around to check on me. I picked up my pace again. That question had never occurred to me. I pondered for a minute.

"It must have been my mother."

"Really? Why—"

Without warning, a blast knocked me ten feet away. Beams of light dug craters and fissures around us. I thanked God for my protective face mask as it was pelted with shards of hard ice.

Montor shouted, "Disperse!"

In situations like these, he was of the thought that huddling together would likely get us all killed in one shot. Better to separate with the hope some would evade the attack and could come back later to help those who might be injured. Adrenaline fueled me to run as fast as I could. Heavy perspiration kicked in despite the cold temperatures. There was no sign of anyone around me when I stopped to catch my breath. I looked around to establish whether there was some sort of direction or pattern to the attack coming from the sky. The beams were creating fissures in an X formation to the right of me about a mile apart from each other. I stopped and waited. Sure enough, the beams continued in the same direction. Of course, I ran the opposite way. There were other types of bombardments that created craters. Those were not coming as frequently and were further apart from each other. I started moving again, maintaining a steady jog for two hours while thanking myself all the way for the rigorous work-out routine that had well prepared me for such a trek.

Thirst forced me to stop and grab a pod from my backpack. I popped it in my mouth and sucked on it slowly while surveying the surrounding area. Wind picked up and blew snow everywhere. The visibility was less than twelve feet. I called out to the others and searched my mind for any telepathic connections.

Nothing.

Then a rumble.

The blasts had triggered some avalanches in the nearby hills. The ground shook. I kept moving, using my *vimor* to leave a trail. The narrow beam melted the snow and left a mark on the ground. I realized new snow might cover the trail, but maybe I'd be lucky and the precipitation would hold off for a while. Night fell two hours later, and temperatures plummeted. I dug a trench with my *vimor* and activated some crystals for heat. Covering myself with a small weatherproof blanket, I took stock of my supplies: six thirst pods, four nutritional bars, two *hanstorics*, a healing pad, some toiletries, a change of clothes, and a force field generator.

So, what are my options?

I could not set up the force field generator or the tablet for fear it could make me visible to any scanners the Lostai might use to sweep the area. The *hanstorics* were a mode of escape. Montor had instructed that anyone who became separated from the team and in danger should return to Fronidia, the one planet in the sector that for sure would not be involved in any battles. I was too stubborn to even entertain the idea. I would not leave this planet without my daughter.

Didn't Montor say we were a mere two days away from where they might be holding Amber? I could be so close. Can't turn back now. There might not be another chance.

Dehydration and the frigid overnight temperatures posed the main hurdles for survival. I counted enough thirst pods and heating crystals for three days. Not sure whether swallowing the gray Lostai snow would make me sick, I resolved not to try it unless it became necessary. The potential of being buried alive by an avalanche was real. There was not much I could control there other than prayer. I slept in spurts of a couple of hours at a time. At daybreak, I was walking again.

The landscape remained unchanged. My view comprised snow-covered slopes and drifts. The temperatures did not warm up that day, and the icy wind cut through my guts. I no longer heard or saw any evidence of bombardments from the sky. Every so often, I used my ocular device to search for something other than dreary gray. During one of those scans, something came into view. Two hills appeared to be separated by an area of flattened snow, as if worn down by some type of transit. My heart skipped a beat.

Maybe the Lostai military base I'm looking for is behind the hills.

No sooner than the thought had formed, my legs sprinted as if they had a mind of their own. The closer I got, the clearer it was to me that the ground had suffered traffic of some sort. My heart exploded with anticipation as I approached what appeared to be a snow-covered road. I slowed my pace to examine the surrounding area. Other than the road, there was nothing different.

I'll just follow the road. It must lead somewhere.

What the heck!

In my next step, the ground gave way. I fell about fifty feet into a pit and landed with a thud. I would have died had it not been for some foamy material softening my landing. Still, pain ripped through my leg.

Damn, I probably have fractured my ankle.

It was the same ankle I injured years before. My breath came in gasps as I tried to compose myself. A creaky noise followed by footsteps alerted me that I was not alone.

Darkness turned to light. My stomach tightened as I faced a large group of Lostai. The only thing that stopped me from immediately using my telekinetic ability to hurl them away from me was their appearance. They were not dressed in military uniform and, other than illumination rods, were unarmed.

And then the other thing. Lights popped into my brain.

My God. Some of these Lostai are Sotkari Ta.

One of them stepped forward, his arm outstretched invitingly. I blocked my mind. He spoke out loud in Lostai, but with a distinct, unfamiliar accent.

"We do not intend to hurt you. We should probably have our doctor examine you for injuries."

Neither he nor any of the others bothered to block their minds. Either they were unconcerned about me taking control of their actions or were untrained. Long past having any moral qualms about using every tactic at my disposal when it came to Lostai, I promptly read his mind.

To my amazement, he was being sincere.

"I believe my ankle is broken."

"It is probable with that kind of drop. We are sorry about that, but it is a security measure against intruders. We are in hiding."

"Hiding? From who?"

"I am not authorized to answer your questions, but I will get you the medical help you need."

"Umm, have any other travelers come by here? I was with a group before the bombardments separated us," I asked while still accessing his mind.

"No one else has come by here."

Again, he was being truthful, but even though he masked any emotion, I sensed his consternation.

With that, he gestured to the two Lostai closest to him. They left and returned after a few minutes with a stretcher, gently placing me on it and taking me through a labyrinth of dark, underground tunnels. There was some ventilation because I could feel cool air. We reached a large chamber lit up with crystals and furnished with a few cots and the most basic of medical supplies, reminding me of nineteenth-century Earth's history. The Lostai who greeted me there was also Sotkari Ta and introduced himself as "the healer." I wasted no time letting him know he could find in my backpack the tools needed to take care of the injury.

"I have a healing pad in my bag. If you help me, I can use it to diagnose whether there is a fracture and repair it."

"No. That type of technology is scannable by certain sensors and is not allowed to be activated here. I seem to have a gift for sensing fractures, so let me touch the area."

He removed my footwear and, using a razor, slit open the

leg of my suit. My ankle had puffed to twice its normal size. The minute his hands touched my skin, I sensed his Sotkari Ta energy, but he clearly was untrained and guided only by instinct.

"Help me sit up and reach over," I said. "I can check on my own."

"Are you also a healer?"

"No, but let us be honest here. I know you are Sotkari Ta, as am I. We can use our abilities for healing purposes."

My words left him flabbergasted.

"Sotkari Ta? What abilities are you referring to?"

Is he trying to mislead me?

I inspected his mind.

He has no idea what he is.

"Umm, just help me."

He sat me up and observed wide-eyed as I examined the area of inflammation.

"Yes, definitely it is fractured, but luckily the bone did not break through the skin."

He was still confused but composed himself.

"OK. No problem. I can align the bones and bandage it up. You will probably not walk on it for about one lunar cycle, but then it should be fine," he said with a smile.

I deflated his presumed medical wisdom.

"That is unacceptable. I am on a rescue mission and must be on my way as soon as possible. I cannot do it on my own, but together we can use our powers to heal it in a matter of hours."

"I still do not know what you are referring to."

This won't be a matter of hours. I'll need to train him.

13

The healer's name was Sharox. I allowed him to wrap my ankle for the time being. I couldn't help but notice the gentleness in his touch.

"I will let you keep your supply bag, but if you try to activate any of the devices, we will be forced to destroy everything you carry in it. Can I trust you with this?"

His voice carried the even monotone sound I had come to equate with Lostai creepiness, but even with the warning, his expression displayed none of the ruthlessness or arrogance I had observed in Zorla and other Lostai military.

He looks almost kind-hearted.

"Yes, OK. Now, can you make me a promise? You cannot understand now, but your healing instincts are no coincidence. You have certain abilities you have not tapped into. I can show you how to harness them. I need you to spend several hours with me during the next few days so I can train you how to speed up my recovery."

"I must admit, I am very curious about this. How would you know what I am capable of? I must consult with my superior on the matter, who most likely will need to check with Madam

Premier Taraxi. In the meantime, I will bring you nutrition and water."

Madam Premier Taraxi? Well, that's a mouthful. Must be a powerful leader.

He brought me a bowl of broth. The pasty, bland chunks that swam in the lukewarm liquid were a mystery to me, but hunger forced me to eat. After I ate, he sat me in a sort of wheelchair and pushed me down another tunnel to a small chamber with a shallow crater in the center. A large vat filled with icy chunks of gray snow sat at the edge of the pit. Buckets, heating crystals, washcloths, and towels were piled against the opposite wall. A shelf carved at an angle circled the inside of the crater for reclined seating.

"You will be with us for a while, so you might as well wash up, get out of all that combat gear, and slip into something more comfortable. You will need none of that here."

I was wary of leaving myself so vulnerable in the middle of a camp full of Lostai, but the idea of a warm bath appealed to me. Sharox helped me out of the wheelchair and on to the sitting shelf. A much younger female Lostai arrived. She eyed me with shy curiosity as Sharox introduced her.

"This is Mexar, my assistant. She will help you."

Once Sharox left, I unbuckled my utility belt, took off my gloves and other gear, and tapped the collar of my suit. It inflated, and I extricated my arms and pulled the now baggy material down over my torso. Mexar helped me pull out my legs, making a point of averting her eyes to avoid seeing my nakedness. After setting my suit aside, she filled a bucket with snow and dumped it in the pit, repeating this several times. As I began to shiver, she added a crystal and handed me a wash-cloth. The snow melted, and I submerged myself up to my waist in the warm liquid.

"The crystals provide both heat and a cleaning and disin-fecting agent," explained Mexar. "I'll leave to give you some privacy, but try to hurry. The liquid eventually drains into the ground."

She returned after a few minutes with a warm, loose-fitting, one-piece garment similar to what she and the others wore. I had a change of clothes in my bag, but the cloth was so soft against my skin that I accepted it.

As she wheeled me back to the infirmary, I asked, "Have you lived here for a long time?"

"Umm, I am not authorized to give you any information."

These Lostai were pale with protruding eyes. Whether she answered me or not, I concluded they had been living underground for quite some time. Before returning me to the infirmary, Mexar asked if I needed a bio break and took me to another small chamber. The room consisted of a narrow but deep pit for squatting over with more washcloths piled on the side. I held on to Mexar's shoulders to steady myself—an embarrassing moment for both of us—and put my weight on my uninjured ankle. When I was done, she grabbed some crystals that were also piled nearby and dropped them into the pit. The crystals ignited once they hit the bottom, and I suppose they eliminated the waste and any odors.

At the infirmary, she set me up in a cot that was only a bit more comfortable than the stretcher they had brought me in on. She extinguished the illuminating crystals and laid down on another cot.

"Get some rest. Sharox will be back soon."

I knew rest was important for healing, but I couldn't help but worry about Montor, Josh, and the rest of the crew. Were they OK?

God, please watch over them.

The pain woke me up. Sharox was mixing something in a bowl. Without turning to look at me, he said, "You are in discomfort. I am preparing something to help with that."

"How did you know?"

How did he even notice I was awake?

"You were moaning and restless."

He walked over.

"Here, eat this. Make sure to swallow it all."

Why is everything the Lostai ingest so pasty?

Thankfully, the thick orange paste didn't smell bad. It had a mild, minty taste, a flavor I had never come across in the food available at the Lostai science station where I was once held hostage.

"What is this for?"

"Inflammation and pain."

"Thank you. Have you inquired with your superiors regarding what I mentioned to you?"

"Yes. I am still awaiting their reply."

After swallowing the last of the medicine, I tried to prod him.

"I can tell you are passionate about your role as a healer. It is a shame you have so little medical equipment to work with."

"I make do. We are a resourceful people."

Who are they anyway...these Lostai Sotkari Ta?

"Are you not even the least bit curious about what I mentioned to you? You have the potential to do extraordinary things. Let me show you."

He stepped away, alarmed.

"Stop. I do not have permission."

Determined to get out of there as soon as possible, I focused my mental energy and accessed his mind to make him do what I wanted. There was a time when I thought this was the most immoral thing to do to a person. Those days were long gone.

Plus, he's just a lowlife Lostai, right?

I would do whatever was necessary to get back to finding my daughter.

It required an extreme amount of mental effort, but I was able to both manipulate his mind and perform telekinesis, levitating the empty medicine bowl. He was baffled.

"How are you doing that?"

I brought the bowl back down on the table beside me.

"Come, get closer to me."

Under my influence, he followed my instructions. I grabbed his hand. His energy was potent. The shock of our connection made him pull his hand away. I grabbed it again.

"Close your eyes. Calm your nerves. I want you to think of nothing other than the bowl on the table. Picture it in your mind. The size and weight of it. The texture of its surface."

He took a deep breath.

"OK, now imagine lifting the bowl without touching it."

We remained still, holding hands, for at least fifteen minutes. I thought I felt an energy surge, but then he yanked his hand out of mine. Our connection broke.

"I said, I am not allowed to do this!" he shouted, his face contorted in outrage and confusion.

Damn!

I wasn't strong or experienced enough yet to manipulate someone's mind for more than that time.

Maybe I'm going about this all wrong.

I remembered I had sensed no ill will from Sharox when I scanned his mind.

"OK. Listen to me. It is time I confide in you." It was a risk, but one I felt was necessary. "The Lostai military is holding my daughter captive. I cannot wait around here for a lunar cycle. Who knows what they are doing to her? Do you have family? Children? Siblings?"

His jaw dropped.

He swallowed hard before asking, "Did you say, Lostai military?"

"Yes, of course. What did you think I was doing in this forsaken place?"

His speech slowed down.

"Are you saying Lostai military is here, in Morzaki? Are those the bombardments we heard?"

"Wait, did you not know that somewhere in this region there is a Lostai military camp? Have you never seen or heard of them?"

Now, I worried that, once again, we had come looking for Amber in the wrong place, although it was possible that two isolated groups in this area might never run into each other. This remote, frigid region of Losta covered a land mass about the size of Siberia. Sharox didn't reply and ran out of the chamber. A few minutes later, Mexar returned.

"Sharox said something important has come to his attention and asked that I stay with you until he gets back. It is late. You should be sleeping by now."

I had no choice but to try to rest. The pain waned, but now my worries kept me awake.

14

W hen I woke up the next morning, I noticed right away that Sharox was back and my backpack was missing. I didn't have to ask for it.

"Madam Premier Taraxi wants to examine the contents of your bag herself."

My stomach churned at the thought of a Lostai leader going through my things. If she broke the encryption on my tablet, she could access confidential information.

"I do not like the fact that she has taken my belongings."

I'm sure he could hear the annoyance in my tone.

"It is only a precaution," he replied.

"I would like to speak to her as soon as possible," I insisted.

"You will, soon enough. She wants to meet you, too. In the meantime, she has authorized your teaching me about these healing abilities you spoke of. You have caused quite a commotion. It is the first time I ever have spoken to her in person."

A million questions ran through my head, but I felt Sharox wouldn't answer any of them. I'd leave those for the Madam Premier...whatever.

"OK. For this to work, you need to commit at least a half

hour a day to meditation and half hour a day to practice. Ideally, it should be even more time than that."

I'd forego having him do the physical workout routine that Sotkari Ta usually also performed daily. That wasn't critical for what I needed him to execute.

"Meditation?"

"Yes, find a quiet place where you will not be disturbed. Repeat this thought in your mind: I have been given total control of myself and my surroundings."

"That sounds a bit presumptuous."

"Trust me. That is also how I felt when I was first trained, but think about this: Your people are here, in this winter wasteland, being resourceful, as you mentioned, surviving in an environment where hardly any living creature can thrive. Imagine what you can accomplish once you unleash your full potential. This meditation builds faith in the extraordinary abilities that are within your grasp. Believing in yourself is the most important element in this process. The next most important thing is to truly desire to learn to use your abilities. What do you want the most in your life right now?"

He paused to think.

"We have lost people to injuries and illnesses I wish I could have repaired. I want to become a better healer."

"Depending on the effort you put in, you will be able to use your mental abilities to correct injuries and illness that normally would require medicines or instruments. Bring me a small object and lay it on the table."

He brought a medical instrument.

I held both his hands in mine. Our energy connection startled him just like the day before.

"You know, I feel a kind of shock when our hands touch. I have noticed that I feel something similar with some of our people, but not with everyone."

"Yes, not all of you are Sotkari Ta. Close your eyes. Focus on what I mentioned to you."

His hands trembled.

"Do not be afraid."

"OK."

"Think about the instrument on the table. Its size and shape. How much it weighs. You can move it without touching it. Do not reach out to grab it, but imagine you are doing so."

After a half hour, he lost his focus, and I decided to stop. I remembered it took me several hours a day for several days before I could execute mind-matter control.

"Do not be frustrated. This takes time."

"When should we try again?"

"Whenever you want. The more time we spend trying, the quicker you will get it."

"How long did it take you?"

"Several days, but I had many other responsibilities at the time, plus the stress of being held hostage. You are in a much better place mentally than I was."

"Held hostage?"

"Yes, by the Lostai military, but that is a long story. Maybe I will share it with you later."

His eyes lowered, and the worry evident in his expression convinced me that he was no more of a fan of Lostai military than I was.

Well, that's good.

He composed himself and said, "You are my only patient today. Let us continue. I do have a question, however. How will levitating objects help me heal your ankle?"

"It is the same concept. You can use your mind to set the bones in position and aid cell division, blood flow, and bone growth. You have the advantage of already being familiar with anatomy and how the body regenerates. Take off the bandages and place your hands there. Think about how things look inside my body. Think about how they appear at a cellular level."

He did as I instructed. We talked about the medical process of how a bone heals.

"We need to get back to meditation and learning how to levitate. You need to master that mind-over-matter control before you can perform any healing."

Time crawled because neither he nor I were willing to share too much information other than the matter at hand. He left mid-day and in the evening to prepare and bring us food. There was not much variety to their diet, but nutrition was an important part of healing.

I suppose there's not much you can harvest in the underground tunnels of a tundra.

I scarfed down everything he brought me without asking what it was. Better not to know.

Sharox also asked Mexar to accompany me to bio breaks and another bath. There was nothing to signal whether or not it was night. My tablet hadn't been returned, so I didn't have a way to tell time. I followed his lead when he called it a day and helped me back to my cot.

The next day went on the same. We practiced, but no progress. As he wheeled me back to the cot, I heard people shouting outside of the infirmary. They burst into the chamber in a rush. Sharox took a protective stance in front of me.

Damn, now I feel guilty for violating his mind.

"Mina!"

I heard both Montor's and Josh's voices at the same time.

"Get away from her," Montor's voice thundered while he used his telekinetic abilities to propel Sharox across the room.

"Wait. These people have not harmed me," I shouted too late.

Sharox crashed hard against the wall before slumping to the ground.

Montor rushed to me. We hugged each other. I tilted my head to see Josh still standing at the entrance staring at us, his body stiff.

Stepping back, Montor looked me over.

"Mina, are you OK?"

"Yes, yes, except I have a fractured ankle."

"OK. No problem, I have my healing pad. Did you lose your backpack?"

Without waiting for a reply, he pulled the device out of his bag.

"No, stop. We cannot. These people are hiding from the Lostai military and do not use any form of technology for fear of being detected. Is Kindor here?"

Montor's face scrunched up, trying to digest what I was telling him.

"Umm, yes. He is outside covering us."

"Get him. He should be able to fix it."

Once Montor was out of the room, Josh took advantage to approach me.

"I'm so glad we found you. We feared the worst."

Emotions got the best of me. My arms reached up. He leaned over, and I hugged him.

"Mina." Josh's voice cracked. He said nothing else.

I gave him a gentle push away before anyone could see us.

A few seconds later, Montor walked back in with Kindor and Lorret.

"It is good to see you are OK," Lorret said.

Kindor was next to me in another second.

"Montor tells me you are injured. Let me see."

It dawned on me that they were acting like we had free rein of the place. A sudden churning upset my stomach.

"Montor, you did not kill anyone, did you?"

He still wore the confused expression.

"Umm, I do not think so. We mostly knocked them out. I cannot believe some are Sotkari Ta, but they did not defend themselves. What do you care, though? They are Lostai."

I lay on the bed, and Kindor wasted no time removing the bandage. We all remained silent as he closed his eyes with both hands around my ankle. The last time Kindor's hands touched my skin, we were making love. That was a year ago, when I was suffering memory loss. Since Josher's *Bendorai*, I had avoided any interaction with Kindor. Even during our recent time together, I kept my distance.

Montor's jaw clenched. He must have been thinking about the same thing. Shuffling sounds distracted me from these thoughts. I turned to see Sharox getting to his feet.

"Sharox, come here," I said. "I am sorry for what happened, but these are my friends. I want you to see what Kindor is doing. He is repairing my ankle fracture."

He walked over, giving Montor a side glance before approaching me. Montor's eyes narrowed as Sharox got even closer.

"Place your hands on my leg, too. I want you to feel this."

Sharox did as I asked.

Everyone became quiet again. Kindor's energy radiated from my knee to my toes. I closed my eyes and focused on the injured area as well, attempting to help him if I could.

Sooner than I expected, I heard Kindor's voice in my mind.

"It is done."

I stood without a second thought. It was as if I had never been injured.

"Amazing," said Sharox, his eyes wider than usual.

The sound of something rolling across the floor caught my attention. It bumped into one of the table legs and fractured like a delicate ornament, releasing a foggy mist. Everything went black after that.

15

I opened my eyes to see Montor, Kindor, Josh, and Lorret still unconscious on the floor. Sharox helped me up. He held a bunch of leaves in one hand. Lined up by the entrance were ten Lostai with more delicate ornament-looking balls in each of their hands.

"I woke you up first so you can help me stabilize this situation. You need to tell your friends to stand down from attacking us again." Sharox gestured towards the ten Lostai. "Otherwise, we will need to use a more potent toxic gas."

"Yes, I will."

"Let us begin with the big troublemaker first," he said, pointing to Montor.

He got on his knees and rubbed a few of the leaves between his hands right above Montor's face. A strong ammonia-like odor made me cover my nose. Montor sat up with a start.

"Montor, whatever you are thinking, do not do it," I said in a rush. "I do not think these people are our enemies."

Montor pursed his lips but nodded while getting to his feet.

As Sharox roused Kindor, Josh, and Lorret, Montor asked

me telepathically, "Mina, what can you tell me about these people?"

"Well, as you noticed, some are Sotkari Ta, but they do not appear to be aware of their abilities and have not been trained."

"Do you know how they became Sotkari Ta?"

"No one has shared much information with me at all, but I do sense from Sharox that they are in hiding and dislike the Lostai military."

"Do they have any idea where the Lostai military camp might be?"

"No. At least Sharox did not appear to even have knowledge that Lostai military might be in the area. That bit of news actually caused quite a commotion, I hear."

"I would not trust any Lostai. Maybe this is some kind of trick."

"I probed a lot of their minds when they first found me and did not sense any treachery."

"Hmm, where is your backpack?"

"Sharox told me that their leader wanted to examine it."

"Some *hanstorics* were lost. I am not leaving without yours. We need as many of them with us as possible."

Montor turned to Sharox to speak out loud.

"I hear you have Mina's belongings. Return them, and we will be on our way." He looked up and exhaled forcefully. "I am sorry for any inconvenience we caused."

Montor wasn't good at apologizing. He didn't do it often, except maybe with his foster parents and me. Sharox squirmed a bit before jutting out his chin. He parroted his next words as if they were memorized lines.

"Madam Premier Taraxi is unhappy about what you call an 'inconvenience.' We have made a point of keeping our existence here a secret. You have intruded and injured some of our citizens. She would like an audience with you before you leave."

Montor glared at the ten Lostai.

"Do these guys think they are intimidating me with those stupid balls? It would take me one second to stop their hearts from beating," Montor said to me, telepathically.

"Montor, we should talk to this Taraxi person. Some good could come of it, and we could get back the *hanstorics* without killing anyone. It is true that we are intruders. They could have left me to die in that pit I fell into."

He let out another deep breath as he replied to Sharox.

"OK, take us to the Madam."

"Madam Premier Taraxi," corrected Sharox.

Montor's voice deepened, and his diction slowed.

"Yes, take us to Madam Premier Taraxi. Now!"

Sharox cleared his throat.

"OK, follow me."

He led us through a long, winding tunnel I had not seen before. While we walked, I asked Montor about the rest of the team. Kindor, Lorret, and Josh followed in silence.

"We lost two of the Arandans. We left the others waiting outside the pit."

"Oh no." Two people had already given their lives to help me rescue Amber. I covered my face with my hand and sobbed in grief for their loss. "Montor, I feel horrible."

"Mina, they were soldiers. This was a mission to them, like any other. They agreed knowing the risks."

"Yes, but still." I wiped my tears and sniffles. "How did the rest of you find each other?"

"The first blast separated you from the rest of us and killed the two Arandans. After a few hours, Josh and I found Damari and the three other Arandans in a crater. They were carving shelves into the ice with their *vimors* to climb out. The next day, we ran into Kindor, Lorret, Kristom, and Komar. You cannot imagine how we all felt when you were missing."

"How did you find me?"

"The trail you left. That was smart, except if Lostai military had come across it before we did."

After about a fifteen-minute walk, the tunnel widened to a chamber the size of a football field with a twenty-foot ceiling. I couldn't believe how large it was and wondered how deep below the surface we were or whether we had reached a humongous cave. Around the circumference of the chamber were compartments sectioned off by rocks. I counted twelve of them.

"Those are homes. This is the first of our three residential chambers," explained Sharox. "We have told everyone to remain inside for the time being."

I got the distinct feeling we were being watched as we made our way across the chamber and exited into another narrow tunnel. We had walked for an entire hour, having crossed two other similar residential sections before we arrived at an area with much larger compartments. He led us into the largest one.

"These are our government offices."

The "government office" consisted only of several tables and chairs, all fashioned of stone. He invited us to sit. Montor refused.

"I will remain standing, thank you."

I rolled my eyes at Montor, but we followed his lead. None of us sat.

Minutes later, a short, elderly Lostai female was led to the front of the room and helped into a chair by an assistant. Her opaline eyes were milky color swirls with no irises or pupils. More importantly, her Sotkari Ta light immediately popped into my mind. I sensed as she blocked hers. Montor's eyes narrowed. Of course, he was thinking the same as me.

Oh shit. This one has been trained!

Kindor, Montor, and I looked at each other and immediately blocked our minds as well. Josh and Lorret could only guess from the looks on our faces that something was up.

"Hello. I am Mina. Your doctor has been taking good care of me. I hope you are feeling well," I said, hoping to strike a positive note.

"I am blind, not sick," she snapped. "Let us get down to business. What are you doing in Morzaki?"

She left us speechless. That lasted only a couple of seconds for Montor.

"That is none of your business. Return Mina's belongings, and we will be on our way."

"First of all, it is my business. I am responsible for this community. You have disturbed our peace and possibly have led our enemies here. Secondly, it seems the contents of Mina's bag are important to you. I suggest you show some respect if you want them back. I gave it to my assistant with instructions that she give it to a third person without telling me who she gave it to. That person handed it over to another unknown person. This has continued until the final person hid it. You will have to go through quite a few of us to find it."

"Montor, let me handle this," I said in Arandan to keep Taraxi from understanding.

"I do not trust her or these people," he replied. "She knows more than what she is letting on."

"With more reason, we should tread carefully."

His jaw clenched, but he gestured with his hand that I should take over the conversation.

"Madam Premier Taraxi, forgive my husband. He is upset because time is of the essence for our mission."

"So, this person is your husband," she said with a huff.

"Umm, yes. To answer your question, we are here to rescue my daughter. Lostai military has kidnapped her. We believe they are holding her and several other children captive somewhere in this region."

She folded her hands tightly. The slow rise and fall of her

chest signaled I had touched a nerve. Her tone became less bellicose.

"I am sorry about your daughter. We have lived in this area in hiding for three generations and have never seen any Lostai military activity in this area. This is the first time we have had bombardments or any kind of disturbance nearby. Was that Lostai military pursuing you?"

"I am not sure, but most probably. This is a vast region. They do not want to be found either, so that might be why you have never run into each other."

"You said there are other children being held, too. Why would Lostai military be interested in children?"

The tremor in her voice made me feel like she was afraid of the answer.

"Madam Premier Taraxi, it is a long story—"

"You may address me as Taraxi and please sit."

She signaled to her assistant.

"Bring us refreshments."

I could tell Montor was about to make another snarky remark. I shot him a stern look.

"Thank you, Taraxi. Yes, refreshments would be nice."

Montor groaned as we all sat.

"So, Mina, in what direction will you be heading when you leave us? Do you have any idea where you are going?"

I turned to Montor, hoping he had the answer. Before he replied, he communicated to me in Arandan again.

"Mina, I am uncomfortable about giving so much information regarding our plans. I still am not convinced this is not some kind of trap."

"I told you I scanned many of their minds."

"Well, this one knows how to block hers."

"Do you know where you are going or not?" insisted Taraxi.

A low growl escaped Montor's throat before he answered.

"I believe the site we are looking for is due northwest from here."

"And you are traveling by foot?"

Montor's lips tightened into a fine line.

"Yes. The Lostai military tracked and destroyed our shuttle."

She steepled her hands and closed her eyes for a minute before replying.

"We have explored the immediate region extensively. I can tell you that there is nothing within one week's walk in that direction."

"I am confident that is the right direction. Perhaps it is farther than a week's hike."

"If you think the weather has been harsh until now, things are going to get worse. No heating crystal will save you from hypothermia. My guess is that you might survive three days more, probably less. The seasonal changes here are extremely consistent. In the last day or so, the temperatures have declined."

I thought about the two Arandans that we had already lost and turned to Montor.

"The rest of our team could be in danger!"

She cocked an eyebrow.

"If you left friends outside, I assure you, they ARE in danger."

Montor jumped to his feet and approached Taraxi. Her assistant obstructed his path.

"OK, Taraxi, you apparently have something on your mind besides informing us about the weather. Speak up."

"Are you always this perceptive?" she said. "Yes, I have a proposal for you."

"Wait," I shouted. "If our friends are in danger, we should take a break and go find them."

Taraxi pursed her lips as she considered my request.

"I will allow it. Go look for your friends, but Mina remains here with me. I will have our guards show your husband an easy way out."

Lorret also stayed with Taraxi and me while Sharox and Taraxi's assistant accompanied Kindor, Josh, and Montor out of the chamber. After a while, she returned.

"They are on their way with our guards, Madam Premier."

"If they hurry, maybe your friends can be saved."

I bit my lip and glanced at Lorret, who shot Taraxi a hateful look. She whispered to me in Arandan.

"Being in the midst of all these Lostai makes me want to vomit." She had also suffered much at the hands of the Lostai military.

I fidgeted the whole time we waited, nervous energy getting the better of me. To distract myself, I tried to make conversation.

"Taraxi, I am amazed how your people have survived here all these years being so isolated. Where do you get your supplies from? You did not even allow Sharox to use my healing pad."

"Well, I was not familiar with the technology and could not risk it somehow making us visible to Lostai sensors. It has been difficult, but we have managed. When my ancestors first arrived here, we were able to salvage a few reproduction devices. The first order of business was to reproduce old-fashioned mechanical machinery and replacement parts needed to manufacture supplies and textiles. You did not get to see it, but we have a miniature factory in one of our larger chambers. We are creating most of our necessities as people did a thousand years ago."

"Amazing. What energy do you use to run the machinery?"

"We brought solar energy cells with us. When the weather warms up, we take the energy cells outside to recharge. We were also lucky to find crystals occurring naturally in the caves and reproduced a mechanical device that changed their molecular makeup to convert them into heating crystals. Later, we learned how to grow and harvest them."

Even Lorret became interested in this survival story.

"Do the reproduction devices still work after all these years?" she asked.

"Some did break down. The remaining ones we use only in extreme circumstances, so they have kept well."

Even with the interesting information Taraxi was sharing, three hours felt like three days. My heart jumped when Montor, Josh, and Kindor returned. I rushed over to them the second they entered the chamber.

"Did you find them?"

"Yes."

"Are they OK?"

"The old Lostai was right. The weather is much worse than before. We found them unconscious, but Kindor stabilized their vitals. Sharox is taking care of them now. Mina, I think if we had arrived even an hour later..." His voice lowered. "They would not have made it."

<h1 style="text-align:center">16</h1>

We all sat again. Taraxi's assistant left for refreshments and brought back a pitcher filled with a thick slimy concoction and served it to us in small stone bowls. The only thing refreshing about the beverage was the temperature. The weird taste lingered on the back of my palate. Montor jokingly told me in Arandan that I'd have a price to pay for making him drink the stuff. At least the serving and tasting of the drink helped diffuse some of the tension. I retook the baton of the conversation.

"Taraxi, returning to our earlier discussion, what would you like to propose to us?"

"These tunnels extend far beyond the area we currently are occupying. There are many branches, some of which we have explored, others we have not bothered with. I propose to grant you permission to travel underground towards your destination. You will be protected from the harsh weather. I can assign some guides to help you. There are underground springs you can use for water, and we can show you which fungi, rodents, and insects are edible."

Ugh! So that's what I've been eating!

This was not a simple act of kindness. Her body language radiated focus and resolution, her fingers jabbing the air as she gesticulated for emphasis.

"That is very accommodating of you. What would you ask in return for this favor?"

Taraxi settled back into her chair.

"Are those children Sotkari Ta?"

My jaw dropped.

"So, you do know about that!"

I side-glanced at Montor, who smirked. Our minds were still all blocked, so we couldn't communicate telepathically, but he had "I told you so" written all over his face.

"Yes," I continued and returned my attention back to Taraxi. "The Lostai military has taken those children because they are either original Sotkari Ta or have embedded Sotkari Ta genes. Their goal is to harness their powers and induct them into the Lostai army. My daughter has been taken to lure me here because I was also once their hostage and escaped from them."

"That is unfortunate," she said, a grim tone in her voice.

The time had come to ask the Madam Premier some questions.

"Taraxi, I know some of your people here are Sotkari Ta. We can sense their light in our minds. It would appear from my conversations with Sharox that they are unaware of what that means. You, however, seem to have been trained. How is this possible? I thought the Lostai did not have the bioengineering technology to embed those genes in their people."

"I suppose they do not. Otherwise, why would they still be kidnapping Sotkari Ta people?"

"Exactly. So, how is it that you are Sotkari Ta?"

She bowed her head.

"As you said earlier, it is a long story, but let us drink some more, and I will explain."

We pretended to sip our drinks as she narrated her people's history.

"An ancestor of mine was the head of a small group of Lostai dissidents that did not agree with the imperialistic turn our government had taken. They were persecuted for their beliefs and fled Losta. About one hundred Lostai dissidents in all boarded a spaceship with the idea of saying farewell to their home world forever. We settled on a planet at the edge of the galaxy populated by a people who were far behind us in technology. The planet, with its humid, tropical climate, was quite out of our comfort zone. We felt confident the Lostai government would never think to look for us there. The natives were an amphibious people, different from any race we had encountered in the sector. They called themselves and their planet, Namson."

"I am familiar with that planet. I spent some time there leading guerillas in liberating their villages from the Lostai," said Montor.

"Their lack of technology allowed us to live there undetected until my ancestor revealed himself to the leader of a nearby village, and they became friends. For several generations, everything was fine until some of our people born there began to exhibit unusual behavior, claiming to feel strange shocks of energy when they touched each other, seeing lights in their minds, and, the most troubling of all, sexual attraction."

Montor found this amusing and couldn't stop himself from chuckling.

"I fail to see the humor in this," said Taraxi, quite annoyed at his reaction. "Lostai mate once each revolution for reproductive purposes only. These Lostai were having sexual relations much more frequently and for pleasure."

Montor laughed even louder, until I reached over and pinched him.

"Sorry, Taraxi, for my husband's childish behavior. Please continue."

Montor rolled his eyes but composed himself.

"My ancestor's Namson friend said something similar was happening in their population. My grandfather was one of those 'special' Lostai children. We dismissed these behaviors as some type of mutation, and life on the Namson planet continued normally. That is, until the Lostai military arrived at the Namson planet two generations later."

Every muscle tightened in my body. I had met the Namson, too. They were a good people. The Lostai had murdered, kidnapped, and enslaved them.

"I was three revolutions old at the time. First, they took several Namson children and young adults. My grandfather learned from our Namson neighbors that Lostai military only took the 'special' ones. They slaughtered any Namson who resisted or tried to fight back. Then, they came for us."

Taraxi covered her mouth with both hands. Montor's eyes grew angry. Kindor looked away, and I couldn't stop trying to swallow the lump in my throat. A shared sadness enveloped all of us.

"I also was one of the 'special' children and they took me, too. Even though I was so young, I still remember my terror. Being blind made it all the more horrifying. The poor Namson had no way to rescue their people, but we still possessed the spaceship on which our ancestors had arrived. Yes, it was old technology, but it still worked. My grandfather and father put together a crew and took off in pursuit of the Lostai military ship. The Lostai military captain tricked my grandfather's crew and convinced them to dock and board the Lostai military ship. They would have ended up as prisoners had it not been for what my grandfather described as a gray-faced alien with blue hair."

We all turned to look at Kindor.

It must have been a Sotkari!

"The Lostai had tasked this alien with training the hostages to harness supposed dormant powers. The gray-faced alien turned against his Lostai employers. He caused the captain and his lieutenants to lose consciousness, like your husband did to my people here. With his help, my grandfather's crew threw them out of the airlock, killed the other Lostai soldiers, and returned to the Namson planet."

Montor couldn't help fist pumping at this part of the story.

"My grandfather and this gray-skinned alien became friends."

I interrupted her.

"We have here with us one of these gray-skinned aliens. His name is Kindor."

She nodded to acknowledge him and continued.

"The alien's name was Korem. He said his people were known as Sotkari Ta and explained that the Lostai had invaded his world and hunted them down. Some Sotkari Ta scientists from his planet who were exiled from their home world were afraid their species was on the way to extinction. They found a way to embed their genes into the embryos of unsuspecting pregnant females on other planets that were in earlier stages of civilization."

A long exhale escaped me.

"Yes, my husband and I are a product of this seeding as well."

"Well, they probably had not imagined there were pregnant Lostai on the Namson planet and accidentally did the same to them. They never would have done that intentionally. The last thing the Sotkari Ta scientists would have wanted was to embed their genes in Lostai hosts. The Lostai were their enemies."

Kindor shifted in his seat. I'm sure the idea of Lostai with the powers of a Sotkari Ta disturbed him.

"Korem trained my grandfather in the Sotkari Ta rituals and showed him how to use telepathy and telekinesis. My father did not have these abilities and did not want any part of it. I was my grandfather's only grandchild, and we were very close, especially since we were both 'special.' He spoke to me about the meditation and exercises he had learned for improving these abilities, and I asked him to teach me. Later, my grandfather learned from a nomad Namson tribe that the Lostai military had returned to another region of the planet. Korem explained to our elders that the Lostai military possessed scanners that detected the brainwaves of the 'special' people in our community. He advised them it would not be long before they returned to take our children again."

By this time, my head was pressed in my hands as I relived my own victimization at the hands of Lostai military. Montor rubbed my back to soothe me.

"The elders decided we could not remain on the Namson planet any longer. My grandfather was a historian. He knew of an ancient Lostai civilization that had once taken refuge in the Morzaki region by creating a series of underground tunnels and villages. We returned to Losta, simulated a crash landing in this area, taking what we could and setting the spaceship to auto-destruct. The harsh winter and constant blizzards soon covered any evidence on the surface of our arrival. We found the tunnels and settled here. Many died along the way, but with hard work, this became our new home."

I understood from her fascinating story why she might be motivated to help us. Lostai military was their enemy as much as they were ours, but there were still doubts to clarify.

"That is an amazing survival story worthy of admiration, but I am curious why people like Sharox do not know about their dormant Sotkari Ta abilities."

"Yes, I imagined you would be curious about this," acknowledged Taraxi. "Although my grandfather was grateful to Korem and curious to learn about Sotkari Ta, the rest of the elders and my father were not. They resented the Sotkari Ta scientists who had embedded their genes into the embryos of expectant Lostai mothers without their consent. Those genes put a target on our heads. It was a curse that they wanted to forget about."

Montor and I locked eyes. We could understand that sentiment. Yet without those embedded genes, we would have never met. I shook off the thought and returned my attention to Taraxi.

"They let my grandfather indulge in his curiosity but forbade him to share those teachings with anyone else. The fact that he taught me was our little secret, but I honored the wishes of my ancestors. I am grooming my assistant, Lanext, to take over my responsibilities when I die or am no longer capable. I have shared the story with her, but she does not have these genes."

Kindor used sign language to communicate with me.

"Tell her that the Sotkari Ta genes will continue to be passed down from generation to generation within this community."

I relayed the information to Taraxi.

"Yes, I have noticed that, but I am the last of those who were not born here. Those born in these caves no longer even call themselves Lostai. They are Jomoloxti, which comes from the Lostai words meaning, the hidden. The new generations of Jomoloxti will know nothing of that part of our history and ignore those quirks."

Kindor's brow furrowed.

I'm sure he doesn't like to hear his abilities being characterized as quirks.

"But they will still be at the mercy of the Lostai military. Is it fair that they be unaware of that danger?" I said.

"Is any of this fair?"

True.

"So why did you allow me to teach Sharox how to harness his healing powers?"

"It was a dilemma, but I decided it was in our best interests."

"Which brings me to my last question. What do you want in return for your help?"

"Yes, right." She straightened her body and returned to her no-nonsense tone. "I suppose once you find the children, your plan is to take them off this planet, correct?"

"Yes, of course."

We didn't know how many children the Lostai were holding and whether there were more than what could be transported via *hanstoric*. Once we secured control of the site, Montor intended to contact the United Rebel Front to come in for a rescue and transport if necessary.

"I want our entire community to be transported off this planet and taken to a place where we can be assured safe haven."

I met Montor's eyes. She was requesting a monumental task.

"Umm, Taraxi, how many people are we talking about?"

"Seventy-seven in total."

Montor stood, shaking his head.

"Listen, Taraxi, I understand you are trying to protect your people, but we cannot even guarantee the rescue of all the children we might find there. How could we commit to transporting your entire community? Our own lives are at risk. I guess you are not aware, but there is a full-scale war in this sector between Losta and a group of rebel planets. We call ourselves the United Rebel Front."

"I am not naive. The truth is, even if you gave me your word, I would still be at the mercy of your sense of honor. I realize you could forget your promise. But know this. If you try your best to save us, you will have our allegiance forever. I might even reconsider my position and agree to have some of my Sotkari Ta people trained. We could infiltrate key Lostai installations."

Montor's eyes widened. I could almost hear the gears of his mind working. We exchanged looks once again.

Could we trust that she'd betray her own people?

Taraxi signaled to her assistant and whispered in her ear. Lanext helped Taraxi up and guided her to where I was sitting. She took Taraxi's hand and placed it on my forearm. Taraxi squeezed. I reciprocated, grabbing her forearm in the traditional Sotkari Ta salutation. A sensation of bonding coursed through me. This type of thing could not be faked.

"I must admit, Taraxi, a group of trained Lostai Sotkari Ta committed to our cause could be an asset like no other."

That was the first time I saw Taraxi smile.

17

I asked Taraxi if we could adjourn the meeting to check on our friends in the infirmary and to discuss her proposal amongst our team. She agreed and arranged for us to be escorted back to the infirmary. All six of our friends were still unconscious when we arrived but had been changed into warm clothing and covered in blankets.

"Will they be OK?" I asked.

"I believe so. It can take a full rotation for the body to rewarm," replied Sharox. "Nothing else we can do other than monitor their vitals."

Montor, Kindor, and I unblocked our minds so we could communicate telepathically.

"I will stay here with Sharox to monitor them," said Kindor. "I am sure you need some time to consider Taraxi's proposal."

"I sensed sincerity in her energy," I said. "What are your initial thoughts on the topic?"

Kindor didn't hesitate in his response.

"Her story is fascinating, but it could be a fabrication to trick us. We need a sign of complete trust. She should unblock her mind and allow us to probe her thoughts. Once we are sure she is being honest, we can move ahead with this partnership."

It sounded more like something Montor would have said. The three of us had changed so much since we first met.

"I agree," said Montor. "And she is not the only one I worry about. What if we train some of her Sotkari Ta subjects and they defy her commands and turn against us? They would have to agree to remain unblocked unless confronted with enemy Sotkari Ta."

"Yes," said Kindor. "Montor, you should be the one to check on them. You do have the most experience in violating people's minds."

Kindor's facial expression didn't appear to reflect malice behind his words, but even I felt the need to shoot him a disapproving look. Montor took a menacing step in Kindor's direction, his eyes narrowed.

"And you, Kindor, would be an expert in taking advantage of people whose minds have been compromised. Do not pretend to be so noble. Remember who you are talking to."

I couldn't afford for them to rehash their differences at this critical time and interjected with a different concern to distract them.

"I am not sure our bodies are suited to travel in small, dark tunnels for long periods of time."

Montor turned his attention back to me.

"Agreed. It seems they have created passageways to the surface. We should probably do intervals of the trek above ground."

Thankfully, we were able to discuss the rest of our concerns without Montor and Kindor getting into an altercation. Our friends were still unconscious when Montor, Josh, and I returned to meet with Taraxi. Lorret remained with Kindor at the infirmary.

Taraxi made a point to address me as the person in charge

of our group. It was clear she was no fan of Montor, and she hadn't heard a word out of Josh's mouth. I explained our terms to her. After thoughtfully considering each of our points, she agreed to all of them, except one.

"I prefer our minds be probed by someone other than your husband."

"Umm, Taraxi, the reason we suggest Montor for this task is that he has the most experience in this particular Sotkari Ta talent."

"Why does this not surprise me?" she replied, a scornful tone in her voice.

"I have no idea, as you barely know me," replied Montor.

I was glad she couldn't see how he glared at her.

"OK, fine, but I have one more request," added Taraxi. "You have shown a high level of distrust by asking that I open my mind for your inspection. I could equally feel threatened by you. I would like access at least to Montor's mind, since he seems to be the most aggressive of your little crew."

Unfortunately, as if to prove her point, Montor jumped out of his seat and growled.

"No filthy Lostai scum is going to read my mind."

"Montor!" I shouted.

"No!" He whirled around, blazing eyes on me, but pointing at Taraxi. "She needs to understand. She is not on equal ground with us. Our people have done nothing against the Lostai other than defend ourselves. On the other hand, we have all suffered at the hand of the Lostai. The Lostai killed my whole family and decimated my people."

Josh, who had appeared disconcerted and frustrated since they first found me in the infirmary, grabbed me by the shoulders and, shaking me, spoke in English through gritted teeth.

"Mina, my daughter's life hangs in the balance. I've done my best to control myself, but I can't keep this bottled up anymore. I hate that I have pretty much zero influence on how we're going to proceed, and I'm getting a little crazy here. There is no chance we will survive outside. We need to use these tunnels. If he doesn't agree with her terms, I swear I will smash his head open with a rock while he sleeps."

"Why is someone speaking in yet another language?" asked Taraxi.

Montor lunged at Josh. Josh got to his feet.

"*Shermont!* Get your hands off her!"

"OK, everyone, just calm down for a moment," I shouted even louder. "Please!"

There was a much-needed minute of silence. I did three deep inhales and exhales before speaking again.

"Taraxi, I will give you free rein to probe my mind. Montor has a long, difficult history with the Lostai. He feels strongly about this. I will not ask my husband to make yet another sacrifice for my daughter."

"Is it not his daughter as well? And who is this other person who suddenly seems so passionate about the topic?"

"No, she is not Montor's daughter, and please do not ask me anything else. I cannot explain now. Trust me. Everyone in our team will follow my wishes. They have all come and risked their lives with only one mission: to help me rescue my daughter. I assure you, my thoughts represent the thoughts of us all. Can we move ahead?"

Taraxi consulted with Lanext in hushed whispers while I gave both Montor and Josh stern looks. Finally, she replied, "OK, Mina, we have an agreement."

I couldn't hold back my extreme sigh of relief.

"Thank you, Taraxi. I would like to start on our trip as soon as our friends in the infirmary can walk."

"That probably will not be until tomorrow. In the meantime, Lanext and I will identify whom to assign as your guides. We also will have your bag returned to you and show you where you can rest tonight."

"Thank you so much."

We all walked back to the infirmary to find Kristom and Komar awake. Damari and the three Arandans were still unconscious. Sharox received two other patients, children who accidentally ingested something poisonous. Kindor requested to stay with Sharox to help with the patients. Lorret said she would stay also, so Taraxi arranged for cots to be brought in for them. Lanext escorted the rest of us back out to one of the large residential chambers and into a vacant compartment.

This gave us a view of how these people lived. The outer walls and two inner walls were constructed with piles of filed-down rocks and stones, stacked about six feet high, and set in place with some adhesive. This allotted enough privacy for the short Lostai, but Montor, at well over six feet, could look over the walls out to the main chamber. The two inner walls created two sleeping sections and a living room of sorts. There were no kitchen or bathroom-like areas. Each residential chamber had communal food preparation, dining, bathing, and toilet areas used by all the families that lived in the twelve compartments within a chamber.

This compartment was empty inside, but I suspected the others boasted little in terms of furniture as well. Our sleeping bags were left behind when we retreated from the caves, but we still had our blankets in our backpacks. Lanext brought in large rectangular chunks of the same foamy material that had cushioned my fall into the pit. These would be our beds. She also brought clean garments so that Montor, Josh, Kristom, and Komar could change out of their flight suits for the night. Montor and I would settle into one room, Kristom and Komar in another, and Josh in the living area.

"Are any of you interested in washing up before getting to sleep? We do not know when we will have a chance again during this trek."

Everyone agreed it was a good idea, especially when I

mentioned the warm water. I showed them where the bathing area was and the process.

"Let them go first so we do not need to be rushed," said Montor, with a naughty smile, having already forgotten his earlier outburst with Taraxi and Josh.

Kristom headed off to have his warm bath while the rest of us stood outside the compartment waiting our turns. I pulled Montor aside and spoke to him in a lowered voice.

"We need to talk."

He cocked an eyebrow.

"OK, go ahead. Talk."

"I have no way to thank you for everything you have done so far to help me rescue my daughter, but if we are going to be successful, you need to control your temper."

His eyebrows knitted in confusion.

"Why are you suddenly talking to me as if I were a stranger? Thanking me as if I were doing you a favor? You are my wife. Your pain is my pain. I could not believe my ears when you told Taraxi that *Aembuh* was not my daughter."

"If she were your daughter, you would not have thought twice when Taraxi asked to probe your mind. If it had been Josher—"

He ran his hands over his head and avoided my eyes.

"If it had been Josher, I would have reacted the same stupid way. I am sorry, Mina. I do not know how you can control your emotions so well surrounded by these Lostai. In this, you are stronger than me. Even Kindor has his reservations with these people."

"If you had squeezed her forearm as I did, you might have more confidence in her honesty. I really sensed her collaborative energy. Anyway, you will have a chance to probe her mind to be sure. I understand this is tough for you." I reached up to stroke his cheek. "It is not easy for me either, but I need us to remain focused, Montor."

He cupped my face in his hands and looked into my eyes, his filled with regret.

"I am sorry, Mina. You are right. I have allowed these people to get under my skin. I need to get back to my unemotional military mode. The days since the bombardments separated us have affected my judgement. The thought of losing you makes me crazy."

Sharing his well-guarded vulnerability with me always softened my heart.

Our eyes locked. Before I could whisper his name, his lips were on mine. A kiss that remained soft and sweet only for seconds, until his hands raked my hair and his hungry mouth demanded more. At times like these, it was easy to forget that others might be watching. He gathered me in an embrace, and his kisses traveled down my neck.

"Umm, next," announced Kristom, looking refreshed and wearing his new garment, which made him look like some alien biblical character.

"I go now," replied Josh, in a raspy voice, avoiding anyone's eyes.

When he returned, he went straight inside the compartment without as much as a "goodnight."

"Should I go next?" asked Komar.

Montor and I replied "Yes" in unison.

After Komar returned, Montor and I grabbed our garments and headed to the bathing area.

Montor looked around and asked, "How do you ensure privacy here?"

"You take three large stones and place them at the entrance. People know not to enter or to continue on their way without looking inside."

"Hmm, OK."

We both hurried to place the three stones in the right spot and fill the pit with ice and snow. I was already wearing one of their garments, so disrobing for me was just a matter of pulling it over my head. Montor looked me over.

"Hurry, it is cold," I said, almost embarrassed at the lust in his eyes.

He tapped the collar of his suit. It inflated, and he made quick business of pulling his legs and arms out. Now, it was my turn to take in his nakedness. I caught my breath. His height, muscular build, unabashed sexuality, and swagger...it all ignited my desire. Even though we had fooled around in our sleeping bag at the cave, we hadn't seen each other like this since leaving the spaceship a week ago. That was a long time for us.

He had brought his backpack with him and found the birth control vial. Instead of having me apply the liquid as he usually requested, he did it himself in a most lascivious manner while I watched.

Oh boy. THAT is hot.

We threw in the crystals. As soon as the ice melted and the vapor convinced Montor the water was warm enough, he grabbed my hand and led me in. He scooted down on the seating shelf to recline and pulled me on his lap to straddle him. With both hands on my butt, he pushed me up until my knees were level with his chest.

"Not fair," I pretended to protest. "I am out of the water, and it is cold."

"Do not worry. I will warm you up soon enough."

He pushed me farther up into position, holding me against his face. Hoping no one would peek in and find us in this most obscene position, I held on to the edge of the pit for dear life as his tongue and mouth pleasured me. My body was already weak with satisfaction when he coaxed me back down, his hands sliding over my body and fondling my breasts as he penetrated me.

"Oh Montor, yes...yes."

The water splashed with our vigorous movements.

"Mina...sweetness..." he whispered. "I would like the other way, too."

I repositioned myself to face away from him, tilting forward. He wrapped his arms around me, holding me in place as he pushed into me from behind. A few deep thrusts and my body melted into orgasm again. He held on tight, grunting as he climaxed. The beating of my heart matched his breathing. He trailed kisses down my back until heartbeats and breathing slowed back to normal.

"I love you more than anything, sweetness. Never forget that."

"And remember that I love you too, Montor."

He grabbed a washcloth we had left within reach on the edge of the pit.

"Tomorrow is an important day. We need to rest," he said as he dunked the washcloth in the water and rubbed it on my back.

"Yes."

The washcloth floated away as he licked my earlobe.

By the time we tiptoed into the compartment, Josh, Komar, and Kristom were sound asleep.

18

———

Damari and the three Arandan soldiers regained consciousness overnight. Thankfully, they didn't lose any fingers or toes to frostbite. After Sharox and Kindor confirmed they were well enough to leave the infirmary, we all assembled for a midday meal in one of the communal dining areas. We ate whatever they served without asking what it was. Lanext and Taraxi joined us.

"Mina, we have identified four guides to accompany you on your trek. Although I am the last of my people who were not born here, everyone here has heard the stories of how our ancestors were persecuted dissidents forced to hide here for our beliefs." Lanext shot me a look as if to remind me that no one else knew about the Sotkari Ta part of their history. "We have a common enemy, and that enemy is the Lostai military obsessed with imperialistic demagoguery. Please know we picked from a group who volunteered for this task. They are clear that their service to you benefits both our groups. They are also aware of the risks involved."

"Thank you, Madam Premier Taraxi. We are honored to accept their help on this important mission. Yes, to be perfectly clear, none of us here are guaranteed safe escape from this planet. We will do our best to protect each other and achieve a positive outcome."

Lanext introduced the four volunteers. The two females were named Bexin and Sostax, and the two males, Axor and Merlis. After the meal, Taraxi invited me into her office. As usual, Lanext assisted her. Josh and Montor followed me in like my shadow. Kindor remained outside, introducing the four Jomoloxti volunteers to the rest of our crew.

Taraxi motioned for all of us to sit and get down to business. As a gesture of trust, I unblocked my mind. Taraxi and Montor did not.

"Mina, the only steps remaining before your team sets out are to collect supplies, set some ground rules, and read each other's minds."

"Yes, so let us begin."

I could be equally efficient.

"Good. I left the volunteers with instructions to work with your team on gathering the needed supplies while we chat here. Moving on to the ground rules. First, you will notice the volunteers are not Sotkari Ta. This was not a coincidence. Lanext and I want to minimize the chance that any of our Sotkari Ta people will be captured and forcibly mated with other Lostai. We do not want to contribute to any more suffering. Those genes must remain contained within our small group. Even though my citizens do not know all the implications of being taken captive by the Lostai military, they have all been taught to fight to the death rather than become prisoners. I hope you will find a place for us where we can be forever separated from Losta."

Montor sat up a bit straighter and nodded at me, lips pursed and approval in his eyes.

"Yes, this is our position as well. We will do our best to achieve this goal."

"Excellent. To that point, if you are successful, as a gesture of gratitude, we agree to later identify a few Sotkari Ta from our group to be trained and integrated into your United Rebel Front. We will need to screen for the most trustworthy and upstanding of our citizens as they will learn a part of their history that we meant to keep a secret. Until that point, under no circumstances are you to divulge our history to any of my people. Do I have your word of honor on this?"

Montor and I exchanged glances again.

"Yes, of course."

"Finally, you know we have purposely minimized using any technology to keep our location hidden. I would like you to continue to honor this practice. Just because I have made up my mind that this place is no longer safe for us, does not mean we should be advertising our location just yet. However, I realize you may come across situations where this precaution is no longer practical. Perhaps when you already have the upper hand, or they have already discovered us, or as a last resort, it might make sense to use technology. I will allow only you, Mina, to make that risk and reward decision."

Montor rolled his eyes but smiled.

"I am thankful, Taraxi, that you trust me with this judgment call. I will not take it lightly. I do suggest we leave you with one of our tablets, so if such a situation should arise, I have a way of communicating with you."

"Agreed. Well then, all that is left is to execute the mind probes."

"Taraxi, my mind has been unblocked this whole time. I give you permission to access my thoughts."

Her voice entered my mind without any hesitation to communicate telepathically.

"Mina, are you ready?"

"Umm, yes."

"Guess what, Mina?"

"Ugh, what?"

"My grandfather never learned how to access people's minds. I was bluffing, but we do not have to tell your husband that, do we?"

We shared a smile. Then it dawned on me.

"But he may find out anyway when he probes you."

"Ah yes. How silly of me. You know, Mina, I have trusted you since we first grasped each other's wrists."

"Me too, Taraxi. However, my husband—"

"I know. I know. He will want to check me. It is fine. Honestly, I do not blame him."

She continued aloud, "OK, Montor. I am satisfied that I can trust Mina. I have unblocked my mind. Go ahead. Let us get this over with."

Montor was very skilled at this. It took him mere seconds to access a person's thoughts and innermost feelings. He stared at his folded hands. When he looked back up, we witnessed a rare sight. All traces of sarcasm, arrogance, and contempt were erased from his eyes.

"Well, what did you detect?" I asked him.

"Yes, she is being truthful."

"So, nothing out of the ordinary, right?"

He narrowed his eyes, and I hoped he wouldn't detect any mischief in mine. "No, nothing."

"Taraxi," I addressed her telepathically, "Montor did not detect that you are not able to read minds."

I heard a rare Lostai chuckle in my head before she replied, "Well then, let us keep that little secret between us."

I couldn't suppress my smile, and Montor eyed me with suspicion before saying, "Taraxi, I am satisfied that we can trust you, too. I will do everything I can to help your people get to a safe place."

"Thank you. Well, it looks like we are all done here. Let us see if the others are ready."

As we walked out, Josh approached me.

"So, Mina, I'm not sure I kept up with everything that was said here. What are your thoughts about all this?"

"I'm feeling very positive. Now, I just want to get going as fast as we can. Our target is more than a week's trek away. Every minute that goes by without rescuing Amber is a minute too long."

"Yeah, I agree."

In the communal area, the four Jomoloxti guides carried large bags on their backs and a ridiculously narrow cart constructed of a pliable metal set on treads of similar material. They piled it high with various articles. Everyone on our team had their backpacks and combat gear except Kristom, who lost his during the bombardments. Those were the two missing *hanstorics*. We also would carry the foamy material we used as beds rolled up and strapped to our backs.

Sharox returned my flight suit. I stepped away for a moment to put it on. The suit's auto-mend technology had repaired the cut in the leg area he made when he tended to my ankle injury. When I returned, Montor was discussing with the Jomoloxti guides where he believed the Lostai camp might be. Manual compasses were the only tools we could use to guide us. I approached Taraxi and extended my arm. We grasped each other's wrists.

"I know my grandfather's Sotkari friend used to say, 'May the Farthest Light guide you,' but we Jomoloxti have different beliefs. Be wise and brave, Mina, and success will be yours. Contrary to what your husband may think, you are the leader of this team. The one that has the most to lose."

Her words made me think of Josh. He also had the most to lose. No one knew what he was suffering in silence.

"Thank you for your help and trust, Taraxi. I hope when we meet again, we can celebrate victory together."

"Yes. Now go."

The fifteen of us soon were out of the Jomoloxti community chambers and down a narrow tunnel. Montor, the tallest of us, barely had a few inches between him and the ceiling. Now, I understood the dimensions of the cart. We only fit walking single-file. One of the Arandans helped to push the cart while two of the Jomoloxti guides led us and the other two took the rearguard. After an hour, we came upon a fork opening to two wider tunnels. Our guides, without hesitation, chose the left one. We all were thankful for the increased space, but I noticed we were on an incline. As we climbed, the surroundings changed appearance. Dark purple growths lined the walls. Insects the size of tarantulas scurried about.

After four hours, the guides recommended we stop for a rest. They scraped the purple fungi from the walls and gathered bugs, collecting them in stone receptacles. I reclined against the wall. Montor put his arm around my shoulder.

"Sweetness, looks like they have decided on the menu for dinner," he said with a smirk.

"Mmmm, I just cannot wait," I replied, rubbing my tummy. "Montor, I have been meaning to ask, why are we traveling upwards rather than towards our target?"

"They said that behind these hills are higher mountains. They believe this tunnel system continues into that area and leads to caverns with exits, so we can access the outside every so often. We should try to climb to a higher vantage point where we can use our ocular devices to get a view of what is out in the distance."

I dug into my backpack and pulled out a nutritional bar.

"Do you want half?"

He took it.

"I cannot decide what is more revolting, this or the insect mush they will prepare for us later."

The break allowed the team time to fall into a camaraderie. I looked around. Josh, Kindor, and the other two Sotkari Ta joked about something. Lorret let her guard down and was in a lively conversation with the two female Jomoloxti. The male guides were showing the Arandans and Damari how to crack open the shell of a certain insect to harvest the soft meat inside. When we started on our way again, there was more chatter among us.

Later in the day, our good mood suffered a setback. Our guides made their first mistake. They led us through a tunnel that became so cramped we crawled for two hours, only to reach a dead end, requiring us to go back and try another route. To make things worse, the Jomoloxti could go an entire day without a bio break and didn't consider the same was not true for the rest of us. Those four hours were very uncomfortable until we found smaller rooms branching off the tunnels where we could relieve ourselves in privacy. The day's travels had been especially tough for Montor, who, due to his size, exerted a lot of energy squeezing through some of the small tunnels. After we doubled back, he shared a few choice words for our guides. He fortunately kept them between the two of us telepathically and in Arandan, so they didn't catch on. After twelve hours, we called it a night in a large chamber where we all enjoyed enough space to stretch our legs.

19

We didn't see the light of day for another one hundred hours. Those of us not used to being in the dark for so long became antsy. The rest of our senses went on hyper-drive to compensate for our eyes' shortcomings. Now, the sounds of crawling insects boomed in my ear.

"These caves are getting stinkier by the minute," growled Montor.

We all were having a harder time waking up in the morning. Even Damari's ever-cheerful personality went dark as he argued with the guide who awoke him for breakfast. I constantly reminded the guides that we needed to designate several spots for taking bio breaks in privacy and that we needed to plan stops for this purpose every three hours or so. Our Jomoloxti guides were so patient with our crankiness. They assured us we had exited the tunnels in the hilly area near their home and were now into a cavernous system within the larger mountains.

Montor was the first of us to detect the draft, a rush of chilly air that roused us from our drudgery. The tunnel widened, and we saw a bit of light in the distance. I couldn't explain it, but my body sped up as if my very life depended on getting to that spot. The closer we got to the light, the wider the tunnel became. Soon, we were in the largest chamber we had come across since starting out. The large opening drew us like a magnet. Even the sound of the whirling wind outside brought a smile to my face. We all rushed to the opening, which led to a narrow ledge. Luckily, we didn't push each other over. It dropped to what appeared a hundred feet.

Once my eyes got adjusted to the daylight, I took in the view. The initial excitement gave way to disappointment. I didn't know what I was expecting, but snow-covered mountains for as far as I could see left me depressed. Discussions about the success probability of our mission were conspicuously absent from our conversation. The possibility that we might not find Amber was a reality that no one wanted me to hear. The guides decided we would camp here for a couple of days to get familiar with the area. We all sat while they set up a pit for heating crystals. They gathered some snow in a stone pot and set it over the crystals, to which they added insect meat, cream-colored balls, and, to my surprise, some green flakes that looked like dried herbs.

"Where did you get those?" I asked.

The oldest female, Bexin, who had assumed the role of leader among the four guides, answered.

"As Taraxi must have shared with you, our ancestors arrived here in a spaceship from another world where plant life was plentiful. Before they destroyed the spaceship, they salvaged whatever equipment and supplies they could carry with them, including seeds and portable gardens. You did not get to see it, but we have a garden we maintain with crystals where we harvest grains, vegetables, and herbs. It renders only a small amount each season that we usually distribute amongst our community to celebrate special holidays. Taraxi allowed us to bring some with us on this trek to help lift your spirits."

We all looked at each other in silence, acknowledging their sacrifice.

"Wow, that is very generous of you."

Bexin didn't reply as she continued to prepare the meal. The tiny balls were made of mashed-up grains. Once she sprinkled in the green flakes, a garlicky aroma filled the cave.

"This is not typical Lostai cuisine. Our ancestors learned these methods from the natives of the planet they had migrated to when they left Losta."

When she served us the soup, we all ate as if it were a feast made for royalty. Even Montor praised Bexin on her culinary abilities. After dinner, Montor pulled out two bottles from his backpack.

"Friends, let us warm up our bones with some of this fine *stampu*."

We wiped out the stone bowls where the soup had been served. These were our only eating utensils. Montor poured everyone some of the liquor.

In consideration of our guides, he refrained from his typical toast of kicking filthy Lostai butt. Instead, he said, "To the safe completion of all our missions."

Afterwards, he taught everyone a rousing old Arandan warrior song and soon everyone was chanting:

Jonjuri, the victors!

Unity, our key!

Oh, Tan Aranda!

Our planet will be free!

The day had been a long one. After cleaning up all evidence of dinner and drinks, everyone laid claim to their sleeping spots. The chamber was about fifty by fifty feet, so there was plenty of space to spread out. Montor and I headed to a corner and unrolled our foamy mattresses. Although large, the chamber offered no privacy, so everyone kept their suits on. Montor still had folded in his backpack the tarp he had used to protect us when we slept outside. He consulted with Bexin on whether it might be a good idea to stretch across the opening to keep out some of the chill and wind. The tarp came with an adhesive that helped keep it in place. She agreed. That and the heating crystals helped keep us warm.

Montor pushed our foamy mattresses together, and we wrapped ourselves in our blankets. He spooned me, as usual. I glanced around. Josh was still sitting, his back against the wall. I didn't mean for our eyes to meet, but once they did, he stared, holding me prisoner. Heat flushed my face, and I shifted my position, which only made Montor tighten his embrace. Shutting my eyes, I fell asleep pondering how I never in a million years would have guessed I'd end up in such an awkward situation.

The Jomoloxti were up bright and early the next day. They removed the tarp from the cave opening and let the daylight and the chill wake us up naturally. Montor and I shared a nutritional bar for breakfast, as did some of our team members, while others ate some fungi porridge prepared by Bexin. As soon as we were done eating, she called us into a meeting.

"We have reached an area unexplored by our people and need to do a bit of reconnaissance. You do not all need to come. A few of us will suffice and the rest could remain here and rest."

I quickly spoke up.

"I do not want the team to separate. Bad things have happened in the past when we split up."

Montor chimed in.

"I agree."

"OK, we would like to see if there are openings such as this one in the direction where we are heading. This way, we can avoid getting lost in the tunnels but have places where we can shelter at night or rest from the cold. Be aware, the ledge outside is narrow. Also, we need two team members to carry the supply cart. We can take turns."

We gathered our things and followed Bexin outside to the ledge. It wasn't snowing, but the gusts were brutal. We needed to tread carefully. Any slip could mean a fatal fall of several hundred feet. After four hours, we came across our first novelty. The ledge was now bordered by a guard rail made of a rope-like material, weathered enough to appear ancient. Also, to our relief, the ledge widened, making it less treacherous of a walk. Two hours later, we found another cave opening.

"We are four hours from nightfall. I suggest we walk two hours more. If we do not find another opening, we should return here to rest the night," said Bexin.

"Let us explore this opening and its nearby tunnels instead to ensure there is no danger," I said.

"Yes, you are right, Mina. That makes sense."

This cave was similar in size to the other. Almost too similar, as if artificially constructed rather than a product of nature. We investigated the main tunnels leading to the cave and concluded they were safe. The Arandans made an additional discovery, a partially submerged den of hibernating rodents. I convinced myself they appeared more like rabbits than rats as Bexin skinned and butchered them.

"Montor, is there any *stampu* left?"

He laughed out loud and answered telepathically, "Good idea. Get drunk before we have to eat those creatures for dinner."

I slapped him on the arm.

"No, silly."

I suggested to Bexin that we add a splash to the dish she was preparing. She was skeptical but went ahead with it.

"Can I see what vegetables and herbs you've brought with you?"

Soon, we were working together preparing the meal. By the time dinner was served, everyone was in high spirits, encouraged by the inviting aroma of the food. Afterwards, Bexin warmed up more snow in a larger pot. We took turns taking the warmed water into the tunnels where we could have privacy to wash up a bit and take any necessary bio breaks. By the time we were all done, everyone was ready to call it a night. If it weren't for the fact that this was a rescue mission, it would have been an excellent, albeit extreme, camping trip.

20

We weren't expecting to come across a bridge, but that's exactly what we found the next day. With the bridge came a dilemma. Bexin pointed across to the next mountain.

"Mina, we need to continue in this direction, according to Montor's calculation of where he thinks the Lostai camp is. That requires we continue on this ledge that wraps around the mountain until we reach the ground, and then hike up the next mountain or see if there is a pass below. Another possibility is to go back to working our way through the tunnels. Either of those options is going to take quite some time. Also, your team was becoming disconcerted with the constant darkness. We understand time is of the essence. We could cover more ground in significantly less time if we used this bridge to get across to the next mountain. I am not suggesting we do that. I am only presenting the different options."

We stared at the bridge that swung in the wind and at the devastating precipice and drop to the gap below. The bridge, including the deck, was made of thick rope tightly woven together. It looked like a gigantic hammock with handrails anchored at each end by stone arches. The textile used in making the rope must have had some interesting properties because no ice or snow accumulated on it; a good thing since frozen material could become brittle and break. I wondered how its makers had constructed it.

"I would suggest someone test the bridge before we attempt to cross it," Bexin continued.

There was movement in the huddle of people. Josh pushed his way to the front of the group.

"I do it," he said.

Confusion hung in the air for a few seconds. The Arandans, with their toxically masculine hive mind, gaped at Montor, an obvious message in their eyes.

This male is trying to upstage you in front of your female. Why is he so willing to risk his life for her daughter?

Montor's jaw clenched. In a moment, he was in front of Josh, staring down at him.

"No. That is quite brave of you, *Joshwar*, but unnecessary. I will do it."

His tone was more confrontational than appreciative. Josh glared back.

"Stop," I said. "We do not have time to spare. I would like to shorten the travel time, if possible, but I will be the one to test the bridge first. You are all risking enough for me and my daughter. Some have died already. This is something I must do."

A cacophony of voices replied, "Mina. No."

Montor pulled me aside. Josh followed.

"This is a private conversation between my wife and me, *Joshwar*."

Josh didn't budge.

"My daughter. My issue."

Josh had the sense to whisper, but the tone was firm.

Montor huffed and turned to me.

"I thought we talked about this. Your pain is my pain. Your risk is my risk."

"I know, Montor. Everyone here is risking their lives to help me, but I need to bear the brunt of this burden. She is my daughter. She is here because of me. I will not allow anyone to face a danger that I do not face first." I looked at Josh. "This goes for you, too. The discussion is closed."

I moved up to the start of the bridge. Montor rushed after me and pulled me into an embrace. He pressed his forehead against mine.

"Mina, be careful. I will stay focused on your movements. If you slip, I will do my best to lock on you and use my telekinetic abilities to pull you to safety."

I gave him a quick kiss and looked the bridge over. Even in the best of conditions, it would take at least ten minutes to get across. I put on goggles, grabbed hold of the handrail, and gave it a good tug. I turned back to everyone.

"It appears sturdy enough."

Montor's face was a slab of stone, and Josh shook his head, raking his fingers through his hair.

There were so many reasons to be afraid. I had always hated heights and narrow spaces. The way the wind caused the bridge to swing also reminded me of an incident that had happened the day before Montor and I got married. We were on a jungle trek where we had to cross a dilapidated bridge, and a strong thunderstorm surprised us. He fell into the raging river below. I had to somehow summon enough courage and focus to continue across without knowing if Montor had survived the fall. He did, but he had also received a severe injury from a wild beast attack. We barely made it out before the river swelled. As if that memory weren't traumatizing enough, the low profile of this bridge's guard rail provided little protection from falling over. My Sotkari Ta training helped me to focus and get centered. I took my first step on to the bridge.

Grasping the handrail again, I stomped hard with my foot to test the strength of the woven ropes that made up the bridge floor.

I might as well find out sooner rather than later.

Hisses and gasps filled the air as everyone held their breaths. To my relief, nothing snapped. I took another step and another, holding on to the handrail as if my life depended on it because, well, it did. After that first test stomp, I wanted to maintain a light pace to place the least amount of pressure, but the winds shifted. The howling gusts forced me to bear down with each step forward. My heart exploded with the fear that any of those steps might cause a break in the rope. I hated the seconds when I released the handrail to move ahead.

Halfway across, the gusts shifted again and tossed me to the bridge floor. If my friends shouted, I was glad they were too far away for me to hear their reactions. My legs trembled as I came to my feet. I needed another meditative moment to overcome my dread.

I can do this. God has given me the strength.

I braced myself and focused on the bridge's swings.

I need to move with it, not against it.

Relaxing my muscles, I focused on envisioning myself as a part of the bridge. When the winds died down, I took advantage to take several steps. When it picked up, I released my body tension, bent my knees, and swayed with it. After the last step, I turned around and raised my arms in the air.

"Yes!" I shouted in English.

They couldn't hear me, but I saw them fist pumping.

Montor was the next to come across. He mimicked what I had done. When he reached me, his hug left me breathless.

"Mina, amazing. You were dancing with the bridge. I am so proud of your strength and courage."

Josh came next. Without thinking, he high-fived me. Montor, still overcome with emotion, didn't question it.

"That was pretty badass, Mina," Josh said in English.

After him, two Arandans managed to cross while carrying the supply cart. One by one, the others came across. Nature granted us more good luck by calming down the winds so that the last few who crossed faced less of a challenge. A rope handrail also protected this mountain's ledge. We seemed to be halfway up the mountain.

"I suggest we walk downhill. At first, I wanted us to get a view of the area from up here, but there does not seem to be anything interesting from this vantage point. We might as well get to lower ground," said Bexin.

It was almost midnight before we found a cave where we could shelter in. After sharing our remaining nutritional bars with our Jomoloxti guides, everyone went to sleep.

It took us three days to reach the base of the mountain. The last evening was difficult because we could not find a cave to shelter in and spent the night outside. There was enough space on the ledge to set up the heating crystals and the foam mattresses. Montor attached the tarp from the edge of the mountain to the ledge. We covered ourselves with our blankets and huddled together underneath. Even with the heating crystals, I knew we couldn't survive another evening outside and prayed we'd find shelter by the next evening.

Once we arrived at the base the next day, we scoped out the area. We were thankful to find a narrow pass in the direction we were headed. Other than that, everything else looked the same. Gray sky, ice, and snow all around us. The pass curved to the right so we could not see too far ahead. When we turned the curve, something startled Bexin.

"Stop. Mina, please hand me your ocular device."

"What is it?"

"I think I saw something shiny, like a reflection. Keep everyone out of sight."

We moved back while she scanned the area ahead of us.

"Mina! Come see."

There it was. Something vehicular was moving in and out of our line of sight.

"OK, so there is some sort of vehicle, but I saw no buildings at all. Whoever they are, they must be in the cave system."

Montor ordered all of us to hide well behind the curve.

"Yes, that is my thought as well," Montor said. "So, we need to consider carefully how we will approach."

We discussed our options. Obviously, we could not just continue and meet them head-on. The element of surprise was critical since we would surely be outnumbered. One possibility would be to turn around and circle the mountain on the opposite side. Another could be to hike up the mountain and see what we could observe on the other side from a higher altitude. The final option would be to enter a nearby cave system and hope to find tunnels leading towards our target area. We couldn't use our *hanstorics* because we didn't have a clear landing destination. Plus, we needed as many fully charged *hanstorics* as possible to escape once we found Amber and any other prisoners.

"I have another concern," said Montor. "If the people in those vehicles are Lostai military, they most likely have the type of sensors that can pick up Sotkari Ta brain waves. Six of us are Sotkari Ta. Moving together as a group will likely trigger their sensors. Perhaps traveling in the tunnels might hide us from their tracking devices."

A gust cut through my chest like an icy spear, bringing something else to mind.

"Also, the caves provide us shelter. We cannot survive another night like the last one," I added.

"OK, the caves, it is," said Bexin.

21

W e spent the rest of the day looking for a cave entrance and were about to resign ourselves to another night in the cold. The clear sky caught my attention. Lostai's nearest moon appeared gigantic, casting shadows and illuminating the icy surface in a way I had not seen before. Too bad it was the home world of people who had harmed me so much. Otherwise, I would have thought it beautiful. As my eyes took in the silvery shimmer, I noticed an opening we previously had missed. It was too small to walk in. We'd have to crawl. Maybe it would lead nowhere, but at least the cave could shelter us for the night.

No one argued when I insisted on crawling in first.

"Promise to give me at least fifteen minutes to scope out the area."

I scooted down the narrow tunnel on my tummy and arrived at an open area with a high ceiling and eyehole above that let the moonlight in. Three openings high enough for me to walk through led away from the chamber. I stood, stretched my arms and legs, and spent a few minutes walking down each tunnel. Nothing spelled danger for me, so I gave the team the OK to enter.

Our supply cart didn't fit, so we distributed what we could among our backpacks. We brought the precious vegetables and herbs that the Jomoloxti had sacrificed for us and most of the cookware. We could not crawl through with the foam mattresses rolled on our backs, so after we all were in the cave, Montor and Damari worked together to push and pull them through the tight space.

Bexin walked around, running her hands on the cave walls.

"These caves look different from the ones we are familiar with. I am not sure what we can harvest here for food."

She was right. Only white, needle-like crystals covered the cave walls. No fungi anywhere. The Arandans didn't find any hidden rodent dens, either.

"The opening up there keeps this too cold and bright for the fungi to grow or the animals to nest. We will probably find something as we get deeper into the tunnel. No problem. Tonight, we shall have vegetable soup."

Although better than spending the night outside, cold air crept in from the opening above. Fortunately, exhaustion helped us fall asleep quickly. The next morning, we picked the tunnel that seemed to head in the direction we wanted, walking five hours in a downward orientation before running into anything of interest.

The chamber we found was quite a discovery and the first in what appeared to be a sequence of dwellings. The rock had been carved into stairs, shelves, horizontal slabs, benches, doorways, and circular receptacles. Hieroglyphic-like etchings decorated the walls.

"Do you recognize this language, Bexin?" I asked.

"No. When my ancestors left the Namson planet, they chose this region as their new home because they knew of an ancient civilization that once lived underground in the Morzaki region. My guess is that all this pertains to that society."

In another room, we found gray liquid trickling out of a circular opening in the wall into a carved-out basin in the ground. A trench parallel to the floor drained the water out of the basin.

"Wow, this is like a pipeline from the surface to capture melted snow."

Before anyone could protest, I cupped my hands underneath and took a generous gulp. Besides the strong mineral taste, it seemed fine. A blessing since we had run out of thirst pods and water. We filled our canisters and splashed our faces with it. In the next hours, we found rooms of different sizes with more elaborate carvings and sculptures. By the end of what Bexin's manual timekeeper showed to be the day, we still had not come across an alternative food source. Bexin prepared the last batch of vegetables and herbs, and we settled in one of the rooms for the night.

The next morning, we heard sounds that were too far away for us to distinguish. Rumbles and grating. Perhaps muffled voices, too.

"From now on, we walk with our weapons drawn," instructed Montor. "Sotkari Ta, divide yourselves. Three in front, three in back."

The noises drifted in and out of our earshot but were louder with each step. Montor, Damari, and I moved up front. Kindor and the two other Sotkari took the rearguard. Josh was right behind me. My muscles became twitchy, and my senses heightened. I caught myself flexing and unflexing my fingers.

I need to calm myself down.

I took a deep, cleansing breath. Then another. And another. Before I exhaled on the last one, everything went silent. Montor turned and signaled that we should stop and remain quiet.

We waited.

No change, so we moved out of the main tunnel into a smaller opening to the side. Only the sound of our footsteps interrupted the silence. Montor turned to look at me, his lips pressed into a tight line. He communicated to me telepathically.

"What do you think, sweetness? Should we continue down this way or get back into the main tunnel?"

Since the bridge crossing, he had shifted from all-powerful leader to sharing that role with me. I scratched my head as I peered down the narrow pathway. The space appeared to get more restricted and curve back towards the way we had come from.

"I say we continue on the main tunnel. It seems there are several smaller tunnels, like this one, branching out from the main one. We can slip into one of those if we hear something approaching. Deviating down this narrow path appears to take us backwards."

He rubbed his chin as his eyes darted around.

"OK. Agreed."

We piled back into the main tunnel and slinked forward. Everything continued quietly for a while until we heard a bump and feet shuffling. As luck would have it, at that juncture, there was nowhere for us to hide. We approached a curve ready to face whatever was coming and met three Lostai in full military uniform. Someone behind me gasped. The Lostai fell to the ground.

"I caused them to lose consciousness," whispered Montor. "Disarm them and take away any devices they might have on them while I run down this corridor to see if anyone else is coming."

As Montor left to investigate, Bexin said with a bit of sarcasm in her tone, "He really is good at that, huh?"

Montor returned.

"OK. I did not see or hear anything else. This is a great opportunity for us to learn more about this place."

He poked a *vimor* against the chest of one of the Lostai soldiers and roused him.

"*Grimah*, what is happening here?" shouted the soldier.

"I ask the questions, you lowly germ." Montor squinted as he accessed the Lostai's mind. "We saw some vehicles outside not too far from here. Who do they belong to?"

The soldier's voice turned flat, a glaze in his eyes.

"Lostai military."

"Is there a secret Lostai military installation nearby?"

"Yes."

"Are you holding children as prisoners?"

"Yes."

Montor's jaw clenched.

"OK, Lostai scum, how do we get there? Can it be accessed from this tunnel?"

"Yes."

"How far from here?"

"Two days by foot."

"What were you doing this far out?"

"Our commander has reason to believe some intruders might be in the area. He ordered us to survey these tunnels."

"*Shermont!*" Montor looked at me with troubled eyes. "If they contacted their headquarters to let them know they heard something, they might send more to investigate."

He returned his attention to the Lostai.

"When was the last time you communicated with your commander?"

"Yesterday."

"So, you did not radio in just now to let them know you heard something?"

"No. We suspected we heard something, but we wanted to be sure before calling it in. Last time we heard something, it turned out to be water trickling, and he said we wasted his time and it was embarrassing—"

"Enough!" shouted Montor.

He continued interrogating the Lostai about the layout of the installation, where the children were being held, their defense and communication systems, and how many soldiers were there. We learned the unit was small. One hundred Lostai soldiers and three Sotkari Ta sympathizers. Not even Lostai found an assignment in this winter wasteland pleasant. We also learned there were twenty young prisoners.

Montor put the Lostai back to sleep while we discussed our plan of action. With our ten *hanstorics,* we could transport up to fifty people if we huddled close together. That would be more than enough for the twenty hostages and the fifteen of us, but orchestrating that while being under attack would be no easy feat. The main tunnel led to an exit on the other side of the mountain. The Lostai installation was in a dome built around the exit point.

"Montor, I have a suggestion," said Bexin. "My co-guides and I can dress in these soldier's uniforms and cause some confusion when we enter the installation."

Montor pressed his fingers against his forehead and shook his head.

"Uhh, Bexin, I was going to suggest you stay behind. You have already fulfilled your purpose."

"What is the problem?"

Montor looked around at nothing in particular and covered his mouth.

"Umm, those Lostai are our enemies. I am not sure how you and your friends will feel when we start killing them."

"You still do not trust us," she replied, outrage in her voice.

Montor's facial muscles strained, and his brow furrowed.

"That is not the only thing."

Only thing?

I gave him a dirty look. He ignored it.

"You do not know how to work any of their technology. We will manipulate the minds of these soldiers, arm them and have them shoot as many of their comrades as possible, as well as compromise their defense and security systems."

I checked Bexin's expression, trying to detect any unease with Montor's plan. There was none.

"Montor, Lostai military terrorized our ancestors. On top of that, they are holding children. We have no qualms about whatever steps you must take to rescue them, and we intend to help," she replied.

Their eyes locked for a second.

"OK, good. However, I just remembered, they have three Sotkari Ta aiding them. Actually, none of you non-Sotkari Ta can go in there until we kill those three first."

Josh brushed past me to address Montor, chin up, and meeting his eyes squarely.

"No way I here stay."

Josh's voice was full of pain and determination. He could be very stubborn.

My thoughts traveled to the previous year. I remembered how Montor's foster father was used by the Lostai when I tried to rescue the *Barinta* crew at Dit Lar. Foxor's intentions at the time had also been courageous, but he foiled my plan when Gio, a Sotkari Ta man from Earth, manipulated his mind. I ended up being taken and tortured by Gio. The memory made me forget my better judgement, and I grabbed Josh's arm to have him turn to look at me. Montor swatted my hand away.

"What are you doing?" he growled.

I glared back.

"I do not have time for your ridiculous jealousy right now, Montor." I didn't even bother to check his reaction as I reached up and grasped Josh by both shoulders, speaking to him in English.

"Josh, I know what you're feeling, but here is the issue. Those Sotkari Ta that are on the Lostai side can manipulate your mind. You could turn against us. Trust me. You won't be able to fight it. We can't risk that. So, yes, you, the Jomoloxti, and the Arandans need to stay back until we neutralize that threat. Then, of course, I expect you to come in and help. Do you understand? You need to promise me that no matter what you see, you will not show yourself until we let you know it's clear for you to come in. Amber's rescue depends on it. Promise me."

Josh's whole face and body contorted into an uncomfortable ball of tension. After a deep breath, he answered, "OK, Mina. I promise."

I turned back to Montor to find crazed yellow eyes.

"Mina, you must love to test my self-control," he said to me telepathically.

"Relax, please. Josh needed to understand the graveness of the situation."

Montor pursed his lips and rolled back his shoulders before addressing our group out loud.

"We need a method to communicate to those who stay behind that we have put down the Sotkari Ta threat and that it is safe for you to join us. Mina, I feel we have reached the point where we need to use technology. Taraxi left that decision in your hands, so let me tell you something else. Before we left for this mission, I put in a call into the United Rebel Front high command. They said they would send in backup if we confirmed children were being held hostage here. Just before going in, I suggest we turn on our tablets so that first you can contact Taraxi and let her know we are calling in for help. Next, I will call my contacts and ask that they come to evacuate the Jomoloxti community. Until they arrive, Taraxi needs to know that her location will be compromised so she can take whatever actions possible to protect her people. We also will need to use technology to communicate with our team here to let them know when it is safe for them to come in and join us. What do you think?"

"Yes, I agree. It is time."

"Good. There is another thing that must be discussed before we move forward. My plan is to manipulate the minds of these three Lostai idiots. Mina and Damari are not skilled enough to keep a prolonged connection. That leaves you three." Montor pointed to Kindor, Kristom and Komar. "Kindor, I know you have reservations about mind control. What about—"

Kindor used his tablet to reply.

"You know I have already used mind control with the Lostai commanders we took from Sotkar. Why are you questioning me? I have no problem with it when it comes to dealing with murderous Lostai military. What is the plan?"

"Umm, OK. What about you, Kristom and Komar?"

Kristom gestured he was the better choice for this task.

"OK, so Kindor, Kristom, and I will control the minds of the Lostai soldiers and pose as their prisoners. We will have them take us to the highest-ranking commander, and I will take control of his mind. I suppose, at that time, I will kill my Lostai."

"No need to kill him so soon. He can still be of use to us," said Kindor.

"I understand, but I am not sure how long I can hold both minds captive," replied Montor.

"That is not a problem for me. I can do it easily."

Montor rolled his eyes and said to Kindor, "You are such a showoff."

Kindor shrugged, trying to muster an innocent look, but the twitch of his mouth betrayed a bit of amusement.

Montor continued explaining the plan. "I will then have the commander take me to where the children are being held and release them. In the meantime, I need you two to kill off as many Lostai soldiers as you can, but prioritize locating and killing the three Sotkari Ta that are assisting them."

Montor opened his backpack. "Who is missing an earpiece?" He pulled out communication devices and handed them out to those who needed one.

"The Sotkari Ta of our team will need to block their minds until we kill the Sotkari Ta assisting the Lostai. This poses a communication problem since we cannot talk to each other telepathically until then. We will all keep in touch using the earpiece devices. Unfortunately, it does not completely solve the problem for you Sotkari who are mute. Using your tablets will not be practical in the middle of the chaos." Montor stopped and thought for a bit. "This is what we will do. As the Lostai Sotkari Ta threat is neutralized, raise your fist in the air like this." He demonstrated. "One finger means one Sotkari Ta down, two for two, and three if all three are down. At that time we will unblock our minds and send a message to our team members waiting outside that it is safe for them to join us."

"And what will I do?" I asked.

"You, Damari, and Komar will need to wait for Kindor, Kristom, and me to complete our charade. Once I have control of the commander's mind and you see the commotion caused by these Lostai idiots turning against their comrades, you will come in to help us. I will have their commander take me to where the children are being held, and you will follow me and help me secure them."

"Before we go in, we will need to teach everyone how to use the *hanstorics*," I said.

"Yes, correct. Kristom, Kindor, Komar, Damari, Mina, and I will each have a *hanstoric*. We each can make the jump with four others. That leaves four *hanstorics* for the remaining nine of you. I suggest we distribute those to Bexin, Lorret, Josh, and Noomar. Decide who of the remaining five will be your partners. We will set the United Rebel Front headquarters on Aranda as the destination on our *hanstorics*. I think that is the safest place to keep the children until we determine the best way to transport them back to their home worlds."

"Why not Fronidia?" I asked. "Aranda is probably being threatened by Lostai battalion crafts by now."

"We do not have permission from the Fronidian government to transport rescued hostages to their planet, and they wish to remain neutral."

"Hmm, OK. I see."

"Now, I have another question to pose to all of you. I think we need to decide one more thing as a team."

We looked at each other and then focused on Montor's next words.

"Do we wait until all fifteen of us can meet where the children are located to make the jump together? This would ensure no one gets left behind. Or should those who reach the children first transport ahead of the rest?"

It was a tough choice. All of us wanted to wait till everyone in the team was secure and jump together, but the longer we waited, the higher the risk that some or all of the children might not make it out. Although we were counting on the United Rebel Front to send in backup, we were not sure when they would arrive. It was more likely we would face this fight on our own. In the end, we reached a compromise. Five of us were assigned to secure the children and leave as soon as we had a chance. Everyone insisted I be one of those five.

"Mina, your daughter will want to be with you," said Bexin, echoing everyone's opinion.

The other four in charge of the children would be Damari, Komar, Kindor, and Kristom, since they would all be among the first group in. Montor would stay until the rest could all jump together to ensure no one was left behind.

Now that the plan was finalized, Montor awakened the

Lostai soldiers and temporarily removed their ability to speak so that they could not shout out. He didn't want to waste mental energy on controlling their minds yet. We resumed our trek down the tunnel, leading them at gunpoint. After seven hours, we came across where they had been camping out. We found food and supplies there. Montor knocked out the Lostai soldiers again, and after we ate, we went to sleep, taking turns keeping watch.

22

———

Before heading out the next morning, we trained everyone on how to use the *hanstorics,* presetting Aranda as the destination so that it would be a matter of just tapping the display to execute the jump. By late afternoon, we saw an artificial-looking light at the end of the tunnel. We knew our battle was less than an hour away. At this proximity, any Lostai sensors scanning for Sotkari Ta brainwaves could detect us. We could no longer wait to put our plan in motion. Montor turned on his tablet. He contacted the United Rebel Front command, and we patched Taraxi in.

"Commander Portars, this is Montor. We are about to engage the Lostai."

"Montor, I am glad to hear your voice."

"Sir, we do not have a minute to spare. Will you be able to send backup here?"

"There is heavy fighting in the Sector. I cannot synchronize with you an exact time for extraction."

"Understood, sir. We have *hanstorics* and will attempt to make it out of here on our own. There are twenty children incarcerated here."

"Those filthy Lostai have no morals," growled Portars. "Now we are more than justified in continuing our attacks on their home world and associated territories."

"Yes, sir, but there is something else. Even if we can make it out using our *hanstorics*, we need your help for another situation we have encountered here."

Montor went on to explain how the Jomoloxti had put themselves at risk to help us and now needed to be evacuated. Portars was hesitant when he learned they were actually Lostai, but Montor insisted they could be trusted and deserved to be rescued.

"OK, Montor. I know you would not make such a recommendation lightly. I give you my word of honor that we will send a ship as soon as possible and attempt to evacuate all the Jomoloxti. I now have Madam Premier Taraxi's location pinned, so we should have no issue in finding them once we land."

"Taraxi, what will you do in the meantime?" I asked.

"Do not worry, Mina. As you well witnessed, we are not defenseless. We will sit tight until your troops come to get us. Montor, thank you for keeping your side of our agreement. Good luck. Mina, I hope we can speak again soon."

We turned off our tablets, and Montor, Kindor, and Kristom took control of the Lostai soldiers' minds.

"Everyone, face masks on, earpieces in, check everything is in order with your battle gear. Draw your weapons and move forward."

"Wait," I said.

I walked to Montor and hugged him hard, my face pressed against his chest. He bent down and kissed me.

"Be careful, Montor."

"Yes, you too, sweetness."

Lorret took advantage of the moment to caress Kindor's cheek.

"May the Farthest Light guide you, my love," she said.

He nodded, took her hand, and pressed it against his chest.

I turned and addressed everyone.

"Thank you all for what you are about to do. I will be forever in your debt. You have become my family."

Josh stepped forward, his eyes glistening. At that moment, I wanted so badly to hug him, but it would be too inappropriate. Except for Montor, Kindor, and Lorret, everyone thought he was just a concerned neighbor who had come to Amber's rescue. Maybe the Arandans also speculated that he had the hots for me, but none of them could imagine he was Amber's father or the emotions he was going through. This time, Montor didn't complain about how close Josh and I were standing to each other.

"Mina, get our girl out of here," he whispered in English, a tremor in his voice as a tear made its way down his cheek. It took only a millisecond for him to wipe it off, but even Montor turned away, surely to hide that, although he didn't understand the words, the moment had moved him.

"Yes, I promise I will."

It was time. We rushed forward. All of us stopped short of reaching the end of the tunnel except for Montor, Kindor, and Kristom. They gave their *vimors* to the Lostai soldiers, who were now under their influence, and, posing as prisoners, let the soldiers lead them forward. A transparent door secured the entrance to whatever was on the other side. We took cover in a small side opening to stay out of sight, but I peeked as one of the Lostai soldiers placed their hand on a panel by the door. I made a mental note that we would need to blast our way in. As the six of them went through the exit, a din of Lostai conversation, footsteps, and the hum of computer systems reached our ears. The door slid closed, and I said a silent prayer.

Waiting to hear back from Montor was agony. We could not even walk up to look through the transparent door. Josh cracked his knuckles. I paced. The Arandans were fixated on checking and rechecking their weapons. Lorret just stared at the exit.

"Mina!"

My heart jumped at hearing his voice in my earpiece. Our earpieces were all connected, so I think everyone must have had the same reaction.

"Yes, I can hear you."

"I have the Lostai commander under my influence. The fight has begun. You, Damari, and Komar can come now. Hurry, we need all the help we can get."

"OK! Please try to stay away from the entrance until we get in. I will need to use shatter pellets to disintegrate the door," I replied to Montor and then signaled to Damari and Komar. "It is time."

Josh and I made eye contact before I stepped into the tunnel. His eyes held so many emotions. He grabbed my hand and squeezed. One of the Arandans cleared his throat. I ignored it.

"It's going to be OK," I whispered in English. I turned to remind everyone, "Stay hidden here until we let you know that we have killed the Sotkari Ta who are assisting the Lostai."

Damari, Komar, and I moved ahead. We reached the transparent door. I looked in. The installation was set up in a typical Lostai military camp format, a large operations center with holographic displays, individual workstations, and meeting cubicles. The room lit up with weapon fire.

"Stand back," I said.

I pulled a shatter pellet from my utility belt and hurled it towards the door. The door disappeared in a burst of blinding light.

At first no one noticed us, allowing me to scope out what we were facing. *Vimor* and phaser fires, people shouting, and soldiers running everywhere overloaded our senses. There were two distinct areas of disruption. Kristom and Kindor, with their three Lostai puppets, were on the right, leaving a trail of Lostai soldiers on the floor. Montor was on the left, heading towards the exits that led away from the operations area. From another corridor, a horde of Lostai soldiers piled in.

I calmed my breathing and focused on the Lostai soldiers entering the room. In an instant, at least twenty soldiers lost their weapons. Next, I hurled the now unarmed soldiers high in the air and let them drop hard. Most did not move after landing. Damari tried to follow my example but didn't have my level of telekinetic skill. He changed tactics, using his strength and agility to bulldoze every Lostai in front of him with his weapons or his body. Komar went to help Kindor and Kristom. Despite being outnumbered, we were holding our own. Yet one thing worried me.

"Montor, Damari and I are behind you, but I do not see any of the Sotkari Ta Lostai sympathizers. Do you?"

"No. I am concerned about this, too. They may have them—"

"Hello, Mina. We have been expecting you. Although we underestimated your resourcefulness."

I almost vomited at the sound of his voice booming from a holographic screen that reached the ceiling.

"Yes, it is I, your former commander, Zorla."

The introduction was unnecessary. His creepy voice was imprinted in my memory.

I remembered how he kept me prisoner on Xixsted.

How he scored my back with electric burns.

How he ordered Gio to torture me.

I wished I could kill him, but the coward was not there physically.

"Oh, and there is your faithful pet, Montor. Where does he think he is taking Commander Vermox? To free the hostages? I will do you a favor and bring three of them out to you."

My heart sank. The holographic image shifted, now

showing three Sotkari Ta walking out of a corridor holding three young people at gunpoint. One of them was Amber. I'm sure my friends recognized her immediately. She looked so much like me. The other two were Arandan children. Zorla's voice boomed again.

"So, you see, we are disrupting your little party—"

A narrow beam of light shot across the room. The Sotkari Ta who held Amber went down. Two seconds later, so did the one next to him. The third one looked around to see where the shot had come from. Montor took advantage of the confusion to shoot a perfect hole between his eyes. His voice in my earpiece distracted me.

"Wow, Mina. Did you ever bother to mention to me that *Joshwar* was a sniper?"

I whipped around. There Josh was, standing high up on some equipment on the other side of the room.

Of course, he didn't pay attention to my instructions.

The hologram turned off and pandemonium ensued as the Lostai soldiers realized they could no longer rely on their Sotkari Ta helpers.

Weapon fire resumed, and I shouted, "Everyone, the Sotkari Ta are down. Come in!"

Josh was now the center of attention, so I took advantage to run forward to Amber and the other two hostages. Damari followed right behind me.

"Mom? Mom!"

I don't think I have ever hugged her so hard. There was no time for words or explanations.

"Honey, we have to run."

Montor reached us, accompanied by the Lostai commander.

"Mina, I have planted a command in this idiot's mind to take you to where the other hostages are being held and set them free so you can begin transporting them. As soon as he does, kill him and let me know so I can refocus my attention on something else. Kindor, Kristom, start making your way over here and help Mina and Damari with the transporting. I will stay behind to ensure everyone gets out."

Damari, Amber, the two Arandan children, and I bolted down the corridor but slowed once we realized the Lostai commander was walking like a zombie.

"Hey Montor, any chance you can tell him to run over there?"

His chuckle transmitted loud in my earpiece.

"I did not want to attract too much attention before, but I suppose it makes sense now."

Now that we had to push ourselves to keep up with the Lostai commander, I couldn't help but laugh.

The children were held in four separate dormitories, a Lostai guard posted at the door of each one. By now, they had guessed the commander was under our influence and shot at us. I shut my eyes and hurled them against the walls.

"What the heck! Who did that?" Amber asked in a shaky voice, her mouth falling open.

"Come on. I'll explain later. Right now, we need to get out of here."

We rushed to each dormitory entrance. The commander placed his palm on a side panel, and the doors opened. Children of all species were sitting at tables. They looked at us with one common factor among them.

Fear.

I didn't speak all of their languages, so I relied on my gestures to make some of them trust me. Damari killed the Lostai commander, and I let Montor know.

"Mina, hurry. Things are getting difficult out here, and some Lostai soldiers might make their way to where you are."

"Damari and I cannot take some children and leave the rest here alone."

"Yes, Mina, I know." I could hear both the worry and impatience in his voice. "Kindor, Komar, and Kristom are making their way over there."

Damari and I moved all the children into one room and closed the door. A bunch of Lostai soldiers stormed our way. I disarmed three of them, but my mental strength was waning. I thought about using a shatter pellet against them, but it was too hectic. If our friends were right behind, they could be disintegrated, too. We'd have to fight the rest the old-fashioned way. Damari and I ducked into one of the empty dormitories and took turns firing against the oncoming threat. After giving my mind a few minutes of rest, I felt able to use telekinesis again.

Time to kick some Lostai butt.

I walked out of cover with weapons in both my hands.

"Hold on, Mina!" shouted Damari.

Ignoring Damari, I focused on the metallic door to another empty dormitory and used my mental abilities to rip it out and hurl it at the soldiers. I raised the door up in the air again and slammed it against the Lostai that were already scrambling on the floor. Taking a moment to refocus, I disarmed the remaining soldiers, their weapons scattered all around, and methodically shot each one in the head. Farther down the corridor, Bexin, Lorret, and two Arandans made their way toward us. I was expecting Kindor and the other two Sotkari Ta.

"Kindor and the others felt it made more sense for them to stay behind and help Montor. We were the first to make it down this way. Now, we must hurry as more Lostai soldiers are trying to come here," explained Bexin.

We brought the children out of the room.

"Montor made us promise you would go first," said Lorret.

I hesitated and looked around. The others were organizing the children in groups to prepare for the jump.

"Mina, we will be right behind you," Lorret insisted.

A part of me felt guilty that I was given the privilege to leave first, but I quickly pushed that thought away.

I need to get my daughter out of here.

I pulled out the *hanstoric* from my backpack, gathered Amber and three other children in a huddle close to me, and tapped the screen.

23

___

"Wow, that was weird," Amber said, observing her surroundings.

We stood in a conference room on the island of Penstarox, the United Rebel Front Headquarters on Aranda. I remembered the place well. Montor and I were married here. The Arandan soldiers were shocked at seeing us appear out of thin air, but some recognized me.

"Mina, is it really you?" one of them exclaimed.

"Yes, we have some more friends on the way with rescued children."

"We will let Commander Portars know you are here."

In a sequence of flashing lights, groups of five appeared across the room. After all five groups arrived, we sat down the children and checked to make sure everyone was fine. Lorret came over to me and grabbed me by the shoulders.

"We did it, Mina. We did it!"

I hugged her and the others. Most of them were not accustomed to friendship hugs, but I hugged them anyway, tears of joy streaming down my face.

"Thank you, everyone, but I'm not ready to celebrate until all of our friends arrive."

They all nodded in agreement. I led Amber aside and embraced her. She wasn't the child I had left behind, yet the young woman in my arms felt so fragile.

"Have you been eating well?"

"Not really."

"Oh baby, I missed you so much."

"I missed you too, Mom. We thought you were..."

Her voice cracked. I kissed her forehead and rubbed her back.

"Oh baby, I'm so glad you're safe. Oh honey, are you OK?"

Quiet sniffles and whimpers soon exploded into loud bawling, a painful crying that hurt my chest and stomach and left us gasping for air. We held each other so tight I couldn't tell who was shaking, but probably it was both of us. Glancing down, I saw she wore the detestable wristband. I remembered it well. The surrounding skin was scarred.

"We'll take this shit off, honey."

"They hurt me with it."

"I know. I'm so sorry."

We shared another round of crying. When we regained our voices, she asked, "Mom, what about Dad?"

"He should be here shortly."

"Mina!"

Commander Portars walked over. Both Amber and I wiped our faces and ran our fingers through our hair.

"Yes, sir."

"I am so glad you made it here safely. And this must be your daughter. She looks very much like you except for the hair."

My hair was curly and matched my eyes. Amber had my honey-colored eyes, but her hair was jet black and straight like her father's.

"I am ordering a feast for you and the children. In the

meantime, we have brought out some refreshments. I see there are several Arandan children among the rescued. Once again, our people are in your debt."

I signaled to Damari. He walked over and gave Amber one of his signature broad smiles.

"Hi," she said.

"Amber, Damari is a good friend of mine. Go with him and get something to drink. Damari, please ask Bexin to come here."

"Nuh problem, Mina."

Portars could not mask the shock of having a Lostai right next to him. I switched to speaking Lostai.

"Commander, this is Bexin. If you want to thank someone, it should be Taraxi, Bexin, and the rest of the Jomoloxti community. Without their help, our team probably would have died in a frozen grave. Also, we must honor the families of the two Arandan soldiers we lost."

Portars nodded to Bexin.

"Understood, Mina. We have already dispatched one of our fastest cruisers to evacuate them. Also, our medic is on his way over here with first aid supplies."

A collective gasp of surprise distracted us. Kristom and Noomar appeared in the middle of the room. Portars, Bexin, and I ran over to greet them. They were both out of breath.

"Where are the others?" I asked.

"Some of our friends were injured. Montor and Kindor are trying to reach them," replied Kristom.

My fingernails dug into the palms of my hand. Lorret joined us. Her expression mirrored my concern once I relayed what Kristom had said.

"Mina, I know you are worried," said Portars. "But there is nothing you can do now. You might as well come and have something to drink."

"I appreciate that, Portars, but really, I cannot enjoy anything until I know everyone has returned safely."

"Very well, Mina. I shall wait with you. At least, sit. You all look exhausted."

We sat at a nearby table. No one said a word as minutes went by at a snail's pace.

Fifteen minutes.

My legs couldn't stop twitching. I stood and tried to walk off the nervousness. Another fifteen minutes went by. Bexin's lips pressed into a fine line. None of her fellow Jomoloxti had arrived yet.

Please, God, let them make it here safely.

A light flashed. Komar appeared in front of us with two Jomoloxti. Bexin let out a sigh of relief and rushed over to greet them. Lorret and I locked eyes. She buried her face in her hands. Montor, Kindor, Josh, and the last Jomoloxti remained missing.

Another flash of light. Kindor appeared with the last Jomoloxti, who was pressing one hand against his arm. When he let the hand drop, we saw that a chunk of his arm was missing. Lorret jumped into action, pulling out a healing pad and placing it on the injury. The medic and his assistants arrived and rushed the injured Jomoloxti to the infirmary. Bexin ran after them.

I didn't respect that Kindor and Lorret were still in an embrace, instead asking him telepathically, "Where are Montor and Josh?"

Kindor didn't reply, but his grim expression was like a chokehold. I gasped for breath and heard a voice say, "Mina, you need to calm down."

I think it was Portars. The room spun around me as the last flash lit up the room. Montor and Josh were there right next to us.

Thank you, God.

Wait. Something is not right.

I never would have imagined the sight before my eyes. Montor carried Josh in his arms, his bloody glove grasping Josh's right leg awkwardly. Josh's face was too pale. A large bloody stain covered a gash across Montor's chest. Then it hit me. Josh was missing a leg. Montor laid him on the floor. The pool of blood that formed sickened me.

"Dad!"

Amber ran across the room. She collapsed on the floor, pressing her face against Josh's chest, screaming at the top of her lungs. Damari was right on her heels. He shot me an odd look as he realized who Josh really was. Even the others who didn't understand English sensed something was off about her reaction. Other than Amber's screams, the room became silent. I tried to pull her away.

"Honey, we need to work on him."

She wouldn't budge, her eyes so wide I could see the whites all around.

OK, I need to compose myself and take action.

"Lorret, please, hurry, give her a sedative. And get that filthy wristband off her arm. Damari, take her to the infirmary."

Lorret rushed to inject Amber, and Damari carried her away.

I got on the floor and pulled my healing pad out of my backpack. There was so much blood. Barely containing the urge to puke, I centered myself and cut open what was left of that side of his pants. A phaser had sliced his leg clean from the mid-thigh down.

"Stay with me, honey. There is a lot of advanced medical technology here. We can fix this," I said in English.

Josh was unconscious.

With trembling hands, I wrapped the healing pad around his thigh. Tears blurred my vision.

"Lorret, please help me."

She sat on the floor next to me and studied the diagnostics on the device connected to the healing pad.

"Mina, his vitals are really bad."

He was crashing. I could no longer hold back my emotions and wailed, "No. No. No."

"Mina, he lost too much blood, but I did not want to leave him there," Montor said in a grave voice.

"Shut up. Come over here and help me. We can use our Sotkari Ta healing power."

Montor's voice deepened.

"I think he is beyond that kind of healing."

I turned and glared at him, baring my teeth like a crazy wolf lady.

"Oh, you and your petty jealousy. I cannot believe you would sink this low."

I disregarded Montor and hunted for someone else who could help.

"Kindor, please, please. You have powerful healing abilities."

Kindor kneeled next to me. I ripped open the top part of Josh's suit. Kindor placed his hands on Josh's chest. He locked eyes with Lorret and shook his head. His abilities told him the same thing the medical device had shown Lorret.

"Mina, I can possibly rouse him for a moment so you can say your goodbyes."

"What? No!"

Josh's eyes narrowly opened.

"Mina."

The room became a vacuum where only Josh and I existed.

"Oh Josh, I didn't want this to happen. Please don't leave us."

His voice was something between a whisper and a grunt.

"Is Amber safe?"

I could barely speak between my sobbing.

"Yes."

"Mina, I want you...want you to know. It's true. I wasn't faithful. I wasn't the best husband, and I didn't deserve you, but I honestly did love you."

"Forget about that, Josh. Listen, we're going to fix you up."

"I don't think so, but Mina, please don't forget about Bobby. Chris is already his own man, but Bobby doesn't deserve to be an orphan. At least he should know what happened. Please don't abandon him. Promise me."

Before I could say another word, life left his eyes, and his face turned a new kind of pale.

No. He can't be gone.

First, I grabbed his shoulders and shook him.

Next, I kissed his forehead.

I kissed his cheeks.

I kissed his mouth and lingered there.

I kissed the palms of his hands.

In my mind, these were not kisses of passion. These were powerful kisses of memories, of grief, of pain, of regret. Maybe they could bring him back somehow.

I let myself fall over him, gathering him in my arms, my face pressed against his chest.

Our life together flashed through my mind.

"No," I shouted over and over until my surroundings blurred and I lost my voice.

This is all my fault. Maybe if I had made other choices, none of this would have happened. Maybe if I had not fallen in love with—

Someone helped me to my feet. I turned to see it was Kindor. I looked at everyone around me.

Montor was nowhere in sight.

Lorret, Portars, Noomar, and the other Arandans stared at me, their expression somber, but also something else.

Disgust? Disbelief? Outrage? Shock?

Kindor's voice entered my mind telepathically.

"Mina, I will accompany you to the infirmary. You need to rest. We will respectfully take care of Josh's body until you can explain to us your last rite rituals."

24

———

I heard Damari and Amber talking, their voices coming in and out of my earshot.

"Yuh parents brave, Amber. Yuh father save yuh life, and me neva meet a woman as determined as yuh mother."

"Who was the person who brought my dad back?"

"I think it betta if yuh mother tell yuh."

It hurt to open my eyes. I sat up in the infirmary cot and called out to her.

"Amber."

She walked over. Damari wisely came up with an excuse to leave.

"Mom, how do you feel?"

"I have a pounding headache, but I'm OK. What about you?"

She sighed, and her eyes filled with tears.

"I can't believe Dad is gone. I just can't believe it."

I extended my arms. She leaned into me as we hugged.

"I know, honey. It's horrible, just horrible." I couldn't control the tremor in my voice. "Before he left us, I let him know you were safe."

"Why did this have to happen, Mom?"

Her high-pitched tone was the precursor to weeping. I rubbed her hair and kissed her head.

"It's my fault."

She pulled back and cocked her head.

"Yours? Why?"

"The Lostai commander who orchestrated your abduction is angry with me. He did it to punish me, to lure me into his clutches. He wanted me to join his military and use my abilities for his plans. I refused and was able to escape."

"Yeah, I know about that creepy guy. Some other alien lady translated for him. But, Mom, that's not your fault. This whole thing is crazy. I can't believe we are galaxies away from Earth dealing with aliens." She shook her head. "I can't believe what I saw you do to those Lostai soldiers."

I glanced at her arm. The wristband had been removed. I kissed the ugly scars covering the skin in that area.

"Amber, I'm so sorry for what they put you through. Did they hurt you in any other way?"

I bit my lip, worried at what her response would be.

"Only the wristband. The one who spoke English said I was lucky because that guy, Zorla, wanted me in good shape for when the time came to negotiate with you. She said you abandoned your duties, but because I hadn't inherited all your Sotkari Ta genes, I couldn't take your place. I was just bait."

"He's such an asshole."

"What's going to happen now, Mom?"

"The first thing I need to do is explain what has been going on with me since I was taken from Earth. Sit, this will take a while."

I steadied myself to have the most difficult conversation of my life. When I got to the part about my relationship with Montor, she became indignant.

"You cheated on Dad...with that alien guy? How could you?"

I didn't want to poison her with stories of Josh's own infidelities. There might be a right time in the future to touch on that topic, but this wasn't it.

"Yes, but I thought I would never see any of you again. It felt like I had died and become a new person. Montor and I both have a full set of Sotkari Ta genes. That was at the root of the powerful attraction between us, but this grew into a bond like nothing I have ever experienced before. I owe him my life. He has sacrificed so much for me. We wouldn't have been able to rescue you without his help." I stopped for a breath. "We are married and have a son."

Her jaw dropped, disbelief in her eyes.

"So, you just forgot all about us, got married, and had an alien child!"

"I didn't forget about you. Not one day went by that I didn't pray for you and hope you all were OK. It's not like I planned all this to happen, but it did. I'd like you to meet Josher. He's your half-brother. You know, he has the same eyes as you and me."

She stood and pressed the palms of her hands against her forehead.

"Mom, what the hell do I care what color his eyes are? This is crazy."

Guilt stabbed me like a knife.

"I know. I know. I'm sorry. On top of your dad's death, this is probably too much to take in all at once."

She glared at me.

"You think?"

Kindor appeared in the doorway.

"Honey, can you give me a moment to talk to Kindor?"

"Sure, whatever," she huffed.

Once she left the room, Kindor approached the bed.

"Mina, how are doing?"

He must have noticed my swollen eyes. I wiped my nose

with my fingers and rambled phrases that bordered on incoherent.

"Oh Kindor, I am so happy we rescued Amber and the other children, and thank you so much for your help, but Amber has lost her father, and I was trying to explain about Montor and me. She was not taking it too well. By the way, where is Montor?"

"Umm, he left."

"He left? Where to?"

"I do not know, Mina. Montor left without a word."

"Really?"

"Umm, Mina, you know I never have claimed to understand Arandan customs, but even I felt uncomfortable with how you handled *Jochuar's* death. Montor may have contacted Portars afterward, although I doubt it. The way the Arandans all looked at him while you were carrying on—"

"Oh, no." I hadn't even thought about it. "I...I lost control."

"I am sure no one in that room had any doubt that he was Amber's father after how both of you reacted. They realized you were not a widow as you have been claiming, and then to top it off, you *kich* him everywhere, like a lover."

"No, no. I did not mean it that way. You know kisses can mean a lot of different things in my culture. I felt so guilty. I just did not want him to die." My heart ached. "What can I do, Kindor?"

"I do not know, Mina." Kindor shook his head. Raised eyebrows made it clear I was in deep shit. "But I think you should talk about it with Lorret. She is female and Arandan. Perhaps she can give you the right perspective."

I jumped off the cot.

"Yes, yes. I need to speak to her, and I need to find Montor right away. Oh Kindor, so many things are bombarding my brain right now..."

The room spun around me, and Kindor grabbed my arm to steady me.

"Mina, do not let yourself become overwhelmed. Your daughter needs you to be well."

"I know. It is just...I am also so heartbroken over my Earthian sons. I cannot imagine how they must have felt when Joshua and Amber went missing. Especially the younger one, Bobby. He is only an adolescent. Joshua told me he was very affected when I was taken. He asked that I not abandon him now. Those were his last words." I covered my eyes as a fresh set of tears streamed down my face. "The truth is, I have failed everyone."

"No Mina. Do not think that. Everyone is emotional right now, but with time, things should settle down. I will tell Lorret to come see you."

"I am not staying in this infirmary room one minute longer. Take me to her."

We walked back to the conference room. Thankfully, not many people were there. Damari and Amber were sitting at a small corner table conversing. Lorret, Bexin, and the other Jomoloxti were eating at a larger table.

"Mina!" Their eyes widened as if I were a ghost.

I forced my body to relax.

"Lorret, can we chat in private?" Her eyes shifted at first, but Kindor touched her arm as if sending a silent message. "Umm, sure. We can sit over there. Do you want to get something to eat?"

"No. I have zero appetite."

One side of the conference room was lined with cubicles. We picked the farthest one for privacy. I didn't wait a second to speak up.

"Lorret, do you have any idea where Montor might be? I know he must be upset about my reaction to Joshua's death."

"We all are lamenting *Joshwar's* loss. He was a brave warrior and a hero."

"Yes, he was, but I realize that the way I behaved put Montor in a compromised position. It was stupid of me. I blamed myself for Joshua's death. I was worried about my daughter. My emotions got the best of me."

Lorret averted her eyes. She took a few minutes, as if searching for the right words.

"Yes, that was a humiliating moment for him. Not only that, but you were vicious and unfair. He risked his life to bring *Joshwar* back. I do not know where Montor went. He spoke to no one."

I pressed my lips together.

No more whiny crying.

"Yes. I was an idiot."

"I will not lie, Mina. You know I care much for Montor. I am not too happy with your behavior. He must feel lost now that everyone knows his marriage to you is a farce."

"I love Montor. Our marriage is not a farce."

Her eyes were like daggers.

"It did not seem that way. Tough situations, like alcohol, reveal our true feelings. It seems like *Joshwar* is the one you loved."

I was worried sick at what Montor might do. My heart was heavy with guilt for putting him in this position but also frustrated at how these people had jumped to conclusions.

"You all are not familiar with my culture. Those gestures were not of passion. If that had been my daughter's body, I would have kissed her the same way."

Yeah, not completely truthful. I wouldn't have kissed her on the mouth.

"Lorret, you are my friend. I trust you. Help me, please. How can I fix this? To be honest, I did still have feelings for Joshua, but more like a family member. We shared almost twenty revolutions of life together. We raised children together. Yet, had he lived, I had no intention of reuniting with him." I placed my hand on hers. "Remember how Montor reacted when you two first reunited on the *Barinta*? You had not seen each other for a long time, and there was no longer love between you, but you were both extremely moved. I remember feeling a bit jealous. Lorret, I am Montor's wife now, and believe me, I love him deeply."

Her expression softened, but she took some more time before answering.

"I hope that is true, because my heart broke for Montor when I saw him walk away from that scene. You emasculated him."

Tears escaped down my cheeks. I looked away and wiped my face.

Damn it! I said I was done with crying.

"He must assume your marriage is over and will most probably seek a divorce." Lorret scratched her forehead. "Although, I do not even know if it is still considered valid since you were married to Joshua at the same time. On the other hand, you are truly a widow now. It is all perplexing."

"I did not mean to hurt him. He does not deserve that. I owe my daughter's life to him. I owe him my own life. I love him so much, Lorret."

I sobbed openly now, having given up trying to control my tears.

She rubbed the back of her hand against my cheek.

"OK, well, obviously you must talk to Montor. He needs to be convinced that you love him and still want to be his spouse."

"Yes, yes. Of course, I do."

"That is not the only thing. Montor must preserve his honor in the eyes of his community. I suggest you find the priestess that married you and get her opinion on how such a matter could be resolved. Priestesses are among the most respected people in our communities. If you get her on your side, she will know how to make your marriage to Montor acceptable to him, his friends, and his family."

"I have her contact codes. She gave them to me at Josher's *Bendorai* and said I should consider her our family's spiritual guide. Montor probably went back to our home in Fronidia to see Josher. Hopefully, there is a *hanstoric* available that I can use to jump there, but first I need to take care of Joshua."

"Portars has placed his body in a preservation chamber awaiting your instructions."

"Thank you so much for guiding me through this, Lorret."

I hugged her and hoped it was another reminder of the quirky human gestures her people might misconstrue.

"I wish you luck, Mina. Hopefully, we will talk again soon."

25

Portars didn't look up when he greeted me, but he mentioned nothing of the incident at Josh's death.

"Mina, we have preserved *Joshwar's* body awaiting your instructions."

I wiped away the tear that had started its way down my cheek before Portars would notice. My grief for Josh's death was still so fresh. I swallowed the sobs that tried to escape my chest.

I'll have to control my emotions if I want to learn about Montor's whereabouts.

I explained to him that cremation was an acceptable way for us to treat Josh's body.

"Good. That is how we honor our dead, too. Josh's quick and brave actions directly saved the lives of two Arandan children, not to mention the others you rescued. We wish to give him a traditional Arandan warrior ceremony, and we will place his remains in an *omori*."

I learned that an *omori* was a special receptacle made of a rare metal used for the cremated remains of only the most honored Arandan soldiers.

"That is very kind of you, sir."

"I suppose afterwards we will give his ashes to you, and you can decide what to do with them."

"Umm, yes, thank you." I looked around his office, summoning up the courage to ask him the question that weighed so heavily on my mind. "Sir, do you know where Montor is?"

His expression revealed nothing, but for the first time during our conversation, he looked me in the eye.

"I do not know, Mina. Why do you not contact him via your tablet?"

"Right," I replied, swallowing against the knot in my throat.

"The ceremony for *Joshwar* will be held in one of the holographic rooms in one hour. We will take care of everything. You and *Aembuh* can meet us there."

"Thanks again, sir."

He resumed reading his tablet, so I stood and left his office.

The holographic room was set up as a temple, automatically bringing back memories of my wedding to Montor. All lieutenants, higher-ranking military leaders, and rescued children in Penstarox attended Josh's funeral service. A priestess officiated the ceremony.

Too bad she's not the one who married Montor and me. I could start working on solving the mess I'm in.

Amber preferred to stay with Damari, who was quickly becoming her shadow, rather than stand by me. People gave me weird looks. As we waited for Portars to arrive, I overheard two Arandan lieutenants whispering to each other. Apparently, they didn't know that I understood Arandan.

"So, she was married to both of them at the same time? No wonder Montor will not show his face here."

"Yes, but the Arandans that were with them on this mission said they saw Montor defeat him in a fighting match, and had the female not intervened, he would have killed him. I guess that would count as a duel. Plus, she is truthfully a widow now."

"She was still married when she was with Montor, though, and she had children with the Earthian male."

"Shhh...she is looking at us."

"And I can also hear you," I said in my best Arandan.

They looked away.

The color of blood dominated the temple. Marble floor, curtains that draped the walls, and the tunic worn by the priestess were all the same deep hue of red. Her thick hair was gathered up high on her head, held up by an ornamental band made of shiny red beads. Portars arrived and handed the *omori* to the priestess.

The priestess called the ceremony to order. Everyone stopped chatting. She recited a poem and chanted a long prayer before addressing us.

"This person whom we are honoring today is not of our world, nor did he speak our language. Yet we choose to wish him success in his journey to the spirit world. His actions embody those of a true warrior, and forever we will speak his name with respect. *Joshwar.*"

"*Joshwar.*" A wave of solemn voices carried his name across the room.

Tradition called for repeating his name several times. By the third time, Amber had buried herself in Damari's arms, her body shaking. I felt alone and incomplete.

"How are you doing?"

The hand on my shoulder and the voice in my head startled me. I whipped around.

"Montor!"

"Shhh. We must mention no other name at this time. We

are cementing *Joshwar's* name in our history." His voice sounded hoarse in my mind.

With a gesture from the priestess, everyone's chanting died down. She asked if anyone wanted to say final words. People looked around. Damari and Amber exchanged words. Amber nodded, and he led her to the front of the room.

"Amber has requested that I translate to Arandan for her."

He spoke Arandan much better than Lostai.

Oh my God. What will she say?

She tightened her fists and straightened her posture before speaking to Damari, who repeated her sentences in Arandan.

"On behalf of Joshua's family, thank you for treating his death with the same honor as you would for any of your own fallen heroes. I am just learning about your culture, but I can see that you are a courageous and respectful people. I also thank my mother's husband, Montor, for risking his own life to bring Joshua back here. Thanks to him, Joshua spent his last minutes among friends and not with those filthy Lostai."

Montor inclined his head, admiration in his eyes.

"The girl certainly takes after her mother."

I couldn't help but smile.

Everyone fist pumped. The priestess asked if anyone had something else to share. Amber had said it all. We filed out to the conference room, where refreshments were being served. As soon as people noticed Montor was back, they whispered and shot furtive glances our way.

"Come with me," Montor said, his voice even deeper than before. "I will not have people gossiping about my family and me behind my back."

He led me to a podium on a stage in the front of the conference room. I remember raising a toast on this very stage the day I married Montor. A quick tap on the console and his voice boomed across the room.

"I would like to have your attention, please."

His voice startled everyone. No one was expecting another speech, and much less from him. As everyone turned towards us, dread crept from my stomach into my throat. Montor and I had not talked about where he had been or his thoughts on what had happened. His expression seemed too serene. It scared me.

"There are some here who attended my wedding at this facility. That day, I shared a secret that had darkened my soul for most of my adult life. You learned I had served in the Lostai army as an influential assistant to a high-ranking Lostai commander. I think it is time I unburden myself of another secret that has been pestering me. Hopefully, it will put an end to your inappropriate comments."

Ah hell. He's going to tell them.

"When I met Mina, she harbored little hope of returning to her planet. You all already knew that when the Lostai kidnapped her, she left behind three children. What almost everyone did not know is that Mina had also left behind a husband."

He rolled his eyes as the expected murmur traveled through the crowd.

"According to our customs, such a situation would require her husband and I to face each other in a duel to the death or incapacitation before I could ask her to be my spouse. Unfortunately, we did not have the *hanstorics* at the time, or I would have done just that, even against Mina's wishes. This type of tradition does not exist in her culture."

Chatter arose across the room, people probably commenting on the lack of decorum on Earth in such matters. That lasted only a few seconds.

"Silence!"

Even I jumped.

"I do not need to justify to you why Mina and I got married anyway. As most of you are already speculating, *Joshwar* was *Aembuh's* father and Mina's first husband. The Lostai targeted Mina's daughter to punish us for having joined the rebel movement and not submitting to their wishes. *Joshwar* tried to help his daughter as she was being taken and was accidentally swept up into the transportal, too. As you can imagine, the events of the last days have taken a toll on *Aembuh* and Mina. Now that you know their relationship with *Joshwar*, there should be no surprise at their reaction to his death. I have consulted with our spiritual guide, who has explained to me that my marriage to Mina is null and void because she was already married at the time."

The collective gasp included my own.

"What we will do about that concerns only Mina and me. Regardless of our relationship going forward, you all owe Mina and her family respect and consideration. Let us not forget that Mina bravely returned many of our children to their homes when we first discovered the Dit Lar transportal. Remember, Mina endured torture instead of divulging United Rebel Front secrets, and she is the reason I am currently not wearing a filthy Lostai uniform. As you witnessed in the words of her daughter and in the bravery of her husband, *Joshwar*, honor runs deep in her family."

Her husband Joshwar? This is not going as I had hoped.

"I have also been gravely impacted by these recent events. Although I am calmly delivering this message to you right now, be sure, I am not in a good mood. Anyone I catch murmuring about this topic will feel my wrath." He scanned the room and even glared at Portars. "I mean, anyone."

He turned to me and asked, "Do you want to add anything?"

I was speechless, shaking my head as tears welled up in my eyes.

He looked out at the crowd.

"OK. That is all. Thank you for your attention."

He tapped the console and led me off the stage, holding my hand, but I detected a chill in his touch.

26

————

The room remained silent for a few minutes as Montor and I walked to the refreshment stand. No one even dared to glance at us. He poured himself a shot of *stampu*.

"I need one too, please," I said.

He served me a glass a tad shorter than his. We both gulped down the harsh liquid without looking at each other. In the distance, Damari was talking to Amber, his speech fast and his gestures animated. I assumed he was explaining what Montor had just said.

"I want to go home and see Josher," I said.

"Yes, so do I." His voice was still in that flat tone that left me so uncomfortable. "What will happen to your daughter?"

"For now, she will stay with us until she decides what she wants to do, if that is OK with you."

Montor served himself another shot.

"Us?" He rolled the word around in his mouth before bringing the glass to his lips.

I dared to look up at him. He stared off at nothing. We needed to talk in a less toxic environment.

"I would like to go home as soon as possible. If there is a *hanstoric* available, we three can make the jump together," I said.

"Yes, I will ask Portars and be right back."

I walked to where Damari and Amber were.

"Hi."

"Hi, Mom. Listen, we need to talk. I was a bit rough with you earlier."

"It's OK. Yes, we have lots to talk about, but right now I just want to go home."

"Home?"

"Well, my home. It's on another planet, called Fronidia. Even though it's neutral in the war, it's the safest place for us in the sector because the Lostai are no longer welcome there. I haven't seen Josher, my son, in two months. We all need to rest and clear our minds. Montor and I have issues we need to discuss, too."

"Umm, Mom, can Damari come, too? He's been really kind and helpful."

I shot him a stern look, forgetting for a moment that Amber was no longer the fourteen-year-old adolescent I left behind four years ago. Damari cupped the back of his neck with his hand.

"Me nuh wah be nuh trouble, Mina," he said.

"No worries. That's fine. I'm sure Montor won't mind."

"Did you mention my name?" Montor's voice startled us all.

Damari's eyes blinked so fast. He understood the unspoken tension that still hung around us. I switched to Arandan.

"Amber was asking if Damari can stay with us for a few days. I guess she is happy to talk to someone from Earth close to her age, especially at this difficult time."

Damari was twenty-two.

Amber looked up to meet Montor's yellow feline eyes and gulped but recovered, extending her arm for a handshake.

"It's good to finally meet you, Mr. Montor," she said in English, which Damari promptly translated to Arandan.

Montor mistook it for the Sotkari salutation and grasped her forearm instead. Amber, always quick on her feet, adapted and did the same.

"Oh, I get it. A special handshake."

She actually got him to smile.

"Please tell her that Damari is a good friend and is always welcome in my home. I have a charged *hanstoric*. We should say goodbye to our friends and leave."

Our farewells were quick business. Everyone either detected the awkwardness in the air or was simply exhausted. Portars gave me the *omori* and wished me luck, as if he knew I'd need it. We picked up Damari and Amber on our way out of the conference room. Outside, the Arandan sun was high in the sky. We huddled together, Montor tapped the *hanstoric* screen, and in a blink of an eye, we were standing at the entrance of our home in the Arandan enclave on Fronidia. Night had already fallen.

Amber rubbed her temples.

"Wow, I still can't believe how that's possible."

We entered and found Lasarta and Foxor cleaning up in the kitchen. Their greeting was not as effusive as I expected.

I'm sure Montor has told them everything, as he usually does.

Amber, not knowing how to greet Lasarta, curtsied. She made a face at Damari, who laughed out loud when Lasarta cocked her head.

"Oh my, Mina, your daughter looks so much like you, except for the hair."

"Yes, everyone says that," I replied.

Usually, I would have added, "She gets her hair from her father."

Instead, I asked for Josher.

"Oh, he is washing up, but he should be out any—"

"*Ro Ma!*"

He ran to me, and I swept him up in my arms.

"*Honey!*"

My heart filled with joy at seeing his smiling face.

"I have been a very good boy. Ask *Lo Ro*."

He kissed my cheek and then extended his arms towards Montor, who took him and lifted him high above his head, causing Josher to giggle.

"*Ta Ri*, can we play *Fastorec?* I have been waiting for you to arrive so we can face the higher-level opponents together."

Montor laughed, but I saw sadness in his eyes.

"It is almost your bedtime, but we can play one round."

Lasarta asked if we were hungry.

"No, we are fine. I see that you have already had dinner and cleaned up the kitchen."

Damari averted his eyes, a disappointed look on his face.

Foxor laughed and pulled Damari by the arm.

"Damari, I have the fresh meat pies and fruit pies you like so much. Come, let us all have some."

"Oh good," said Josher.

"No, no. You already have had enough," admonished Lasarta.

Montor came to the rescue.

"Come, Son, let us play that round of *Fastorec.*"

"What about you, Montor? Are you not hungry?"

Lasarta touched his arm, her face a picture of motherly concern.

"No, I am fine."

Her brow remained furrowed as she watched Montor and Josher go to the recreational area. She licked her lips nervously and turned to me.

"Mina, you look so tired."

I was sure she was referring to my eyes swollen from so much crying.

"Yes, we all need a good night's sleep, but I will have one of your dessert pies."

"These are good," commented Amber and then thanked Lasarta and Foxor in Arandan.

"Oh, speaking Arandan already? How wonderful," said Foxor with a broad smile.

Amber probably didn't understand everything Foxor said, but she got from his expression what he meant and offered a shy grin in return.

"Yes, I have been teaching her some Arandan words," said Damari, looking proud of himself.

Lasarta and Foxor insisted they finish cleaning up so we could get ready for bed. They lived in a home nearby. Before leaving, Lasarta pulled me aside and caressed my cheek.

"Mina, I know you have gone through a difficult time. If you think talking with me helps, you know I am always here for you."

"Thank you, Lasarta. I know I can count on you."

I showed Damari and Amber to each of their guest bedrooms, spending some time showing Amber how to use the reproducers and other advanced technology she wasn't familiar with. She needed toiletries, clean pajamas, underwear, and casual clothing for the upcoming days. Each bedroom had its own bathroom, so I showed her how to manage the controls there as well.

"Mom, I'm sorry I was so judgmental when you told me about Montor. Damari has explained so much to me about what you both have been through, and truthfully, I know Dad was no angel either."

"It's OK, honey. I understand your reaction."

"We were tough on Dad, too, when Laura moved in. There was something just too familiar about them. Dad explained he knew her from his military days, but Chris told me they had been seeing each other for some time."

"Chris? How would he know?"

"One day, a few years before they took you, he used Dad's phone without permission to buy something online and he saw messages and pictures."

"Oh my God. Chris never spoke about that."

"Dad convinced him that telling you would only make you sad. Did you not suspect anything? Seriously, Mom. Even my friends check their boyfriends' phones."

"We need a lot of time to discuss this, but our marriage had a rocky start. We did the best we could to hold up the fort for you guys. And we did love each other, in a way, but definitely something was missing. I should have cared more, but I didn't."

"When you disappeared..." She looked away to hide new tears. "That's when Chris shared with me and Aunt Sonia what he knew. We thought...we thought you left us because you were upset about Dad's affair. That's when we all really got mad at him."

I pulled her into an embrace.

"Oh honey. I'm so sorry for everything you've suffered, but we'll figure out how to make things better from now on."

"Mom." She looked at me through determined, teary eyes. "I know you have a new family. I realize you are not going back home, so I want to stay here with you. Please."

I kissed her forehead and cupped her face.

"Look at me. I would love for you to stay here with me, but you should take some time to think about it. Keep in mind, things are dangerous here. There is a war going on, and every-thing is different from how it is back home. There's not a bunch of people from Earth around the block that you can hang out with."

"You've made a new life here. So can I. Plus, you know how interested I was in astronomy. Now, I can study it up close and personal."

"I have enemies here."

"I'd rather face them with you than worry someone is going to steal me away again. And do I have powers like you do? Maybe you can teach me."

"I can show you how to communicate telepathically, but I don't think you have my other abilities."

"Still, that's super cool."

"Well, take your time to think about it. Honey, I'm just so happy that we're together."

Sadness crept into her eyes. I knew what her next word would be before she uttered it.

"Bobby."

She grasped my shoulders.

"Mom, we have to bring him here. He got really weird when you disappeared. I can't imagine how he must feel now with both Dad and me gone, too." She pressed her fingertips on her lips, becoming thoughtful, and shook her head. "Chris won't come. He's doing well at college and has had some good internships. They are already offering him jobs. He has a girlfriend, too. But Bobby, Bobby needs us. Aunt Sonia has taken good care of him, but maybe that creepy Zorla guy might go after him now."

"Yes, I worry about that too, but what if Bobby doesn't want to come?"

"Mom, I'm sure he will."

———————

27

By the time I was done talking with Amber, Montor had tucked Josher in, and Damari had settled down in his bedroom. I found Montor outside on the balcony, staring at the darkness. I touched his back. He stiffened.

"Montor, maybe now is not a good time to talk, but I need you to know that I deeply regret my behavior during the last moments of Joshua's life. I was rude and unfair with you. I did not stop to think how you might be affected by how I was acting. I should have known better. I am familiar enough with your customs and have no excuse other than I just lost control. My emotions got the best of me, but I hope you do not doubt that my love for you is as strong as ever."

No reaction.

"Please, what can I do to make this better? I will do anything."

I squeezed between him and the balcony railing and placed my hands on his chest. He looked down at me. I still could not read his eyes.

"I am reporting for combat duty in the next day or so," he said.

"Combat duty. What do you mean?"

"I will lead a fleet of United Rebel Front battleships to invade Losta. We need to move from defense to offense and destroy the Lostai military once and for all. It is the only way to force the Lostai government to stop endorsing their military's imperialistic and criminal activities."

"Montor, before all this happened with Amber, we had agreed we were going to focus on our family. You said you wanted us to have another child."

"Our family?" His breathing became shuddered.

Finally, some emotion.

"Yes, our family. You, me, Josher, now possibly Amber, Lasarta, Foxor. Just because our marriage has been nullified does not mean we cannot get married again. We still love each other."

He bent down and kissed my forehead and my cheeks. When he kissed my lips, I leaned into him, wanting to demonstrate my love, but he did not linger. He took each of my hands in his and kissed my palms. Mortified, I realized he was mimicking what I had done to Josh and pulled my hands away. His eyes narrowed and his voice became a growl. He pinned me against the edge of the balcony.

"I have each *kix* you gave him burned in my memory."

"Montor, those were kisses of grief, not of passion. You see how I kiss Josher. Let us go to bed. Things will be better in the morning."

He smirked, and I had before me the arrogant, acerbic Montor I had met for the first time on Xixsted four years ago.

"Are you suffering from *jomeney*? I can fix that."

He took my hand and rubbed it against his crotch. *Jomeney* translated to "widow's syndrome" and was a vulgar and derogatory way of saying I was horny and desperate. I knew he was trying to hurt my feelings and push me away. I didn't play into it. Instead, I grabbed him there and looked into his eyes.

"Maybe I am, and yes, I expect my spouse to take care of that."

He kissed me again. This time, it was the real thing, ripe with angst and longing. I vamped up my sexual energy, and he groaned.

"Mina, you know I cannot resist you, but this does not solve our problems."

"Maybe not, but it's a start."

I showered first and waited in bed while he double-checked the security system. After showering, he slipped in next to me, with a clean scent and a hint of a fragrance I had gifted him while we were on vacation. He lay on his back, facing up and getting that blank look. Not wanting to chance him going cold on me again, I straddled him. Our eyes locked, and he caressed my butt, coaxing me to rub up against him. No further foreplay was necessary. We were both ready. With my hand, I guided him into me. His hands moved to either side of my waist. They slid up to cup my breasts. My hips moved to the same rhythm as his thumbs circling my nipples. I had intended to go slow and make it last, but once he was inside of me, it was hard to hold back. Our bodies in sync, screaming for fulfillment, we raced to an intense climax. Spent, I laid my head against his chest to hear the thumping of his heart.

"Montor, I open my mind to you. Read it and you will see how much I love you."

He ran his fingers through my hair. After a few minutes, he broke his silence.

"Mina, no matter what happens, I want you to know..." He continued to twirl my curls around his fingers. "The day we were married was the happiest day of my life."

He wrapped his arms around me even tighter. I reached up to caress his cheek and allowed myself to relax. We fell asleep, but when I awoke and rolled off him, he turned, cupped my face in his hands, and kissed me fiercely. After thoroughly bruising my lips, he moved down to my breasts, his mouth hungry. I twined my fingers in his hair, encouraging him.

"Oh Montor, take me completely."

He growled something imperceptible and continued further down. My breath came in gasps now as I predicted each step of his journey, each kiss a testament to our special bond. Soon his warm breath tickled the insides of my thighs. I wrapped my legs around his neck. Sounds of love-making filled the room. His tongue, my wetness, the mattress creaking, our moans.

"Montor, I need to feel you inside. Don't make me wait any longer."

He pulled up, eyes wild with desire, and pushed into me hard. I found the roughness thrilling even as he continued thrusting way beyond my climax.

"Turn around," he whispered.

I obeyed and turned face-down. He reached underneath to tantalize me with his fingers while he entered me from behind. Another orgasm built up inside me like a volcano. I erupted in cries of pleasure. He let himself go and climaxed amid grunts and panting. I turned to him and pressed my face against his chest. He kissed the top of my head.

"I love you, Mina," he whispered.

"I love you, Montor. You see? We will be OK."

He didn't answer, his breathing still so heavy. I fell into a delicious slumber.

The next morning, I reached over to Montor and instead found my tablet with a notification signal. I grabbed it and saw it was a video note from him. He never looked directly at the screen.

"Mina, I made a last-minute decision to leave you this message. You do not deserve that I go without an explanation, although I doubt you will understand. We come from very different worlds. We never should have come together as a couple."

Hot tears welled in my eyes. I couldn't believe I still had tears left to cry.

Oh no. What the fuck is wrong with him? Damn you, Montor.

"I have lived most of my life in dishonor, first as a filthy Lostai soldier and then marrying a female who already had a husband before he even had a chance to defend his position. I expect to lay my life down as we attempt a last stand against the Lostai military. Hopefully, in death, I can accomplish what I did not in life and be remembered as an Arandan of honor like my father and brothers before me. Our marriage is null, so you are free to do as you please with your life. If you decide to go back to Earth..."

He stood, hiding his face from the screen, but he could not mask the tremor in his voice.

"I have left instructions to Kindor and Lorret that they adopt Josher. They seem to be building a strong relationship. I know we assigned Colora as his *Ro Masa*, and she can continue in that role if something happens to Lorret. I think that, as an Arandan, Lorret can better help Josher learn about his heritage and our traditions."

He cracked his knuckles and sat again.

"Last night, I probed your thoughts as you asked and sensed sincerity in your feelings towards me, but this is something I must do. I am empty inside. If you decide to stay here and remarry, I hope you select someone worthy to be Josher's father...someone better than me."

Without wasting a moment, I recorded a reply. I didn't bother to wipe my tears.

Let him see how he's left me.

"Montor, you are mistaken when you say I could not understand you. My people have a sense of honor as well, but we recognize everyone makes mistakes. It is what we do with ourselves afterwards that marks who we are. You are wrong when you say you have led a life of dishonor. I have witnessed your integrity and honor in so many ways since we have met."

I pressed my fingers on my eyes as if that could stop the steady flow of tears.

"I know I cannot attempt to make you change your mind via a message, so I will make it clear to you what I intend to do. First, yes, I need to go to Earth and hopefully bring my younger son back here with me. Amber assures me he must be in a bad way now that half of his family has disappeared. My older son is an adult now and seems to be stable. I doubt he would leave Earth. This will be a quick trip, and I am not leaving Josher behind. Never again will I separate myself from my children. He will travel with me to Earth and back."

I stared at the screen. The hard lines of determination etched in my jawline and brow almost hurt.

"When we return, I will find out where you are and will join you. I will bring our children with me, and we will face this final battle together. There is nothing you can say or do that will change my mind, other than returning home, of course. Call me irresponsible or reckless for bringing our children into a war zone. I do not care. Our place is by your side."

I could almost hear his deep voice cursing in my mind.

"*Shermont*! That female is so stubborn."

28

———————

I needed to recharge before making the trip to Earth, emotionally even more so than physically. Amber tried to appear strong, but I'd catch that vacant expression of grief when she thought I wasn't paying attention. Damari was a godsend. They told each other stories of their experiences and the things they missed from home. He consoled her, and she seemed to trust him.

After a few days, I asked Lasarta to accompany me on a shopping trip to a traditional Arandan fresh market, an activity we had often done together in the past. Foxor took Damari, Josher, and Amber to visit the recreational holographic rooms that Josher enjoyed so much.

Lasarta's motherly love for Montor was unconditional, but she had become a trusted ally and mother figure for me as well. I was unaware of exactly how much Montor had shared with his foster parents regarding what had happened on Penstarox. He usually was very open with Foxor, who shared everything with his wife, Lasarta.

The market was bustling with Arandans of all ages, a piece

of old Aranda, so out of place amid the technologically advanced Fronidia. I loved how it reminded me of the fresh markets in the Caribbean, a part of my diverse ancestry. Smiling vendors shouted their sales pitches from carts of all sizes painted in showy colors. Aromas of pungent spices and sweet fruit filled the air. As we looked over the produce, fowl, and fresh fish, I brought Lasarta up to date on everything that had happened in the two months we were away.

"Mina, it saddens me that Montor has left his family behind to take on such a dangerous assignment, but I am not surprised. Remember, I warned you about what a jealous Arandan male is capable of and how much our culture's principles of what is dishonorable means to Montor."

"You have always been honest with me, Lasarta. Do you blame me for what happened?"

"Well, had you exercised some restraint, perhaps things would not have escalated into what you are facing now. Still, it is not the first time that Montor's relationship with you has prompted him to unburden himself of secrets. Remember your wedding, when he confessed to everyone of his role in the Lostai military?"

"He said it was hard at first, but afterward he felt relieved."

"Yes, and I suspect he feels that now, too. At that time, taking on an important role in the United Rebel Front was the remedy to having served in the Lostai military. The problem now is that he does not have an answer on what his penance should be for behaving like a coward."

"Montor has never been a coward."

"In the eyes of other Arandan males, he shied away from confronting the husband of the female he desired to make his wife."

"But he explained what happened. I would never have condoned him going to Earth and confronting Joshua, but even if I had, there was no time. After we first discovered the trans-portals, he went to help the Namson guerilla against the Lostai. Then he was injured in the mission to rescue the *Barinta* crew and retake Dit Lar. After that, he helped the Sotkari deal with a Lostai invasion and a pandemic. In the meantime, I was being tortured by Gio." Outrage entered my tone. "What do you people want from us?"

She cocked a brow at the words, "you people," but let it slide, bending down, instead, to meet my eyes.

"Is Montor supposed to have this little chat every time another Arandan male looks at him with disrespect?"

She had done this before. Used a simple conversation to help me understand Montor's point of view. I focused on the fruit in my hand.

"I see what you mean, but is he now doomed to live alone and depressed until he can find a way to die in battle? Is that his only solution?"

"Just because I have helped you understand how Montor is feeling right now, does not mean I actually agree that it is a rational response." She tapped my shoulder and winked at me. "I think he needs time to realize that he is overreacting."

I couldn't believe she admitted he was being a bit of a drama queen.

"OK, but who knows how long that can take? Maybe he will get himself killed in the process."

"So, what are your plans now, Mina?"

"Amber has decided to stay with me here, but I need to go back to Earth to get my younger son. I am taking Josher with me. I will have to disguise him somehow, but anyway, I hope it will be a quick trip to my sister's house. When I return, I intend for our family to be with Montor wherever he is and whatever he is doing."

She shook her head.

"That sounds radical and dangerous, Mina. Taking your children, too? Are you sure that besides Sotkari Ta genes, you do not have some Arandan ones?"

"Well, after being married to Montor for two years, something is bound to rub off."

We laughed.

"Will you and Foxor come with us?"

"Of course."

Besides the chat with Lasarta, I needed a good massage to release all the tension that had built up in the previous months. I usually relied on Montor for those and briefly, at one time, on Kindor. Since neither of those options was available, my next choice would be my friend, Colora. She owned spas, boutiques, and other recreational venues and was back living at her home on Fronidia, not too far from mine. After the massage, we went out to dinner and drinks at the Arandan enclave. I told her about everything that had happened with Montor and Josh and my conversation with Lasarta. She eyed the male waiter with lustful eyes.

"Oh, these Arandan males. Hard not to love those tall, muscular bodies, but sometimes they overdo it with all this concern about honor and respect."

Colora knew about Arandan males. Her deceased husband, Jortan, was Arandan. She'd had a brief fling with Montor before we were married, and I suspected she had something going on with Commander Portars.

"To top it off, Montor has all this self-loathing and guilt. Mina, he once told Jortan that he should have died as a child with the rest of his family at the Lostai labor camps."

"Yes, I know."

"So, did you get some action before he left?"

That was a weird segue.

I rolled my eyes, but my smile gave the answer away.

"That must have been odd, Mina, your current and ex-lovers all together. So, who was the best in bed?"

"Colora!"

"I can speak for Montor." She pretend-fanned herself. "With all that strength and stamina, I am sure he never leaves you wanting, but I have often wondered about Kindor. I could never get his attention. He was so obsessed with you. I can only imagine the explosion after keeping all that passion bottled up inside."

"Colora!" I shouted again, but the drinks had gone to my head, and I giggled. It was the first time I had reflected on my brief love affair with Kindor without regret and anger. Still, it should have never happened.

"I must ask Lorret one day. I hear the Sotkari Ta are very good with their hands and fingers."

"Colora, you are incorrigible."

She was the typical Fronidian, flirtatious and liberal when it came to sexual and romantic liaisons.

"If Montor says you are free to do what you want, maybe you should try a Fronidian." Her eyebrows rose suggestively. "We are a lot of fun, and you will always have plenty of sex."

"No, Colora, I have other ideas."

I told her my plans.

"I see. Well, let me know when you return from Earth. I think I might tag along."

"It is not a vacation. It will be dangerous."

She waved me off.

"I know, but I think Jortan would have wanted me to join you, and maybe you might need someone to help knock some sense into Montor's thick skull."

"Oh Colora, you are a true friend. I will need all the help I can get. You know how stubborn he can be."

Before going to bed that evening, a call came through. I put it on the viewer in the dining room.

"Kindor, how are you?"

He had not reached out to me on a personal line in a long time.

"Good, Mina, and you? I know this must be a surprise. I hope I am not bothering you. To be honest, I have been concerned how things are going for you and your daughter. Montor left me a strange message and instructions about Josher."

"Yes, I imagine."

I explained everything to him.

"Kindor, if I eventually head out to be with Montor as he battles the Lostai, I could use some help."

We smiled at each other in a way we had not in a long time.

"It sounds like you are trying to get the *Barinta* crew back together. I will see what Lorret thinks and let you know."

"OK."

"Mina?"

"Yes."

"I have never really had a chance to say..."

"Oh, Kindor, not now. I am trying to get a handle on my emotions. Rest assured, I know."

He looked down.

"OK. Well, I hope you have a safe trip to Earth and back."

After the call ended, I made myself some tea and sat at the dining table, lost in my thoughts.

I wonder what Montor is doing right now.

The tracker on the reply I sent to him showed he had received my message and had viewed it...more than once.

"Mom."

Amber's voice startled me.

"Oh hi, honey."

"How was your evening?"

"Fun. My friend Colora is a riot. You'll get to meet her one day."

"You look kind of sad, though. You miss him, don't you?"

At another time, in another place, in another situation, there would be no doubt who she might be referring to. This time, I wasn't sure.

"Huh?"

"You miss Montor."

"Oh yeah. I do."

"Has he called?"

Disappointment slipped into my tone.

"No."

"I feel bad. Coming to rescue me caused you problems with him. The whole thing with Dad...Damari explained to me—"

I pointed my finger at her, my tone perhaps a bit too harsh.

"Don't think that for one minute. You know, I felt guilty too, but this has got to stop. I didn't ask for these genes. We were taken from our home. We have nothing to feel guilty about. I've decided that the sooner I get that straight in my head, the sooner I can do what I need to do to be happy."

Amber bit her lip and averted her eyes. I didn't mean to, but I think I made her feel worse. "Yeah, I guess you're right."

I cocked my head in a suggestive way and, adding a silly smile, changed the topic.

"You've been spending a lot of time with Damari."

She blushed.

"He's so nice. I feel comfortable with him. Josher is so cute too, but Mom, I can't believe how he already knows how to fight so well at that age. We went to this place where they have holographic games. I mean, he's really skilled at some kind of martial art. Josher was facing a much taller opponent. It all seemed very realistic to me. Damari said the safety setting was pretty low."

I made a mental note to discuss the safety setting, yet again, with Foxor and Josher.

"Yes, Montor started teaching him as soon as he could walk. It is typical of Arandans. By the way, where is Damari?"

"He told me he was going to do his Sotkari Ta meditation. Mom, are you guys in some kind of weird alien religion now?"

"Not really, but the Sotkari Ta do have a regimen they stick to throughout their entire lives. It's how we keep our skills honed. If you want to learn telepathy, you'll need to do it, too."

We continued to chitchat. I made her a cup of tea, and as she sipped it, Damari walked in.

"Damari, would you like some tea?" I asked.

"Yea, please."

I poured him a cup. Once we all were sitting at the table, I brought up the subject of the upcoming trip to Earth.

"I've been giving myself some time to prepare emotionally and physically before making the trip to Earth. Montor and I have always stored several charged *hanstorics* here in case of an emergency. My intention is to bring back my younger son, Bobby. Josher will travel with us."

"Mom, people are going to notice he's, umm, different."

"We won't be walking around. This will be a quick trip. You said Bobby is at Aunt Sonia's. We'll just go there, but I'll need some help with keeping Josher occupied and hidden while Amber and I deal with Aunt Sonia, who I'm sure will have a hard time when she sees us." I turned to Damari. "I was thinking of asking you, Damari, to come with us."

Damari was caught off guard. He fidgeted in the chair and cleared his throat before replying.

"Mina, Me can't go Earth. Me promise Portars say me would a stay til the war done. Me nuh know how me would a react if me find miself home again."

"Yes, I remember, but you're older now. Plus, your Sotkari Ta meditation should provide mental strength even for such a matter as this one."

"I'm going, but I'm coming back," Amber blurted out.

Damari's eyes lit up.

"For real?"

She toyed with her fingers and nodded.

He tried hard to hide the broad smile this news provoked. Once he erased emotions from his expression, he said, "A true, Mina. Me supposed to can handle it. Me wish me could a see mi family, though."

"You could do a FaceTime or something."

He pressed his face into his fists and shook his head before replying, "No, dat wouldn't work. Mi family big. I don't think even mi mother could a keep dat secret."

"Why does it have to be a secret?"

"No, Damari has a point, Amber. Can you imagine if images of us appeared on social media or if the authorities traced back to where a video call originated? They would hound our families for information. Maybe just an audio call, but we'd have to make sure that person didn't tell anyone. I think I might try to call Chris. We'll see how it goes."

"Yeah. I didn't think about that."

"There's something else I'd like to discuss with you. When we get back, I intend to go support Montor in whatever he's doing. I miss him, and I know he misses me, too. Amber, I plan for you, Bobby, and Josher, to come with me. I'm not separating myself from my children again. The thing is, we'd be going into a war zone. It might seem selfish and reckless, but I feel like bad things happen when we're apart."

Amber placed her hand on mine.

"Mom, with everything you've been through, you deserve to be happy. I support you."

"Mina, mi wah go pon this mission wid Montor too."

I smiled at them both but couldn't hold back my tears.

"Thank you."

"Mom, when are we leaving for Earth?"

"The day after tomorrow."

29

———

My sister, Sonia, and her family lived in an upscale neighborhood about an hour north of Tampa, Florida. We landed in the middle of her backyard. I was glad to feel the chill in the air.

It must be January or February.

The light jackets we wore suited the weather perfectly. I had reproduced something like a hoodie for Josher and pulled the hood well over his head so that it concealed most of his face.

"Is everyone OK?"

Damari's brow furrowed as if he were in pain, his eyes glistening. I gave him a side hug.

"I know. The first time I came with Marcia was very emotional for me, too."

Amber scrunched her face in confusion. "You've been back to Earth before?"

"Yes, honey. I was the guinea pig for the Dit Lar transportal. The first time we used it was to return a kidnapped child to her parents. I took a risk and, after taking her home to New York City, made another jump to our house here in Florida to get a glimpse of you and your brothers. Instead, I found your father and, uhh, Laura. I had to rush back because I didn't know how long the *hanstoric* would remain charged. It was a gut-wrenching decision for me, but that's a story for another day."

Her eyes gave away that she was trying to decide how she felt about that piece of information. We didn't have time for that now. I looked at the sky. From the position of the sun, it appeared to be midday.

If it's a school day, the kids and Rodney should not be home yet.

"OK, Amber, I know this is tough, but I think you should be the first one to get Aunt Sonia's attention. It will be a shock for her to see any of us, but I've been away for much longer."

We walked to the covered patio at the back of the house. Damari, Josher, and I hid in a corner not visible from the sliding glass doors. I heard barking and recognized Coco, our pet labradoodle. A memory of when Josh and I first brought her home at eight weeks flashed in my mind. It was Damari's turn to hug me.

I need to keep it together.

"Amber, I think it's best you don't go up to the front door because anyone walking on the sidewalk can see you."

"She usually leaves these sliding doors unlocked during the day."

"I think sneaking in is not such a good idea, either. We don't want her to have a heart attack. You should knock on the sliding door first."

She made that face that said I was focusing on unimportant things.

"Mom, either way, this is going to hit her hard."

Amber took a deep breath and walked over to the sliding door by the family room and knocked. Nothing happened. She knocked harder the second time and whatever she saw prompted her to shout, "Oh my God."

With one hard tug, Amber slid the door open and said, "Aunt Sonia, are you OK?"

Damari looked at me wide-eyed. It took all my self-control not to run in with her. I signaled to Damari to stay put.

Sonia must have fainted or gone hysterical. If I go in now, I'll make it worse. Let Amber calm her down and break the news to her, nice and slow.

I don't know how long Damari, Josher, and I cowered in that corner. It felt like an eternity.

"*Ro Ma*, what are we doing here? I want to sit. My legs are tired."

"Shhh."

My knees almost buckled when Amber popped her head out and signaled for me to come in. At least an hour had transpired. Not knowing how much Amber told Sonia, baby steps were still required.

"Josher, stay here with Damari."

I entered the family room on jelly legs. Coco greeted me first, taking long deep sniffs before running around me in circles, tail wagging joyfully. Contrary to Coco's ecstatic movements, I walked like a robot but bent over to pet her.

"Oh Coco, I've missed you."

She behaved as if a day hadn't gone by since she last saw me. A piece of my heart broke.

My sister was sitting on the sofa. Her whole body shook like a leaf fluttering in the wind, causing another rip through my heart. I was glad she stood and ran to hug me because my legs went from jelly to stone. I couldn't move. For a long while, sobbing sounds filled the room. Amber embraced both of us, and somehow, we found our voices. Sonia spoke in the high-pitched voice of someone on the verge of tears.

"I can't believe what Amber explained to me, but I'm so happy you are alive."

"Me too. I wish I had more time. Unfortunately, we don't, plus we need discretion. I don't want people driving you crazy. Has Amber explained why I can't stay?"

Sonia buried her face in her hands. They slid down until her fingers covered her mouth. It took her a few moments before she replied.

"She did, but it sounds to me like one of those space opera shows you loved so much. Sorry, Mina, but I'm still trying to wrap my mind around all this. Is he outside...your son?"

"Yes, with a friend, but before anything else, where is Bobby?"

She checked her watch.

"He's in school but should arrive any minute now. He gets out earlier than Sam and Rosalind."

"Did Amber tell you about Josh?"

Her face crumpled in sorrow.

"Oh my God, yes. This is all so crazy. At first, we thought you were angry with Josh and had left for a while. As time passed, we feared you were dead, the victim of a crime or an accident. There was no trace of you. Once Josh and Amber went missing, the local news stations came up with a new theory and speculated that maybe you all were part of a witness protection program. Police and detectives came here often to interview us. We didn't know what to think. Laura is still living at your old place, hoping Josh will contact her. She's called me a couple of times. I didn't like that Josh brought her there, but now I feel bad for her."

I looked down. "Laura."

Sonia touched my arm.

"Sorry, maybe I shouldn't have mentioned her."

"It's fine. I always suspected that Josh..." I stopped and sighed. "Our marriage had problems that we never made a point to address."

A long silence followed, so I changed the subject.

"Amber has decided to come back with me. I intend to take Bobby with me, too, unless he really rejects that idea."

Sonia's brow furrowed in a deep crease.

"I don't know. He's been with us for four years, Mina."

"I want my children with me, Sonia. Even if I stayed here on Earth, he would come back to living with me."

"Yes, I suppose so, but in that case, we would still visit and see each other." Her lips trembled. "You're leaving to another galaxy."

I showed her the *hanstoric*.

"Don't worry. I will be popping in, literally, from time to time, to visit."

"Will your new husband be all right with that?"

"He will have to be."

Sonia rubbed her forehead, looking frazzled.

"OK...well, would you like something to drink? I have that freshly squeezed lemonade you liked so much. Bring your son and friend in. I'll have to hurry and watch for when Bobby gets home so I can have a talk with him before he sees all of you."

Damari's steps were slow and cautious as he walked in holding Josher by the hand, but once he tasted Sonia's lemonade, he gave her a thumbs-up and flashed his signature friendly grin. Sonia bent down to get a good look at Josher. Her eyes were like saucers, and her hand went to her chest as if to control her heavy breathing.

"Mina, I...I don't know what to say." She grabbed Josher gently by the shoulders to study him closer. "If I wasn't seeing him with my own eyes, I wouldn't believe it."

I could tell Josher was feeling more uncomfortable by the minute. Sonia, being a mother, picked it up as well. She stood, and Josher ran back to me.

"Well, I guess this is my first alien contact," said Sonia, trying to make light of the moment. "Maybe I should contact NASA. His eyes look like yours, though."

I spoke to Josher in Arandan.

"This is my sister, your *somasta*. Her name is Sonia. Greet her in the Earthian language I taught you."

"*Hallo, Xonia.*"

"Hi there, kiddo," she replied, walking over to pat his head.

We all heard the click of the front door lock.

"It must be Bobby."

She ran over there. I bent over, hands on my chest. The ache caught me by surprise.

"What is it, Mom?" Amber whispered.

"I think I'm the one who's going to have a heart attack."

Sonia spoke to Bobby in hushed tones. His voice sounded nothing like the child I remembered.

"What? What are you talking about, Aunt Sonia?"

Their muffled voices carried over to where we were sitting, but not enough to catch the actual words.

A gasp.

Silence.

Footsteps.

"Mom!"

Standing in front of me was an adolescent, several inches taller than the boy I remembered.

My God, he's already taller than me.

Unprepared, I stood motionless, my arms limp at my sides. He hugged me and cried, deep gasping sobs originating from his gut. My heart continued to rip apart. I lost my voice and dizziness washed over me.

"Mom, sit down," said Amber.

After hugging Amber long and hard, Bobby sat next to me.

Josher tapped my leg. "*Ro Ma*, why is everyone so sad?"

His lips pouted and twitched. He was about to cry, too. I caressed his cheek.

"Do not worry, *honey*. We just have not seen each other in a long time."

Bobby's jaw dropped when he got a better look at Josher.

"Bobby, this is your brother."

"What?" Bobby dragged out the question and searched the room as if looking for an answer. "Is that a costume?"

"No, honey. He's not from..."

Bobby's incredulous expression made it even harder for me to explain.

"Umm, he's not from Earth. Sit down so I can explain."

My heart sank as Bobby stared at Josher and grimaced.

"Is this some sort of sick joke?" Bobby shouted, doubt merging into outrage.

I held his hand. "Let me explain."

Sonia went to get a glass of lemonade for Bobby, and when she came back, we were a bit more settled down. I explained to Bobby the main points of my situation. He cycled through expressions of disbelief and confusion as I spoke about being abducted by aliens and forced to train in the Lostai bootcamp, spaceships, portals, Montor, Josher, and rescuing Amber. Amber jumped in every so often to confirm what I was saying.

"Where is Dad?"

I tasted blood and realized I had bitten my lip too hard. Bobby looked at me and then at Amber. She covered her face.

"It's bad news, huh?"

I pulled him close to me and barely whispered my reply.

"I'm sorry, honey. He was so brave. He saved Amber's life but was badly injured and didn't make it."

We cried again, swaying in our sad embrace. When he pulled back, he tried to hide his face crumpled in grief.

"I can't believe all this," he said. "Now what?"

"Bobby, I can't stay here."

He looked at Josher with contempt.

"Because of him, right!"

"Yes, and because I'm married to somebody else now. Amber has decided to come back with me. I want you to come with me, too. A lot of bad things have happened to me, but not once did I stop hoping that I could find a way for us to be together again. We will be able to come here and visit Aunt Sonia occasionally. I know this is a lot of pressure, but I don't have too much time." I looked at my sister. "Sonia, how long before the rest of your family arrives?"

"About two hours."

"I think it's best if I leave before they get here."

"If Bobby goes with you, what will I say to explain that yet another member of the family has gone missing?" asked Sonia.

My temples throbbed. I didn't have a good answer.

"Say whatever you think will cause you the fewest problems. I don't know, say you sent him to a family member out of state—"

"I'm not going."

"What?"

He stood and shot me a cold, hard glare.

"I said, I'm not going with you. I don't want to be a part of your new alien freak show." He pointed to Josher. "This thing's father is not going to be my dad. I'm staying with Aunt Sonia and Uncle Rodney."

Stunned, I looked at Amber and Sonia, my mouth open, but no words came out.

"Bobby, don't be so hard on your mother," said Sonia.

He rolled his eyes and walked away. The last piece of my heart disintegrated. Josher stared at me with wide, sad eyes as he watched me break down into tears yet again. Sonia placed her hand on my shoulder.

"It's too much for him to digest in such a short time. You said you'd be visiting. Maybe later he might change his mind."

I wiped my face and nodded.

"Yeah, it was stupid of me to think I could drop in for an hour and fix everything. I have no way to let you know ahead of time when I'll be coming back, but rest assured, I will. Talk to Chris and explain what happened. The next time I come, I'll give him a phone call. Josh and Amber have told me he is doing very well."

"You know, he's planning to visit and spend a few weeks with us here in the summer. Maybe you can come then."

"There's no way I can target a particular timeframe. There are still many things about how this portal works that we don't understand."

Damari stood to place his empty glass on the counter. We looked at each other, knowing that the time to say goodbye was quickly upon us. My mind went through an exercise of the most important questions to ask in the little time remaining.

"Sonia, how is Dad doing? Josh told me he got cancer."

"Yes, prostate cancer, but they caught it early. He responded well to the treatment and moved to a new senior adult neighborhood on the east coast that has a lot of amenities and activities for people his age. He even has a lady friend who stays over his place often. Her name is Lydia. She's very nice and full of energy. They seem to be a good match."

"That makes me happy. What about Lizzy?"

"She and Antonio divorced."

"Yeah, I always had a suspicion things would end for them."

"It's been tough for her. She's been depressed. I have her over often, and she's started to see a therapist. I think she's finally turning a corner."

"Does she still live in Ft. Myers?"

"Yes."

I happened to glance to the kitchen and noticed the digital clock on the microwave. We were running out of time.

"Ooh, I need to give you something."

I went into my bag and got the *omori*.

"Here, give this to Bobby later. It's Josh's ashes. I want to talk to Bobby before we leave, but I don't want to give this to him now when he's already so upset," I said.

"His room is the first bedroom to the right."

I walked over there and found the door locked.

"Bobby, I want to talk before I leave."

I knocked again and waited, choking back new tears.

What if he doesn't even want to say goodbye?

The doorknob turned. He avoided looking at me, but his red, tear-streaked face and puffy eyes let me know he had been crying some more.

I need to be the strong one here.

I sat on his bed and gestured for him to sit next to me.

"Bobby, I know it's crazy and unfair for me to expect you to go with me somewhere unknown when everything that I just explained sounds like a bad dream. I understand your anger. You've suffered so much since I've been gone, and then I dump on you the news about your dad and my new family. I'm so sorry. I just wanted so badly to get back what I had lost."

He leaned his head on my shoulder, and I stroked his hair.

"I can't say when, but I'll come back again soon. In the meantime, you can think about what I proposed to you. If you still don't feel comfortable leaving with me, that's fine. We can spend some time together here. I'll be in less of a rush because by then Aunt Sonia will have talked to your cousins and uncle and prepared them for the shock of seeing me."

He released the tension in his body. I reached around with my other arm and clutched him for fear he might slide to the floor. He pressed his head against my chest.

"I missed you so much, Mom...so much."

Although my eyes blurred with hot tears, I was determined to be strong for him.

"I know, honey, I know. At least now you've seen that I'm OK. I want you to be happy and continue to do well in school. Tell me, are you into any sports?"

He sniffled and straightened up.

"I take martial arts classes. I'm already a brown belt in the adult class."

"Wow, you'll be a black belt soon, and training with adults. That's impressive."

"Yeah, it's really helped me."

We chatted some more as I tried to get to know the man my son was turning into. A knock on the door interrupted us.

"Mina, I think the kids will arrive shortly."

"All right, thanks."

We both stood, and our eyes met. He had his dad's gray eyes and long, dark lashes. He would grow up to be a handsome man. I hugged him, rubbing his back, committing to memory what it felt like to holding him this close.

"I love you, Bobby. We'll see each other again soon."

"I love you, too, Mom."

We both walked back to the family room. Before leaving, a thought occurred to me. I pulled out my tablet and set it to selfie mode.

"Everyone, gather around."

"Mom, that's way too close," Amber said.

"No, this thing corrects the distance. Remember, this is an alien tablet." I finally remembered what a laugh was like. "It's far more advanced than a cell phone."

"Oh, let me get my cell phone so I can keep a picture of you, too," Sonia said.

"I don't think it's a good idea to have a picture of us on your phone. If that image got into the wrong hands, I'm not sure how that would impact your life. I'll do something better," I said.

I transferred the image to my portable holographic viewer and showed everyone.

"That's amazing," Bobby said. "It looks so realistic."

Sonia's jaw dropped. She was still speechless when I showed her how to work the device.

"Keep this private, sis. Only share with our immediate family. I'm not even sure you should show your kids. One slip and you'll have CIA, FBI, NASA, and who knows what other government agency hounding you."

Sonia met my eyes, silently acknowledging the gravity of my warning, and looked at her watch again.

"OK, time to go."

Bobby hugged Amber and me again.

"I prefer to do this outside. For some reason, initiating the jump from indoors gives me the heebie-jeebies, plus I don't want to risk transporting you guys by mistake."

Sonia and Bobby watched from the patio as we walked farther out into the backyard.

I set the destination on the *hanstoric*. Amber, Damari, Josher, and I huddled together. Before tapping the display, Bobby waved. In that moment, he shouted out in a voice that sounded like a child's again.

"Mom...maybe next time."

"Yes, honey. Love you. God bless."

30

We arrived outside of the entrance to the Penstarox operations center. I remembered the days when I marveled at how an airplane ride could put you in an entirely different country, time zone, or climate. Using the portal was a thousand times more disconcerting. Amber cocked her head to check my expression.

"Mom, I know the whole thing with Bobby must have been rough. Are you OK?"

I caressed her arm and gave it a squeeze.

"It was hard, but I'm so glad we went and saw them. I'm going to focus on the fact that everyone seems to be healthy and well. That will help me until we can visit them again. By that time, Sonia will have already explained everything to Chris and the rest of the family. We'll be able to spend more time with them. I just hope the wrong people don't find out where we are and how we traveled back to Earth. I'm concerned about what that would mean for our family. What about you? How are you holding up? This has all been a lot for you to handle, too."

Grief collapsed her face. Her teeth dug into her bottom lip.

"Yeah, Mom, I won't lie. I'm sad, and I wish this were just a bad dream, but I'm glad to be with you."

I hugged her. We shared another moment of sorrow.

"*Ro Ma*, where did *Ta Ri* go? Are you still sad?"

Josher's wide eyes begged for attention. I got on one knee and kissed his forehead.

"Honey, are you feeling OK?"

"Yes, but *Ta Ri* is gone again, and you have been crying so much."

"Do not worry, honey. Everything is OK. *Ta Ri* had an important job to attend to, but we will be with him soon."

I grabbed his hand and gestured to Damari and Amber.

"Follow me."

I led them straight to Commander Portars's office, where his assistant greeted me with a curious look on his face.

"Mina, I was not expecting to see you back here so soon."

"I need to talk to Commander Portars, please."

"Did you make an appointment?"

"No, but it is very important."

"I will see what he says."

He left to go to Portars's office and was back too soon.

"Unfortunately, Commander Portars is busy and cannot see you now."

"Really? Damari, take Amber and Josher to the resting area and make sure they get something to eat and drink." I shot the assistant an impertinent look. "I will stay here until Commander Portars has some free time to talk to me."

Damari chuckled on his way out. If Amber would have been skilled in telepathy, he probably would have told her privately that her mom was on the rampage again.

The last time Montor separated himself from us, he asked Portars not to divulge anything about his whereabouts. This time, I'd have to be firm. At least three hours went by before

Portars came out of his office. He gave his assistant a nasty look when he saw I was still there.

"Hello, Mina. I am sorry I could not see you earlier. You should have let me know you were coming. I am on my way to get something to eat, and then I will have to get right back to work."

"If you do not mind, may I accompany you? You can just listen to me while you eat. Please, Commander Portars. This is important."

He had a soft spot for me, but I didn't know whether recent events had changed my standing with him.

"Fine, Mina, but you will need to be concise. I am very busy."

He used the condescending tone that came so easily to Arandan military leaders. I still considered it a victory for me. I followed him to the conference room, which was full of soldiers.

Portars looked around, catching some of them giving us side glances.

After picking up his food, he said, "Mina, instead of eating here, I will take this back to my office, and we can talk there."

In his office, I wasted no time telling him what was on my mind.

"Commander Portars, where is Montor?"

"Mina, this is the second time recently that you ask me about Montor's location." He looked down his nose at me. "I dislike getting into other people's personal matters."

"I understand, but I know he was on his way to lead a fleet of battle crafts to engage the Lostai and attempt an incursion on their planet. Let me be frank. He left with a bad attitude and ideas about dying in battle. As far as I am concerned, he is still my husband. I am not content to wait at home to receive the bad news that I am once again a widow. I want to commission a ship and go where he is and help him in his quest. The old *Barinta* crew is ready to leave with me."

First, he laughed.

"The old *Barinta* crew?"

Then he smirked and leaned forward, looking at me like I was a child.

"You were just a few civilians under Montor's leadership going on diplomatic missions."

I didn't let his tone intimidate me.

"Remember, under my guidance, that crew played a critical role in taking Dit Lar from the Lostai."

Reclining back in his chair, he replied, "Some of Montor's cockiness seems to have rubbed off on you."

His voice was stern, but admiration flickered in his eyes before morphing into what looked like heartache.

"Anyway, Mina, I have bad news. Montor's fleet has taken heavy losses, and Lostai ships surround the few remaining. I fear he is close to achieving his death wish."

My stomach twisted. I did my best to control my breathing.

"Are you not going to send reinforcements?"

"We can, but it will take a few days for them to get to where Montor is. I think it is a matter of hours before his ship and the remaining others succumb to their Lostai opponents."

"No! We must not allow that to happen. How were we so unprepared?"

"Mina, has someone named you High General and forgotten to tell me?" The stern tone resurfaced.

"Sorry, sir."

"Both sides in this war are constantly figuring out how to crack the encryption in the enemy's communication systems. Perhaps they intercepted our messages and learned of our plan."

"Are you sure there is no way to get another ship there sooner? Do we not have any friends in the area?" My façade of strength fell apart. I shuddered and broke down. "Portars, I cannot lose him."

A notification appeared on his viewer. He was kind enough not to send me out as he took the call. A female and a male Arandan appeared on the screen.

"Officer Xartor, this must be something urgent if my assistant has patched you through without announcement."

Officer Xartor and Officer Na Nar were an Arandan couple, scientists, who had become experts in the transportal technology we found on Dit Lar. They were the ones who trained me how to use the *hanstorics*. I had affectionately nicknamed them, in my mind, the Transportal Nerds.

Xartor cleared his throat and appeared to shrink in his chair.

"Sir, to be honest, we hacked your system and bypassed your assistant because he would not transfer the call."

"This is an outrage! Has everyone lost their minds here?"

"Sir, it could not wait."

"What is it?" snapped Portars.

"Our simulation worked, sir. We are ready for a test run."

Portars rose from his chair and fist pumped in one swift movement.

"Oh, that is excellent news. I will immediately assign a test pilot."

"Sir, what are they referring to?" I dared to ask.

Portars rolled his eyes and grunted an Arandan sound of disgust.

"I might as well. All protocol has been lost today. Officer Xartor and—"

"Oh, hello Mina, I did not see you there."

"Is everyone going to continue to disrespect me and this office today?"

Xartor grimaced and shrunk even further. Na Nar turned away, I suspect to hide a smile.

"Sorry, sir."

Portars continued, but not before giving us each a warning look.

"As I was saying before being rudely interrupted, Officer Xartor and Officer Na Nar have applied the *hanstoric* technology to a spacecraft. If it works, we could jump spaceships through the transportal across the galaxy just as we are doing with people."

I shot up out of my seat as well.

"My crew and I will be the test pilots. I am sure I can gather them here in an hour."

"Mina, you are not a ship captain, nor do you have a crew!"

"Sir, can we continue our conversation in private?" I said.

Portars's loud exhale let us know he was becoming more annoyed by the minute.

"Xartor, thank you. I will be in contact with you shortly."

As soon as the viewer switched off, I spoke up.

"Sir, please let my team and me take the test ship to where Montor is. I can coordinate with Xartor and Na Nar to fortify the shields, augment the weapons system, and optimize propulsion. Maybe taking the Lostai by surprise and adding one more ship to the mix could gain our comrades some time until you can send reinforcements."

"I do not know why I am even indulging such a crazy idea, but who would be with you?"

"Damari, Foxor, Lasarta, Kindor, Lorret, Colora, Josher, and Amber."

"Damari is a fine soldier and Kindor a powerful ally, but the rest...and why do you need Colora?"

"She asked to come."

His jaw clenched.

"And you plan to take your children into a battle that is more like a suicide mission? Even if I were to entertain this idea, which I am not, but if I did," his voice softened. "Perhaps you should leave Colora here with your children."

"Sir, I promised myself I would not separate from Josher or Amber again. My daughter, Amber, is just as stubborn as I am. She would not stay even if I asked her. I suspect I will not be able to change Colora's mind, either. Her knowledge of the civics, languages, and species of this sector has been helpful in the past. To be frank, her personality also helps lighten things up for us when we are stressed."

He looked at his lap.

"Yes, she does have a wonderful personality."

Portars pinched the bridge of his nose before making eye contact and crossing his arms.

"Mina, I cannot in good conscience let you do this. Montor would not want his friends and family, much less his son, risking their lives for such a hopeless case. This is brand new technology. Our intention was to do several tests before using it in official military business. Even if the jump is successful, you will still be outnumbered."

I wasn't about to be dissuaded so easily, and I argued with Portars that my experience with the *hanstoric* qualified me for this mission.

"Commander, let me do the test. We can avoid risking the lives of soldiers that we need for our fight against the Lostai. It would not be the first time you have used me as a lab rat."

He flinched a bit after that comment. Eventually, I begged him to let me try to save Montor. My persistence paid off. Portars agreed to let me use the United Rebel Front's latest military technological invention to help Montor and his crew. He had one condition.

"You need an Arandan male to serve as captain on your ship."

I rubbed my face with my hand in frustration.

"Sir, this reminds me of when you sent Sortomor to lead us.

He did not have Montor or my family's best interests at heart. This is a rescue mission."

"I will allow you to select the captain this time, and Mina, you better not tell anyone that I am being so forbearing with you."

My mind raced, thinking of who I could work with the best.

"Is Junior Lieutenant Noomar here on Penstarox?"

Portars's mouth curled into a knowing smile.

"Yes, he is here. That is a tall order for him to go from Junior Lieutenant to Captain, but I will maintain a direct line of communication with him. Do not think you will manipulate Noomar because he is young and inexperienced or because he helped rescue your daughter."

"I do not want to manipulate anyone, but he knows my family. We all bonded on that mission, and I have no doubt we will be like-minded in our decisions."

"Fine, I will contact him." He stood, crossed his arms over his chest, and bowed. "Mina, good luck."

I rushed out, grabbed my tablet, and started making calls. Within the hour, Kindor, Lorret, Foxor, Lasarta, and Colora were in Portars's office. We had left *hanstorics* in each of their homes for emergencies. In the meantime, I checked on Damari, Amber, and Josher and updated them on what was happening.

"Amber, please keep an eye on Josher. I need Damari to come with me."

Damari and I met with the Transportal Nerds. They took us outside to inspect the spacecraft. Noomar joined us there. Damari and Noomar got familiar with the ship's navigational system while the Transportal Nerds gave me a crash course on everything I needed to know about the new technology. We also worked on the sensor, weapons, and other upgrades.

"It is much smaller than the *Barinta*," I noted. "Hopefully, that means it has better maneuverability."

"Noomar, you are its first captain, so you get to name it," said Na Nar.

Mellow for a male Arandan soldier, Noomar fostered no hidden agenda or power greed, which was one of the reasons I liked him.

"Mina, do you have a suggestion?" he asked.

"I would like to name it *Torixa*."

"A word that means family?" asked Xartor, not hiding the fact that he found the name odd.

"Yes, it is the perfect name for the spacecraft I hope will bring my family back together."

31

That same evening, we gathered on the bridge of the *Torixa*. Captain Noomar and I had met earlier to talk about my opinions on everyone's strong suits. Based on my input, he assigned Kindor to the defense and sensors station. We put Lorret in charge of the weapons array. Foxor would monitor the ship's operating systems. Damari was at the helm and controlling the traditional navigational system. I'd oversee the new transportal technology and help Kindor on his station. Colora would take care of communications. We assigned Lasarta the important duty of keeping us fed and comfortable. I asked Amber to help me with Josher's care, which provided a perfect opportunity for her to get to know her brother.

Noomar activated a holographic star map to display Montor's current position.

"Our latest information is that only two of the ten ships in Commander Montor's fleet remain," said Noomar.

Everyone's face reflected the somber news. Those were heavy losses for our side. I also noted that they had promoted Montor to commander.

Noomar continued with his debrief.

"The information is sketchy, as they seem to be in a fierce battle with several Lostai ships and cannot keep central command updated as they normally would. Kindor and Lorret, your execution in those first few minutes will be critical. We must take advantage of our surprise arrival. You will need to detect the best targets and fire before they get wind of what is going on. We want to hit as many of their ships as possible at least once and, if time permits, a second time. Damari, the minute their sensors pick up our signature, we will need to outmaneuver them. Our small-sized craft is well suited for this strategy, but we must be aware of this asteroid field."

He highlighted the relevant area on the map.

"It appears they are trying to pin our ships against this area to limit their mobility. Mina, that is why it is important that we arrive outside of this perimeter with the Lostai battle crafts between us and our ships. We will draw at least some of their attention and give our comrades a fighting chance. I commanded our scientists to revamp our encryption codes once again, so hopefully we can send messages to our ships that the Lostai cannot intercept. Mina, is there anything you want to share with us about the transportal and making the jump?"

I stood in front of the crew.

"If I may, Captain Noomar, before getting into that, I want to take a moment first to thank you all for coming on this dangerous mission. Once again, you have answered the call to help a member of my family."

"We are all family here," Lasarta interjected.

My face flushed with emotion.

"Yes, thank you. OK, regarding the jump we are about to make through the transportal, everyone here has traveled using the *hanstoric* before. As you know, there is a moment of disorientation upon arrival. We do not know how it will feel using this new technology on a spacecraft. Before we execute the jump, commit to memory the exact actions you will take when we arrive to help compensate for this."

Everyone reviewed their station controls before strapping into their seats. Meanwhile, Lasarta, Amber, and Josher strapped into their passenger security seats behind the bridge.

"One more thing," I said. "For those of you who pray, now is the time."

I closed my eyes and said a silent prayer. Lasarta chanted out loud in Arandan.

"Everyone ready?" asked Noomar.

We all nodded.

"Mina, on my mark."

As I steadied my nerves, Noomar fist pumped, the signal to engage.

I tapped the controls.

A flash of light.

Screeching, bending metal sounds.

I opened my eyes to find the bridge spinning around me as nausea churned my stomach. The ship rocked before stabilizing. This jump was more disconcerting than any I had experienced before. I unstrapped and willed myself to my feet to look around. Kindor and Lorret were already standing behind their stations. Noomar, Damari, Colora, and Foxor were still unconscious. Lasarta was slumped in her seat, too. Amber side-hugged Josher, whose face was scrunched up in confusion.

"Mina, I have already fired on and destroyed three of the Lostai ships," said Lorret, laughing. "They never knew what hit them. Three remain. Apparently, one was destroyed before we arrived. Kindor has activated the new shields modulation, which will confuse their sensors for only a few minutes more. We need Damari to get us moving!"

"Excellent, Lorret," I said as I ran over to Damari and roused him. He awoke with a gasp. Noomar also regained consciousness. I spoke to Damari in Arandan so that everyone could understand.

"Damari, we soon will attract their fire. Be ready to zip between them and the United Rebel ships."

"Yes, Mina," he answered, now fully alert.

"Mina, there is only one United Rebel Front ship left," Kindor communicated to me telepathically.

I tasted bile in my mouth.

God, please let Montor be on the surviving ship.

By then, everyone was wide awake and at their stations. Noomar took over command, so I rushed over to Lasarta, Amber, and Josher.

"Everyone OK over here?" I asked first in Arandan and then in English.

They all confirmed they were fine, although Amber's pale face concerned me. Noomar was shouting orders. I'd have to check on her later.

"Stay strapped in," I said and rushed to Kindor's station.

Having fulfilled my first assignment of getting us here safely, my next duty was to help Kindor on sensors while he kept changing the configuration of our shields system to confuse the Lostai.

"Colora, send the United Rebel Front ship an encrypted message, letting them know we are here to help. Inform them that our plan is to draw the attention of the Lostai battle craft to give them a chance to recover. If they find an opening in the Lostai blockade, they should retreat while we try to keep the Lostai occupied. Let them know of our jump capability. Also, send an encrypted message to Commander Portars and let him know the jump was successful," ordered Noomar.

"Yes, sir."

My heart ached as I studied the readout on my console screen.

"Sir, my sensors show that the United Rebel Front ship's

shields are down by half portion," I said, trying to shut down any emotion in my voice. "They probably have some *hanstorics* over there that they may be able to use."

"Colora, hail the United Rebel Front ship. Lorret, fire at will! Damari, I want us moving at top speed while circling their ships."

Noomar had not finished uttering his orders when we received the first bombardment from a Lostai ship. Kindor's manipulation of the shields system protected us. Only a slight thud let us know that we'd been hit.

"Sir, the commander is on video."

A tiny sound of relief escaped my throat as Montor's image appeared on screen. He could see all of us. Josher, who was still strapped in his seat, recognized his father and shouted to him while flailing his arms and legs. Montor's jaw clenched and the look in his eyes made me gulp.

"Captain Noomar, I am happy to see you, but whose idiotic idea was this?" Montor growled.

I imagined everyone controlling the urge to look my way.

To Noomar's credit, he held his ground.

"We are here on Commander Portars's orders, sir."

"I doubt Portars would send civilians and children to a war zone. Mina, when I received your message, I never believed you would actually drag my family on this senseless endeavor. The only thing you have accomplished is that we now will get to see each other perish."

After an awkward silence, Noomar cleared his throat and spoke up again.

"Sir, our sensors tell us that your shields are compromised. Do you have enough *hanstorics* to jump all your crew over here?"

"What do you think? Would we be here if that were the case?"

Montor's sarcasm cut like a knife. Noomar rolled his shoulders, and I felt bad for having put him in this uncomfortable position. Montor took a deep breath and his expression softened.

"Captain Noomar, I am sorry. I appreciate your help. Because of your crew's brave actions, we are facing three Lostai ships instead of six. We offered the youngest soldiers and those with children to use the *hanstorics* to jump to safety. As you can imagine, no one accepted."

Noomar nodded. No honorable Arandan soldier would accept such an offer and leave their comrades behind to die.

"Sir, our plan is to continue to draw the Lostai fire and keep them occupied. We have upgraded all our systems and can outmaneuver their large battle crafts. Our hope is that we can hold off the enemy until our reinforcements arrive."

"OK, Captain Noomar. I don't know what you did to that ship of yours, but let us see if you can pull off another miracle. Montor out."

Noomar pressed his fist into the palm of the other hand and took a minute before addressing us.

"All right, team. We will continue with the same strategy as before."

Everyone echoed, "Yes, sir."

Damari proved to be an excellent helmsman. Sensors showed that as we zipped around each Lostai ship, they attempted to fire on us and missed each time. Montor's ship took advantage to score hits on the Lostai ships, causing some damage but not enough to disable, much less destroy them.

"It is obvious Montor is having to divert power from his weapons system to compensate for the weakened shields," I said.

"Captain Noomar, we should coordinate with Commander Montor's weapons control to focus firing on the same Lostai ship. Maybe with simultaneous hits, we can pick them off one by one," suggested Lorret.

"Good idea. Colora, please send a message to Montor's ship. Tell them to contact Lorret directly to coordinate our targeting. Lorret, do not wait for my orders to fire. Every second is critical."

Lorret took Noomar's instruction to heart, leaving us only guessing what her and her counterpart on Montor's ship were up to. Her face was a picture of concentration as her fingers flicked across the controls like someone playing a musical instrument.

The explosion surprised the rest of us as she shouted, "Yes!"

We found ourselves surrounded by a debris field amid flashes of red and orange. The ship jerked as Damari reacted to evade fragments of what used to be a Lostai ship.

"Well done, Lorret," shouted Noomar. "One down. Two more to go!"

Cheering with renewed confidence, we geared up to circle the remaining two Lostai ships.

Then our luck ran out.

A photon blast knocked us all to the floor. Josher laughed, thinking it was hilarious for a second, until he heard Lasarta and Amber shout out in fear. He began to cry and call for me. I shuddered, struggling to ignore his cries so I could remain focused on the sensors.

"Mina, thank you for letting us know that one was coming," said Noomar, clearly annoyed.

"Sorry, sir, but they have enabled a masking program that is blocking our sensors. I have lost view of their weapons array and directional systems," I replied.

"One of our thrusters has been damaged," announced Damari. "I cannot execute flight maneuvers as well as before."

"Lorret, what is your counterpart on Montor's ship saying?"

"They are saying the same as Mina. We can continue to fire on the Lostai ships, but now we can only guess at how they will counter. I assume they know they have crippled us a bit by knocking out one of our thrusters."

"Foxor, divert power from propulsion to the weapons system. No use for so much speed now that we have lost the ability for Damari's flight tactics. Lorret, make good use of the additional power I am allotting to the weapons array," shouted Noomar.

"Yes, sir!"

Everyone's tone sounded a bit more frantic. Josher was still wailing, and Noomar glared at me.

"Mina, I cannot concentrate with that," Noomar said, poking the air with his finger as he pointed to Josher.

I ran over to Josher and kneeled on one knee.

"Honey, we are just playing a game for training. Remember the *Golorax* game you like to play at the holographic rooms? This is similar. Please stop crying and relax, or we will lose."

"*Aembuh* scared me," he said, sniffling. "And *Lo Ro*, too."

I shot them both exaggerated admonishing looks.

"They are being very silly. Please, ladies, we are trying to win this game."

Lasarta patted his head and came to the rescue.

"Josher, explain to me how this game works."

Josher launched into his typical detailed explanations, and I turned my attention to Amber. I took her hands in mine and switched to English.

"Sweetie, I won't lie. This is a very dangerous situation, but I need your help to keep Josher settled and calm."

"Mom, are we gonna die?"

"I sure as hell hope not, but Noomar needs everyone to be focused. I can't be distracted."

"I'll try to control myself."

I kissed her forehead and rushed back to check the sensors. Before I reached Kindor's station, another blast rocked our ship. Lights flickered, alarms blared, and I saw smoke outside one of the side windows. Dread choked me.

What have I done? I have brought my kids here to die. Montor is right. I'm an impulsive idiot.

"Sir, one of the Lostai battle crafts is hailing us," said Colora.

"Ignore them. Damari, execute evasive maneuvers but maintain our position between the Lostai ships and Commander Montor's. Lorret, keep firing on them."

Lorret scored a couple of hits that gained us a reprieve, but a few minutes later we were hit again. I looked back at Lasarta, Amber, and Josher. They were engaged in a lively conversation, but Amber's eyes shifted and met mine.

She's terrified.

"Captain Noomar, it seems they are ignoring Commander Montor's ship and are only targeting us. Why do you think that is? They would have much more to gain in terms of prisoners or death toll from the other ship."

The Lostai battle craft hailed us again.

"OK, Colora, put them on audio only. I do not want them to see us."

"Unidentified Arandan ship, this is Commander Leenox, representing the Lostai Empire. I will be brief and to the point. You apparently have a technology that Lostai military is interested in learning more about. You have trespassed on Lostai space and have fired upon our ships. Therefore, we lay claim to your craft and your crew. We will employ our tug beam to pull you into our docking station, where you will be boarded and taken as prisoners. If you fire on us again, we will destroy the United Rebel Front craft you seem so intent on defending. Our sensors detect their shields will not withstand another photon blast. However, we will allow it to leave our space unharmed if you shut down your propulsion system and comply."

Commander Noomar did not reply. Instead, he contacted

Montor's ship. Montor appeared on screen. Noomar rushed to explain to Montor the message from the Lostai commander.

"Noomar, as an ex-Lostai soldier, I can assure you that the Lostai commander has no intention of letting my craft escape. Once they have your ship in their clutches, they will destroy ours and we will both be lost. The time has come to end this madness. Use your technology to jump through the transportal back to safety. I am honored by your crew's courage. I hope history records your brave acts."

Josher noticed his father was on screen and called out to him again. Montor turned away from the screen. When he faced us again, he said, "Son, I am very proud of you." He covered his mouth, and his eyes seemed to search the screen, as if he was staring straight at me. "Mina, you have been the love of my life. Thank you for that. Captain Noomar, I hope you heed my advice. Montor out."

32

I buried my face in my hands, no longer able to control my emotions. As I wept, the sound of Noomar banging his fists on the console and roaring a string of vulgar curse words filled the room. I lifted my head to see Colora's eyes glistening. She gulped before saying, "Sir...the Lostai commander is hailing us again."

"Mina, you have the most to lose here. What are your orders?" said Noomar. "I will follow them exactly, no questions asked. Do you all agree?"

They all nodded, their silent consent weighing on my soul like a thousand bricks.

If I allow our ship to be captured, I will put my children and everyone else in danger. To top it off, we'll be giving up an important piece of secret technology to the Lostai military. Montor is right. There's no way the Lostai commander will honor his promise. It will all be for nothing.

Just as I was about to reply, something caught my attention on the sensors.

"Sir!" I shouted.

Noomar jumped out of his skin.

"Yes, Mina?"

"There are now three Arandan ships in our vicinity."

Sparks and flashes of light illuminated the darkness.

"Sir, they are firing on the Lostai ships!"

"Lorret, join in. Fire at will!" ordered Noomar. "Damari, keep us at a safe distance from any debris."

"Sir, one of the Lostai ships has been destroyed!"

We didn't even stop to cheer as we focused our attention on the last remaining Lostai ship. A phaser beam originating from Montor's ship took out the Lostai ship's shields. All five of our ships fired on the Lostai ship simultaneously. It broke in half before exploding. Debris, smoke, and electrical fire remained in its place.

We finally allowed ourselves a moment of victory. Cheering and shouts of "*jonjuri*" rang across the bridge.

"Mina, are there any Lostai ships approaching this area?"

"No sir, but I am picking up a United Rebel Front fleet heading this way."

More cheering.

I ran over to Lasarta, Josher, and Amber and hugged each one of them once, and then again and again.

"*Ro Ma*, you are squeezing me too tight," Josher complained.

"Sir, Commander Montor is hailing us."

"What are you waiting for, Colora?" Noomar chided her, but in a good-natured tone. "Put him on."

Montor appeared on screen, fist-pumping.

"Noomar, congratulations. You have well-earned your captain's uniform."

"It was only for this temporary assignment, sir," replied Noomar in a humble tone.

"Are you kidding? I personally will see that Portars makes it a permanent promotion. May I use my *hanstoric* to come aboard your ship? I would like to embrace my son and spouse."

Everyone looked at me and beamed. Tears of joy replaced those of sadness that I had cried moments before.

"Of course, sir."

A burst of glowing light blinded us. Once our vision cleared, we saw Montor among us on the bridge. Lasarta unbuckled Josher, and he darted across the bridge into his father's arms.

"*Ta Ri, Ta Ri*! We won the game, right?"

Montor dabbed at one of his eyes and lifted Josher in the air.

"Yes, we did, Son. An astounding victory."

He placed Josher down and examined the room until our eyes met. Three long strides and he stood before me. His large hands grasped my face, thumbs wiping my tears, before his mouth claimed mine. We forgot the people around us, our bodies and souls surrendering to relief, joy, and desire. I don't know for how long we kissed before Noomar distracted us.

"Err...Commander Montor, Commander Portars is on the viewer and has asked to speak to you."

Montor licked his lips. Our eyes remained locked for a moment more before he attended the call from Portars. He stood tall in front of the viewer.

"Commander Portars, I am ready to be stripped of my rank of commander."

"What are you talking about, Commander Montor?"

"I do not deserve it after the losses suffered under my command."

"It is a sad day for the United Rebel Front. We will honor those lost and adequately compensate their families. But let us remember your fleet of ten destroyed thirty Lostai ships. Your name once again will be recorded in the battle chronicles of this war."

Montor bowed his head in deference.

"Thank you, sir. Captain Noomar's crew destroyed three of

those on their own, and without them, my ship would have been lost, too."

"Yes, every person under Captain Noomar's command will receive a commendation."

Lasarta smiled, her patriotic soul proud that she would be one of very few civilian female Arandans to have such a recognition.

"Sir, may I ask, where did those ships come from? How did they arrive so fast?"

"They were waiting to be retrofitted with the new transportal capability. Once we confirmed that Captain Noomar's crew executed the jump safely, we quickly upgraded these ships. We will soon have a full fleet of these *hanstoric* spacecrafts and have also begun research on applying the same technology to larger crafts. The bravery of Captain Noomar's crew has allowed us to be well ahead of schedule in implementing this mode of space travel."

Noomar cleared his throat.

"Commander Portars, I think it is fair to say we owe this advancement to the one person who insisted you allow us to take the test ship on this mission."

Portars sat back in his chair and folded his hands on the desk.

"I have heard Mina being described as stubborn. Thankfully, she is as persuasive as she is determined. We are lucky to have her on our side. Her name will go down in our history books as a pioneer in military transportal travel and, as such, will receive a special honor."

Everyone fist pumped and cheered while I saluted Portars. Once they quieted down, Noomar asked, "Commander Portars, what are our next orders?"

"One of our fleets is headed your way. Montor's ship and the *hanstoric* spacecrafts should join them. Their mission is to create a blockade around Losta and cut off any travel to or from the planet. Hopefully, through this measure and diplomatic discussions with parties of dissent within the Lostai government, we can pressure them into a treaty where our demands are met. Captain Noomar, use one of the *hanstorics* you have on board and take command of Montor's ship. Montor, take the *Torixa* back home with your family and friends. You all deserve some time off."

Montor's lips pursed, his eyes shifting.

"Sir, I would like to discuss with my family what will be our next course of action and get back to you. In the meantime, we will continue with the other ships to meet our fleet."

"OK, Montor, but remember, while you accompany our ships, the Lostai will target you as any other United Rebel Front craft. You would officially be part of our fleet and will need to adhere to military protocols. We need to avoid our new jumper technology falling into the hands of the Lostai at all costs." Portars's voice lowered. "Keep that in mind as you make your decisions."

"Understood, sir."

"Portars, out."

We all sported faces of expectation as Montor turned to look at all of us.

"I need to think," he said, cracking his knuckles. "Captain Noomar, jump to my ship and assume leadership there. Lasarta, I would love one of your special meals. Damari, contact the other ships and, for the time being, follow their navigation plan. Kindor and Lorret, continue to monitor sensors and shields. Colora, please can you watch over Josher for a while? Mina and I have some catching up to do."

Colora shot me a mischievous look.

"Of course, Montor," she replied.

"Mina, please can you show me to your quarters so we can speak in private?"

Colora snickered when he said "speak." As she walked by

me toward Josher, she whispered in my ear, her tone full of innuendo.

"Do you think it will be a long conversation?"

"Colora, shhh."

She giggled again before she headed to the observation deck with Josher. I signaled to Amber that she should join them and then turned to Montor.

"Umm...it is this way."

My cabin only accommodated a bed, a toilet and shower, and a tiny storage unit. As soon as the door closed behind us, in one swift movement, and without saying a word, Montor wrapped his hands around my butt and picked me up. I didn't think twice, wrapping my legs around his torso. He turned and pinned me against the wall, kissing my lips. Feeling mischievous, I tapped the collar of his suit. It inflated, and I laughed as he was forced to set me down.

"What is so funny?" he said with a sly smile before tapping my collar.

As both our suits opened down the middle, we tugged in a frantic rush at the arms and legs to undress. Once our flight suits and undergarments were off, the sight of his strong physique made me playful. I decided to stroke his ego a bit.

"Wow, Montor, have you been putting in extra workout time?"

Of course, he ate it all up.

"I needed a distraction," he said, his voice a low growl.

His pumped-up pecs and biceps and rippled wall of hard abs made it difficult to choose where to kiss first. I settled on his chest. He grabbed a fistful of my hair and, with a gentle tug, had me looking up at him. Our desperate mouths and tongues met again.

"Mina, how I have missed *kix* you."

He coaxed me into bending back even further, continuing his kisses down my neck and collarbone. Desire flooded my every nerve like a drug. We stumbled a few steps and fell onto the bed. I straddled him, and in a frenzy of lust, he grabbed me by the hips to position my body and push inside of me. As we moved in sync, I leaned toward him, my palms on his chest. He moved his hands from my hips to my breasts.

"I want to taste them," he whispered.

Given our height difference, it was impossible to accommodate everything he desired at the same time. He grimaced as I pulled off him and moved forward to press my body against his face. We rolled over; our limbs entangled. His hands and his mouth took what they wanted. Hungry for the taste of his skin, too, I kissed and licked him everywhere I could reach. Soon he was inside me again, his breathing ragged with each deep thrust. I called out his name, pleasure building more and more until orgasmic contractions left me out of breath. Our Sotkari Ta connection made every joining and separation of our bodies moments of sweet agony and bliss. He ran his fingers through my hair, twirling the curls.

"Mina, I was chasing death because I cannot live without you."

My breathing finally returned to normal.

"Oh, my king, there is no need for us to be separated. Let us speak to the priestess to renew our commitment."

"It is hard for me, Mina. There are other considerations for an Arandan male."

"I know. I know. Lasarta explained it to me, but have I not proven my devotion to you? And have you not proven your honor and courage yet again through this battle? Let nothing fog your mind. We belong together, Montor."

The back of his fingers gently skimmed my cheek.

"Let us go home, Mina, to meditate on where we go from here."

33

———

I would have loved to stay in bed with Montor the rest of the afternoon and continue our sensual reconciliation into the night. We couldn't do that to Lasarta. She had worked hard to prepare a proper feast using only the reproducer, since our small ship provided no space to store produce and grains, much less livestock.

We set the navigation systems on autopilot and linked sensors and communication systems to our tablets so that everyone could enjoy the meal together. Montor sat next to me. Lasarta served a casserole dish made of thin layers of mashed tubers, meat, vegetables, and a grain similar to barley. A side salad and plenty of *bomar* completed the dish. The reproduced *vormey* didn't compare to the old-fashioned aged version but was good enough for us to toast to the reunion of the *Barinta* crew. The only one missing was Marcia, the child I returned to Earth two years before.

"I wonder how little Marcia is doing," mused Foxor.

"She was so happy to be back with her parents. I hope she is doing well," I said.

"Mina, how was your recent trip to Earth? I thought your plan was to return with your son?" asked Lasarta.

Whatever she saw in my expression sparked one of regret in hers.

"Oh, sorry, Mina, if I was indiscreet."

I patted her arm.

"It is fine, Lasarta. I was naïve to think I could resolve my family problems on such a quick trip. You can imagine the shock it was for him to see me again, learn of his father's death, and meet Josher, all within a few minutes. He has been living with my sister's family for four years now and decided he was not ready to come back with me. I promised I would visit again soon." I nodded to no one in particular. "He is growing up to be a strong, handsome male."

Lasarta and Foxor's eyes were full of sympathy and genuine affection.

"I am so happy to see you and Montor seem to be reconciling," noted Foxor. "Have you agreed on what you will do next?"

Montor poured himself another glass of *vormey*. His eyes met mine before he spoke.

"A part of me would love to join the fleet and bring the battle to the Lostai's doorstep, but I know it is time to focus on my family. We will go back to Fronidia, where our family can be safe. I can retake my position as Strategic and Liaison Officer and execute my responsibilities from our Embassy Office at the Fronidian capital. Mina and I will speak to the priestess about how best to reconfirm and announce to our community our lifelong commitment to each other."

"That is the best news I have heard in a long while," said Foxor.

Everyone cheered, and Montor brought my hand to his lips. Our joyful moment was short-lived. As Foxor got up to serve dessert, a notification beeped on most of our tablets. Montor read the screen and rushed to his feet.

"We have been boarded!"

We all stood. Adrenaline filled my veins.

"But how?" said Foxor, dropping a plate in confusion.

"Damari, take Amber and Josher to one of the cabins and lock yourself in."

"Yes, sir. I will take them to my room," replied Damari.

Before he finished the last syllable, the small dining area lit up. The now familiar blinding light made it clear. Whoever was here, came using *hanstorics*. When I opened my eyes, four Sotkari Ta in Lostai uniform, one female and three males, appeared before us. Two of them had already grabbed Amber and Josher and were pointing *vimors* to their heads. The other two held phasers in each hand aimed at the rest of us.

I blocked my mind and sensed that Montor, Kindor, and Damari had done the same.

"Josher, block," I shouted in English.

Thank God I trained him how to do that.

He was an excellent student.

The chance of the intruding Sotkari Ta controlling our minds was a larger risk than the disadvantage of no longer being able to communicate telepathically amongst ourselves. Kindor was relegated to sign language.

"Think before you make any move," said the tallest of the Sotkari Ta in a robotic voice.

At Montor's height, he was intimidating and wore a device that looked like a headset microphone. Being Sotkari Ta, like Kindor, he should have been mute. Apparently, the device connected to his brainwaves and translated his thoughts into audio. I had not seen this technology before.

"We have zero qualms about killing these two." He tapped the gun hard against Josher's head.

"Owww."

The color drained from Amber's face. My blood boiled with the fierceness of a mother bear.

"Stop it, you filthy bastard! If you hurt them, I will tear this ship's hull apart, tile by tile. I swear I can do it. We can all die here," I screamed, lifting my hands as if summoning some magical power.

Montor could not help but cock an eyebrow, and Kindor's jaw dropped.

The tall Sotkari Ta nodded to his companions. In a swift movement, they each gave Lasarta and Colora a phaser. The females' eyes glazed over, and they pressed the weapons to their own chests.

"Save me the theatrics," said the tall Sotkari Ta, making eye contact with each of us. "My name is Kentar. If everyone calms down, we can all survive the day. Make no mistake, we are in control here. Our commander is on your bridge with ten Lostai soldiers. Now that we have the situation secure, I will tell him it is safe to walk over here to address you. My comrades each have planted a command in these females' minds. Those of you who are Sotkari Ta better not even think about manipulating our commander's mind. If he displays any odd behavior or is harmed in any way, your friends will shoot themselves, and I will personally take care that the boy dies painfully."

A helpless shudder of rage rocked my body.

"Only my comrades can delete the command from your friends' minds. You kill them, and your friends will remain in this state forever. And if anything happens to me, my comrade here will kill the Earthian girl. Of course, we have all blocked our minds, just as you have, so there is no way to incapacitate us with telepathy. Remember, anything that you can do to us, we can do to you, but your non-Sotkari Ta friends here will suffer for it. I suggest you heed our orders."

"Let me go!" Josher shouted in Arandan, struggling against Kentar's chokehold.

The rise and fall of Montor's chest matched the loud breathing sounds coming from his nose.

"Son, be still." Montor's words were almost as robotic as Kentar's.

Kindor looked at Kentar with contempt and signed in Sotkari, "You are a traitorous germ, an embarrassment to your race and the tenets of Sotkari Ta."

Kentar rolled his eyes and tapped a band he wore on his wrist. "What I do here saves my family and ensures them a comfortable life. Everyone has a price."

He took several steps away from us with Josher in his grasp and spoke into his communicator. "Sir, the situation is under control. You are free to come over and address the prisoners."

The commander walked in, flanked by four well-armed Lostai soldiers. I couldn't control the hatred that flooded my mind when I saw his face.

"Zorla, you bastard," I shouted in Lostai.

"It is nice to see you again, too, Mina. You think you are the only one to master the trick of jumping in unexpectedly? I know you probably think it odd that I would be here in person, but sometimes a leader must take matters into their own hands." He held an extra-long *zirem* that he tapped as he spoke. "You keep slipping away from me. Well, not today."

Zorla gestured to the Lostai soldiers. After they cuffed Amber, Lorret, and Foxor, Zorla pointed at Kindor, Montor, and Damari.

"Do not bother cuffing these three. They can easily break them, anyway," he said, poking me in the back with the *zirem*. "Although, I think they will cooperate."

Lasarta and Colora, with phasers in hand, were in a catatonic state and didn't require further attention.

"Mina, you will come with me to the bridge and program this craft to jump to the coordinates I give you. We are all going back to Losta. If you try to escape, your loved ones will suffer for it, starting with your son." He poked me again. "Go."

Zorla turned to Montor, Kindor, and Damari.

"I suggest you behave. The minute any of these guards radio me that there is trouble. I will kill her and the boy."

Zorla prodded me in the back again, and I locked eyes with Montor before heading down the corridor toward the bridge.

"You know, Zorla, taking a spaceship through a transportal feels a lot different from what you're used to with a *hanstoric*," I said, louder than necessary.

"Stop trying to delay, Mina. Move on," he barked.

Kentar followed with Josher, as did another of the Sotkari Ta soldiers with Lasarta and Colora walking in front of him like zombies. The two remaining Sotkari Ta and the four Lostai soldiers stayed to guard Kindor, Montor, and the rest of our crew. As I walked away, I hummed an old Arandan folk song that Montor had taught me, the chorus being:

Take me back to Aranda
Where my friends take care of me
Take me back to Aranda
Where my spirit can run free

34

______

When we arrived at the bridge, Zorla asked me to show him the transportal controls. Six armed Lostai soldiers huddled around the navigation and weapon stations. He called one of them over.

"Study what she does," instructed Zorla. "Mina, here are the coordinates. Remember, no funny business."

"There are several steps that need to be taken to charge the system," I lied to my newly appointed student. "First, you need to adjust the magnetic field. A precise calculation needs to be done considering the dimensions of the craft and the number of passengers. We have more passengers now, so I will need to recalculate. May I use my tablet?"

"Go ahead."

My Lostai student's brow furrowed in concentration as I explained complex, fake calculations and made up a reason to go check the environmental controls. I darted across the room. He rushed to keep up with me. I took advantage of that moment alone to flick my fingers across my tablet, sending an encrypted message to Commander Portars.

Be aware. Enemies on board.

"Oh, I almost forgot. You pointing that weapon at me makes me nervous. I need to check one more datum point," I said, running back to the transportal station.

OK, Mina, now is the time. You'll need to somehow keep your wits about you. You've done so many of these jumps. You can do it!

Before the Lostai soldier could catch up with me, I tapped the transportal screen, hitting the Return button that would take us back to our point of origin, Aranda.

"Josher, *Xarim!*"

I was referring to a defensive move his father had taught him during their holographic martial art games. Josher did me proud as he tucked his chin, stepped sideways, and elbowed Kentar twice hard in the groin. Kentar doubled over, and Josher slipped out of his grip. As my brain fought the vertigo caused by the jump, I focused my telekinetic power on Kentar and hurled him across the room, slamming him against a wall. The transportal jump brought Zorla and everyone else in the room, including me, to the ground. A noise that sounded like wind trapped between tall buildings assaulted my ears. I ignored it and used telekinesis to bring one of the Lostai soldier's *vimors* into my hand. Fighting against debilitating dizziness and wasting no time, I shot Kentar dead while focusing on the weapons in Lasarta's and Colora's hands, causing the phasers to fly across the room. The momentary blindness was coming on. I scrambled to Zorla and pressed the gun to his chest.

The bridge lit up with what felt like lightning strikes.

Then nothing.

I opened my eyes.

Zorla was unconscious. I still had my weapon on him. The second Sotkari hadn't awoken either. My idea was to use Zorla as a negotiating chip. Two of the Lostai soldiers jumped to their feet and lunged at me. With my mind, I caused them to collide and tossed their weapons far out of their reach. They passed out. The other four soldiers were waking up. I heard footsteps coming from the corridor that led to the bridge.

If those are Lostai soldiers, I'll be in trouble. Maybe my best bet is to run with my weapon and hide. And where did Josher go?

I stood and bolted away from them all. To my relief, I saw Montor coming on to the bridge armed with a *vimor*.

"Mina, where is Josher?" he shouted across the room.

"I killed Kentar and Josher ran, but I am not sure where he might be hiding."

By now, the four Lostai soldiers, Zorla, and the Sotkari were on their feet, armed and shooting at Montor and me. I took cover behind a console and prayed Josher would stay out of the line of fire.

"Remember, we cannot kill the other Sotkari. We need him to snap Lasarta and Colora out of their trance," I shouted.

Unfortunately, that gave away my position. An invisible force, most likely the Sotkari soldier's telekinetic abilities, ripped the weapon out of my hands. Being worried about Josher's whereabouts waned my mental strength. The Sotkari soldier pointed his weapon at me. Trapped, I thought I was taking my last breath. A beam of light zipped toward the soldier, and he went down with a leg injury. Montor had carefully aimed to only incapacitate him.

Kindor, Damari, Amber, Lorret, and Foxor burst onto the bridge, all armed. They kept turning around to fire behind them.

My God, what is Amber doing with a vimor?

Moments later, two Lostai and one Sotkari soldier ran onto the bridge. My heart dropped as I saw Foxor fall to the ground. I couldn't tell from my vantage point if and where he had been injured. Lorret turned and shouted something. Kindor ran back to help her pull Foxor to a corner while Damari and Amber continued to fire at the oncoming Lostai soldiers. Kindor tugged at the magnetic strips running down the front of Foxor's flight suit to rip open the top portion. I said a prayer as I watched Kindor shut his eyes and place his hands on Foxor's chest. Montor's face contorted as he agonized between running to help Foxor, too, or facing the Lostai soldiers. The veins on his neck and forehead appeared ready to burst.

"*Shermont*, you filthy scum have pushed me to my limit," he roared with the angst and fury of a wounded animal.

The six Lostai and one Sotkari soldier flew high in the air. The sound of their bodies slamming to the ground made even me wince. After hitting the floor, they cried out in pain while their bodies convulsed. Montor enjoyed using telekinesis to sever all his enemies' bones from their joints before stopping their heartbeats—a painful way to go. Perhaps that's what he did because a few seconds later, they all were immobile.

The two Lostai soldiers I had dealt with earlier woke up hearing the bloodcurdling cries of their comrades. Montor glared at them. They suffered the same fate. Zorla's eyes darted around the room, a *zirem* in one hand and a *vimor* in the other. Montor charged toward him. The *vimor* flew out of Zorla's hand and exploded midair. I focused on the *zirem,* and in seconds it was in my hand.

"It is over, Zorla." Montor pointed a weapon at him. "There are no other Lostai soldiers to defend you. The ones that are missing here on the bridge, we killed back in the dining area. All your soldiers are dead except that injured Sotkari scum we need for now."

Zorla shot his hands in the air.

"I claim my rights as a prisoner of war."

Montor grabbed him by the neck and lifted him at least two and a half feet off the ground so that he could look him in the eyes.

"And I claim my rights as an Arandan warrior. You ordered Gio to torture my wife. I made him pay and now so will you!"

I heard the din of what sounded like a thousand marching

feet. Commander Portars and a squadron of Arandan soldiers spilled onto the bridge.

"Montor!" shouted Portars. "Let him go. He is a valuable prisoner to be questioned and perhaps used in prisoner trade."

"You promised me, Portars. You promised me I could have his life," Montor cried out in a high-pitched, wounded voice, eyes glistening. His whole body trembled.

Portars reached Montor, placed a hand on his shoulder, and spoke in a low, fatherly tone.

"I know, Montor, but there are things in play here that transcend personal matters."

Montor covered his face in grief at being denied his right to revenge and dropped Zorla to the floor.

I stomped over, *zirem* in hand.

"Commander Portars, have you seen my back?" I demanded.

Portars glanced at Montor, wide-eyed, shaking his head and raising his hands like someone making sure not to touch something forbidden.

"Why would I ever have occasion to do that, Mina? You should not say such things."

Once again, the Arandan male psyche made me roll my eyes.

"Right. Of course you have not. Well, if you had, you would have seen the scars this piece of crap left on my body. I claim the right to reciprocate, and I do not care whether or not you agree."

"You would not dare," Zorla said, his chin lifted in arrogance.

Montor looked at Portars, flaring nostrils and bared teeth betraying his emotions.

Portars nodded.

Montor's eyes filled with gratitude.

"I will hold him down for you, sweetness."

"Let go of me. Portars, this is an outrage," shouted Zorla.

Portars snickered.

"We will add prisoner treatment to the treaty proposal presented to your government."

"Remove his shirt," I said, ice in my veins.

Montor ripped the shirt open with his bare hands and tossed it. With the *zirem* on its highest setting, I worked on Zorla's back. His cries of pain brought on memories of the torment he had inflicted on me. I wanted to be free of emotion, but tears filled my eyes as the stench of burned flesh permeated the surrounding air.

"Stop it. Stop it!" Zorla shouted, tremors of pain ravaging his body.

I leaned over to get close to his ear and whispered through clenched teeth, "Did you have mercy on me? No, you did not."

After those first few clamors, his mouth gaped silent screams, much as I had when he used the *zirem* on me. I considered carving the Lostai symbols for the phonetic spelling of my name into his back. He left his mark on me. I would do the same, but another thought came to mind. I rubbed the area on my bicep where Montor's name was tattooed. Montor had my name tattooed on his arm, too. It was a part of our wedding ceremony.

No, only Montor should have my name branded on his skin. I should brand Zorla with another word. Maybe a message or reminder of some sort.

I concentrated to make sure the Lostai characters seared on his skin were legible. By the time I was done, the scorched skin on Zorla's back spelled STAY AWAY FROM MY FAMILY, and he had fainted in shock.

"When he punished me with the *zirem*, he never gave me anything for the pain and purposely did not erase the scars. He only ordered I be administered an antibiotic to avoid infection.

Portars, please give the same instructions to your medical staff," I said, dropping the weapon, exhausted.

"Yes, Mina, it will be done as per your request. I promise," said Portars in a grave voice.

He gestured to one of his lieutenants, who sent soldiers to cuff Zorla and take him away.

Every muscle in my body ached. I thought I might pass out, too, until I heard Montor shout, "Portars, Foxor needs a medic."

Wait. Oh my God, where is Josher?

"Montor, Montor, we need to find Josher," I said, my eyes darting across the room.

"Portars, please have the soldiers search for my son. He is probably hiding somewhere. We will join the search as soon as I check on Foxor."

Portars called over a few soldiers. To my surprise, one appeared to be human, a young man who looked about twenty years old.

"Are you from Earth?" I asked.

"Si señora," he said in Spanish.

"Do you speak English?"

"Más o menos," he replied, waving his hands to show that he meant more or less.

I stuck with Spanish and explained that we were looking for a child who looked like a mini-Montor. He acknowledged my instructions and headed off with the others to start searching.

Montor pulled me close. His shuddered breathing exposed his dread. He glanced towards Foxor.

"Come with me, Mina, please. I do not think I can face on my own what might wait for me there."

When Montor and I got to the corner where Kindor and Lorret were still working on Foxor, Amber rushed into my arms. Damari was there also, his arms folded across his chest with worry painted all over his face.

"Honey, are you all right?" I asked, holding her shoulders with outstretched arms and stepping back to inspect her.

She said, "Yeah," but started to cry. I pulled her back into an embrace, rubbing her back.

"Everything is OK now, honey. Everything is OK. But listen. You should have taken cover immediately. What were you thinking trying to handle that weapon?"

She pressed her lips together and then offered a shy smile.

"Mom, I know how to shoot a gun. Dad taught me a year ago. After you disappeared, he got this idea in his head that we should learn how to defend ourselves. He was planning to have me get a license as soon as I was of age."

I couldn't remember her ever wanting to use a gun. Another reminder of how my abduction had impacted my family. I shook off the thought and turned to look at Foxor. His eyes were still closed. Now that we were near, I saw the trail of blood from where Foxor had been hit to the corner where he now lay. Kindor pressed a torn piece of his garment around the wrist area of Foxor's left arm. It also was saturated in blood.

Oh God, please don't let him be dead.

Montor's face was a slab of stone as he asked, "What is his status?"

"He lost his hand and a lot of blood," replied Lorret. "Kindor stabilized his vitals, but we almost lost him. He is still in delicate condition."

Montor let out a long exhale of relief.

"Kindor, once again, I am in your debt."

"Say nothing of it," signed Kindor.

Portars's soldiers arrived with a cot and whisked Foxor away.

"Now we need to address Colora and Lasarta and then go find Josher," I said.

Colora and Lasarta were still in the same spot where they fell during the transportal jump, sitting on the floor with blank looks on their faces. I helped them to their feet and led them to the Sotkari that Montor had injured. Montor followed right behind me.

The Sotkari sat propped against the wall with a nasty gash on the thigh. Montor pointed his weapon at the Sotkari's injury and gestured towards Colora and Lasarta.

"OK, Sotkari scum, I will be quick about this. If you want me to spare your life, you will unlock their minds immediately. Otherwise, prepare for a slow, painful death."

The Sotkari's head hung low in defeat, the rest of his body limp, misery in his eyes. He wasted no time in granting Montor's request. Both Lasarta and Colora reacted the same way. Startled, their eyes opened wide like someone awakened from a nightmare. Colora pressed her fingertips against her temples. Lasarta grabbed Montor's arm.

"What happened, Son?" asked Lasarta. "Is everyone OK?"

"Yes, but I would like a medic to evaluate both of you to be sure you are fine."

Montor called over soldiers to escort Colora and Lasarta to the infirmary.

"We will join you shortly," I said.

As they walked away, I couldn't wait any longer.

"Montor, I need to go now and look for Josher."

"Yes, I am going with you. Did you see in which direction he ran?"

"Not really. He escaped from Kentar's grip during the trans-portal jump."

Montor grabbed me by the hand, and we ran toward the dormitory section. Other soldiers were looking for him as well.

"Josher, *honey*, it is *Ro Ma*. Everything is fine. You can come out now," I shouted.

He wasn't in any of the quarters or the Engineering room. I figured he'd be smart enough not to run back to the dining area, and no one from our crew being held prisoner there had seen him. Soon, everyone was looking for him, and my mind played out horrible scenarios.

Could there have been another person with Zorla's crew we didn't know of? Have they taken Josher away?

I searched my mind for any clue of where he might have hidden, and it came to me. In one of Josher's favorite holographic adventure games, the protagonist hides from his enemies in an escape pod. Those were in the airlock.

"Come, Montor, I think he might be in one of the escape pods. He cannot hear us in there."

"I hope he did not actually activate one," said Montor, cracking his knuckles.

We scrambled to the docking station and inspected the airlocks. He wasn't in any of them.

"Montor, I am getting worried."

"Wait, he also likes to hide in storage cabinets," said Montor.

"Engineering has several, and the humming equipment will have drowned out our voices," I said, already heading over there.

When we arrived, we found a soldier with a wide smile holding him up.

"Look who we found hiding behind a panel. I do not know how he squeezed in there."

"*Ta Ri, Ro Ma!*"

The soldier put Josher down, and he ran into my arms.

"Oh, *honey*, we were calling you. I was worried."

"Are those bad people gone? I did like you taught me, *Ta Ri*." He showed the elbow-to-the-groin move.

"We defeated them. You did an excellent job, Son," said Montor, fist pumping. "Let us check on our friends. Then we can all go home and relax."

35

———

We remained on the Arandan military base for a few days. The Penstarox medic discharged Colora and Lasarta after a quick examination, but Foxor remained in the infirmary. When Montor and I arrived to visit, we found Lasarta feeding him her famous "warrior stew," a hearty combination of vegetables, various meats, and seafood, in a thick, starchy broth.

"Foxor, how are you feeling?" asked Montor.

"Like a baby," he said, rolling his eyes, shaking his head, and pointing his thumb at Lasarta.

"After this, you will feel like a young king," she said, smiling.

"When will the doctor clear you to go home?" I asked.

"He says he wants to observe me for another day or two. The prosthetic hand has merged fine with my forearm, but the blood loss exacerbated an old genetic circulatory system ailment. If it were up to me, I would have left already. I feel fine."

Lasarta caressed his cheek. "He is a terrible patient."

He flexed and wiggled the fingers of his prosthetic, which looked almost identical to his other hand.

"This feels better than the original. Maybe I should have them cut off the other one," Foxor said, laughing until Lasarta rapped him on the head with her knuckles. "Owww."

"Stop saying silly things and eat," she said.

Montor and I laughed, relieved to see they both were back to normal.

"Well, we have an appointment with the priestess, and then we are going back to our home at the Arandan enclave on Fronidia. It is still the safest place for us, and I will go back to working at the Arandan embassy there."

"OK, we will see you soon. I hope your meeting with the priestess goes well," answered Foxor.

Before leaving to meet with the priestess, we wanted to leave Josher and Amber in good hands. First, we asked Kindor and Lorret to stay at Penstarox and take care of Josher while we were away. Of course, they had no problem with our request. Kindor and Josher loved spending time together. Next, we looked for Colora and found her in the recreational room chatting with Portars.

"Hello, you two," she said with a wide smile. "All ready for your trip?"

Portars nodded to us, always a bit befuddled when we found him with Colora.

"Yes, Colora. We wanted to ask a favor. Please, can you keep an eye on Amber and make sure she is comfortable and entertained until we get back?"

"Sure, but I do not think she will need my help for entertainment," said Colora.

When I cocked my head trying to understand the cryptic tone in her voice, she discretely pointed to the other side of the room, the typical mischief in her eyes. There, I saw Amber in an animated conversation with the young Spanish-speaking soldier who had helped search for Josher. Montor and I walked over.

"Mom, meet Miguel. He's from Argentina."

Miguel and I smiled at each other. I was so stressed when we first met that I hadn't noticed his Sotkari Ta light in my mind.

"Yes, we already have met. He was part of the squadron that came to our aid when we arrived."

"Miguel lost his family in an airplane accident. It's a long story, but like Damari, he decided to stay and join the United Rebel Front. He's helping me practice my Spanish, and I'm helping him with English," explained Amber.

"And...where is Damari?" I asked, checking the room.

"He said he needed to do his meditation thing but that he'd be back soon."

"OK, well, please check in with Colora. She'll show you where the dormitories are and help you with anything else you need until we get back."

"Sure," she said and gave me a hug. "I hope everything goes well for you."

She smiled to Montor and said, "*Himaney*," which meant good luck in Arandan. Apparently, her Arandan language lessons were going well.

The priestess asked we meet her off-base at a temple located in Montor's ancestral territory. The temple was an hour from Penstarox by transport pod.

"I wonder what her approach will be?" I said.

"You look worried."

"Honestly, I am. You said you would abide by her counsel. What if she rules against our marriage?"

"Worrying will not help our situation. How about you come sit on my lap instead?" said Montor, with a libidinous smile.

My pulse sped up. I knew what he had in mind. It wasn't the first time we'd made love in a transport pod set on autopilot, and I liked the idea of doing it again. He stood and pulled me towards him, our mouths meeting in hungry kisses as his fingers unfastened the clips that ran down the back of my dress.

"Mina, you are so tasty," he groaned.

I wriggled out of the dress and disposed of my underwear. He pulled down his pants and sat in the pilot's seat again, pulling me onto his lap. I straddled him and kissed him softly on the lips. He smiled and pulled me closer, nibbling on my mouth until our lips parted and his tongue found mine. I leaned back, loving how his kisses traveled down my neck and farther. His hands roamed, caressed, and squeezed me everywhere I liked. Our bodies connected slow at first but soon escalated to vigorous gyrations. The hour went by too fast.

The temple stood in a secluded area of woods close to Montor's birthplace. We dressed in a heated rush while the pod descended to a nearby clearing. I tidied my hair as we stepped out of the pod. We followed a dirt trail that led to the temple. Constructed in stones of different shapes and sizes, it appeared ancient. Montor must have read my thoughts.

"This was built thousands of revolutions ago."

Two doors, surprisingly light considering they were made of a copper-colored metal, marked the entrance. They swung freely, like saloon doors. Large, dark metal knockers decorated each door.

"I am announcing our arrival out of courtesy, but these doors are purposely constructed this way to provide protection to the interior while still allowing free entrance to anyone," explained Montor.

We took a step back just in the nick of time. The doors swung open, and the priestess walked through.

"Greetings. You are early. That is a good thing. Follow me."

The priestess, named Noroma, held one door open for us. The interior brought back memories of the holographic representation of a temple where Montor and I were married. Striking red marble tiled the floor. Huge red scrolls with black writing draped the white walls. Other than a center table, there was no furniture, sculptures, paintings, or decoration of any kind.

"Let me invite you to my home."

Arandan priestesses lived in their temples in a series of rooms constructed on the right side of the building. We followed Noroma into a room that represented both ancient history and current advanced technology. The yellowed scrolls and worn leather-bound books on the bookcase appeared as ancient as the building. Conversely, I saw a tablet, a portable holographic viewer, and data files on the desk. Chairs surrounded a table in the center of the room.

"Please sit and be comfortable," she instructed. "So, Montor, I read your note and did some research to prepare for this meeting. I think we will need to have a long discussion. I would like to hear all about how you two met and everything that has happened between you until now."

Montor and I looked at each other, not able to hide how her words put us a bit on edge.

"Yes, that is fine. I suppose it will take some time," Montor said. "But I am curious why you did not ask such questions the first time we got married."

"Before, I was only officiating your wedding, but now you are asking me to take a position on your relationship, make a recommendation, and speak to your community on your behalf. For that, I need to understand the details of your situation and get to know you better. No worries. I have cleared my afternoon schedule. Let us have some *yomoso*."

"Err, I would prefer not—" I started to say, remembering

how I never had been able to stomach the bitter coffee-like beverage.

Montor grimaced and cut me off.

"One does not refuse the priestess," he said under his breath.

"What is the problem?" the priestess asked.

There was no annoyance in her expression, so I spoke up.

"I appreciate your hospitality, but *yomoso* is too bitter for my taste."

"Oh, that does not surprise me. Most aliens find it too strong, but I also have cookies you can dip in to sweeten it. They are very sweet, indeed. You might like the combination."

I gagged the first time I tried *yomoso*. That night was full of bad memories. One of Montor's ex-girlfriends made fun of me, and that evening also happened to be when I first met Gio, the person who later tortured me. I associated the beverage with these unpleasant memories and never tasted it again. The kindness in Noroma's eyes made me want to give it another try.

"OK, I will try it. Thank you."

"Wonderful. Grimor, please bring *yomoso* and *hemilta* for three," Noroma shouted towards a doorway in the room that led to the rest of her residence. "By the way, I must compliment you. You have made a point to learn Montor's language."

"Yes, I apologize for my heavy accent, but I am trying to improve."

She patted my knee.

"No need to apologize. I am sure Montor finds it endearing. Has he learned your language?"

"Only a few words. Our young son knows more than him."

Noroma turned to Montor.

"What are you waiting for?" she said in a mock-rebuke.

I giggled, but Montor seemed to take her words more seriously.

"Yes, I do need to make an effort to learn Mina's language so

I can communicate more with *Aembuh* and help her feel welcome," he said with an earnest expression.

Grimor turned out to be a teenaged male Arandan. He served us and stepped away with a quick nod. Plumes of steam rose from the large mugs of *yomoso*. The aroma of something like a mix of espresso, dark chocolate, and Campari liqueur filled the room. I tasted the icing-coated crisp wafers first. The sweetness was so overpowering, I couldn't control smacking my lips. Montor's lips tightened, I'm sure embarrassed by the look on my face.

Wow, this is almost as bad as the drink. Let me dip some in like she suggested.

Some of the wafer disintegrated in the hot beverage. I blew off the steam, took a sip, and was pleasantly surprised.

"It tastes completely different with the wafer. I like it. Thank you!"

"You see? Everything is worth a second try," Noroma said with a wink.

36

"Let us begin at the beginning," said Noroma, smiling to herself at her play on words. "Now remember, I need honest answers from you, or this will not work. Trust me, I will know if you are not being sincere. Tell me, Mina, what was your impression of Montor when you first met him?"

A tough question right off the bat.

"I thought he was arrogant and unpleasant. I was scared of him, too, but over time I realized it was a tough exterior for someone who held a lot of pain inside."

"I see, and what about you, Montor? What did you think of Mina?"

"I thought she was a weakling I would have to babysit and help escape from the Lostai because my mentor, who was like a foster mother to me, had taken a liking to her."

Yeah. I remember how rude he was.

I made a fist at him, and we all laughed.

"But your feelings toward her quickly changed, correct?"

"Yes, very quickly." He took my hand in his. "And it did not take long for me to realize that Mina is a powerful female of conviction. She is a survivor, and I admire her."

Noroma continued asking us questions about the early phase of our relationship.

"You both have embedded Sotkari Ta genes. I have done some research on the Sotkari race and those among them who have evolved traits. These genes predispose a Sotkari Ta to have a potent sexual attraction toward others with the same genetic makeup, correct?"

I didn't answer. Montor simply said, "Yes."

"So, that is a big part of your relationship. Sooner or later, I would think that will cool down a bit."

Montor's cocky voice entered my mind telepathically.

"Sweetness, that will never happen."

I swallowed the urge to giggle as Noroma continued with her line of thought.

"You will need more than sexual chemistry to survive the test of time. Tell me, Montor, how did your pre-wedding trek in the jungle go? That is something unique to our culture. Did Mina agree to it?"

"Yes, she did," replied Montor.

We told her how, while crossing a dilapidated bridge, Montor had fallen into a raging river and was injured by a wild creature.

"Later, I was attacked by the same type of animal. We ended up nursing each other's wounds that day," I said.

"Did that anger you, Mina?"

"Not at all. In the end, it made me feel like we could always count on each other."

"I see. Mina, has Montor ever broken your heart?"

I pressed my fist against my mouth as I thought about the question. Montor's forehead creased as he waited for my answer.

"Yes. The times he has separated himself from our son and me. I know he thought it was for our safety, but I missed him so much. Our time together has been challenging, with the Lostai constantly chasing us, but worse things seem to happen to us when we are apart. One of those times, he was trapped in a Lostai craft. He told me that our love was a farce, that we only shared a physical attraction, and that he did not love me. It was like a stab through my heart. Then he manipulated my mind so I would be angry and willing to abandon him. Also, I was hurt when I learned of his fling with Colora. In his defense, we were separated at the time, and he thought I had died."

"Colora? Jortan's wife? Ahhh...the Fronidians...another interesting race," Noroma said, almost to herself.

"And what about you, Montor? Has Mina broken your heart?"

I stared at my lap because I knew the answer.

He hesitated.

"Montor?"

After a long, deep inhale and exhale, he replied, "Yes, twice. First, when I found her living with Kindor. They had become lovers during the time of her memory loss, but it was not her fault. Kindor had always pined for her and took advantage of her—"

"Kindor, the person who delivered your wife to you at the wedding?"

"Yes."

"And he still lives today? Why did you not make him pay with his life for touching your spouse? Do you fear him?"

Montor jumped from his chair in anger.

"Of course not! There have been so many times I have imagined my fingers around his neck squeezing out his last breath." He ran those same fingers through his hair in frustration and pointed at me. "But she would not allow it."

"That is right. I did not. I would not permit them to destroy each other over me."

"Montor, I cannot believe you designated him as your *Ta Masa*," Noroma said. "That is the role of someone who should be like a brother to you."

Montor got that crazy look in his eyes, so I jumped in.

"Kindor has helped me in some of my most difficult times. He is a powerful, pure-blood Sotkari Ta who loves Josher and would give his life to protect him. Even Montor's foster parents agreed it was the best choice given the enemies we have. Kindor and I enjoyed a close bond, but all I ever felt for him was friendship."

"Except when you were lovers," Noroma interjected.

"Yes, but I did not even remember Montor then. At the time, I did not even remember being Josher's mother."

"And what are Kindor's feelings now?"

"He and Lorret are together. I truly believe it when he says he is over me."

Montor smirked.

"What do you think, Montor?"

"He still cares for her, but out of respect, he is moving on with his life. He and Lorret seem to be getting along."

"So, you do not worry that he will challenge you for your wife one day."

Montor's eyes turned fierce and his laughter bitter.

"Ha. I just wish he would." He shook his head. "But that will never happen. He respects Mina and knows where she stands. I think he is honestly trying to forge a strong relationship with Lorret."

"OK, and what was the second time Mina broke your heart?"

This time Montor turned away from us and covered his mouth, taking a moment before facing us again.

"Her reaction when the father of her Earthian children died."

Noroma was still seated and tilted her head upwards to meet Montor's eyes.

"You mean, her husband."

Montor acknowledged with a nod but didn't say the words. Tears welled in my eyes.

"Well, what was her reaction?" pressed Noroma.

He cleared his throat, uttering each word with a shudder.

"Grief-stricken, she lost control. She tried to rouse him. She used a physical display of affection that appeared passionate, like how one acts with a lover."

"Let me explain—"

Noroma raised a finger to stop me.

"Montor is not finished yet. How did that make you feel, Montor?"

"Disrespected and embarrassed in front of the other Arandans who witnessed it. But the worst was feeling like I had only been a substitute for the one whom she truly loved."

"That is when you consulted with me, and I advised you that because Mina was married at the time I officiated your wedding, your marriage was not valid."

"Yes."

"You decided to separate from her and your son yet again and put yourself in danger. I suppose you were hoping to die in battle."

"Yes. At least my son would have one reason to be proud of me."

"Yet, here you both are asking for my blessing for your marriage once again. Why?"

"She keeps coming for me," he blurted out.

Noroma couldn't contain her laughter.

"Explain."

"I do not know. I tell her it is best we be apart, but she is so stubborn, she keeps looking for me."

"And finding you. Why do you think that is?"

Since Noroma had shushed me earlier, I said nothing.

"She is a very obstinate female."

"Yes, and what else?"

He looked at me.

"She loves me."

"Yes, I believe she does."

Montor reached down to caress my cheek. I placed my hand over his and gave it a gentle squeeze. Noroma pretended to be distracted with her *yomoso* as Montor and I shared that intimate moment.

"Montor, according to our culture, once you fell in love with Mina knowing she was married, you should have sought her Earthian husband and challenged him to a duel."

"Yes. That is why now I feel like any of my fellow Arandan soldiers who know our story may view it as cowardice. I feel that they have a right to mock and disrespect me."

Noroma pursed her lips and became thoughtful.

"Montor, the day you came to consult with me, you explained why that never happened. At first, you were not aware of any easy means to reach her planet. By the time you discovered the transportals, your priority was to evade your ex-commander, Zorla, and protect your son. Later, you led the Namson guerilla. In the interim, Mina was kidnapped and lost her memory. Although I believe you should not have pursued her at all until you found a way to surpass these obstacles and confront her husband, I know it was not cowardice on your part. You should not label yourself that way."

Thank goodness she set him straight on that.

"Changing subjects, I learned that all the ships under your command, except the one you captained yourself, were lost facing a Lostai fleet."

Montor sat and, looking down, pressed his forehead against the palm of his hand.

"Yes."

"But not before your soldiers bravely obliterated a Lostai fleet three times the size of yours, correct?"

"And had Mina not convinced Commander Portars to allow her to come after me in a craft with untested new technology, I would not be here today."

"Montor, let me be clear. No one can question your courage, or Mina's. I am sure your son will be very proud when he learns of everything you both have done for our struggle against the Lostai."

"Thank you," Montor and I replied in unison.

"Speaking of your son, everyone I talked to only said good things about him. I hear he is a disciplined, healthy, and happy child. I guess being surrounded by so many loving caregivers has negated the instability he has lived through until now. Tell me what your plans will be if you get married as opposed to if you do not."

Montor jumped to reply for both of us.

"Either way, we will move back to my home in the Arandan enclave on Fronidia, and I will go back to work at the Arandan Embassy in the Fronidian capital city. Fronidia has severed all ties with Losta, and they use their advanced technology to protect their citizens at all costs. Josher was born on Fronidia and is entitled to that protection. While we are still at war with the Lostai, it is the safest place for us. Perhaps, eventually, I will purchase a plot of land somewhere else on Fronidia. I enjoy being able to hunt, fish, and spend time outdoors. Honestly, I had not considered Mina and I not being together."

"I see," replied Noroma.

"Mina, tell me about your Earthian children."

I described Chris, Amber, and Bobby and explained each of their situations.

"So, your daughter will live with you and, maybe in the future, your younger Earthian son as well. Montor, do you accept the children of your rival in your home?"

"Of course. He is dead, anyway. Mina now is truly a widow. If I want to have a stable relationship with Mina, I need to be a good stepparent."

Noroma continued to ask questions. She learned about every major event in our relationship, all the highs and lows. I remained seated, but Montor stood again, pacing as he told his part of our stories, accompanied by animated gestures.

At one point, she asked him, "When were you proudest of Mina?"

He sat yet again, leaning forward, forearms resting on his legs, and hands folded in front of him.

"Mina went through a very painful process of recovering her memories, especially those related to what she suffered at the hands of the Lostai military and the family she left on her planet. She pushed through it all with the valor of an Arandan warrior while remaining a loving mother and spouse to Josher and me."

"Mina has suffered a lot since she was taken by the Lostai," stated Noroma.

"Yes. Also, she is an excellent and devoted mother. When I first saw Josher as a strong and healthy baby, I was proud of how, despite being much smaller than our people, she had nourished and cared for him so well. When the Lostai kidnapped her Earthian daughter, Mina would stop at nothing to rescue her."

"Mina, when has Montor made you proudest?"

"So many times." I took his hand in mine. "He led the team to help me rescue my daughter as if she were his own. As he mentioned, he has gone against his nature and culture to grant my wishes. Montor is brave enough to share his vulnerabilities with me. He has risked his life so many times for his family and for his people. He even risked his life so my Earthian husband —his rival, as you refer to him—would not take his last breath among filthy Lostai scum."

Noroma leaned back in her chair and steepled her hands in front of her lips.

"This conversation has been quite enlightening. I had already planned that we share a dinner here. No more questions. Let us enjoy a nice meal together. Then go home. In three days, I will reply with my decision."

37

———

When Noroma gave Montor and me her approval to get remarried, we celebrated the good news at Colora's Members Only on Fronidia, a luxurious lakefront venue that offered fine dining, entertainment, and lodging. The breeze from the lake merited a second light layer of clothing, but not enough to make us shiver. We started off with cocktails and dancing. Colora signaled for the band to play Montor's favorite bluesy ballads. Our last visit here was for Josher's *Bendorai*, a blessed night in more ways than one since it marked the beginning of my memory recovery.

Treated with a mineral that caused the water to change color, the lake mimicked the red oceans on Aranda. It shimmered with the reflection of the large moon hanging low in the night sky.

"This is wonderful, Montor," I whispered.

He gathered me even closer in his arms. His hand traveled up my back as we swayed to the music. Soon, his fingers were running through my hair, massaging my scalp in a way that made me want to kiss him. He bent down to grant my wish, a delicate meeting of the lips that in a fraction of a second morphed into a frenzied make-out session. My legs weakened, and I imagined his mouth somewhere else on my body. Other couples and some loners were on the dance floor too, but in my mind, we had the place all to ourselves.

"Montor, if we keep this up, we might have to forget about dinner," I said, barely catching my breath.

His lips curled in that mischievous way that always made my heart skip a beat.

"But Mina, Colora has asked the chef to prepare a sampling of all my favorite Arandan staples," he said in a mock-childlike voice.

"OK, I guess I will have to be patient."

He kissed my forehead, and I pressed my face against his chest as our bodies fell in step once again.

"Montor, I am so happy. Everything is finally working out for us."

"Yes, in three lunar cycles, you will be my bride...again."

"I wonder why Noroma specified we wait till then?"

"She said it is good for couples to have time to prepare mentally."

"But we have been through this before. We are living together. Is it not just a formality?"

"No, it is much more than that. She will formally announce that we have her blessing and we are to be respected members of the Arandan community, despite whatever happened before. The guidance of a priestess is essential for our people, even for those like me who do not believe in deities."

The first time Montor and I were married, he observed the Arandan custom that required the couple to abstain from sex from the moment a wedding place and time was set until the wedding night. Back then, it had only been a matter of days. This time, it would be months.

"Oh, I almost forgot. We will need to sleep in separate rooms until the wedding night," I reminded him.

He bent over to lick my earlobe and nip my neck.

"That, sweetness, I assure you, is not happening."

Losta agreed to a ceasefire after the second month of a successful United Rebel Front blockade around their planet. Their citizens were spoiled and not used to suffering even the most minimal inconvenience in their daily lives. Once we took the war to their doorstep, the Lostai constituents rebelled against their government and demanded the war be over.

Too bad for them. The war was far from over. The ceasefire only allowed for basic supplies to be delivered to the Lostai cities and territories until a full treaty was signed. A long list of demands would require lengthy negotiations. Planets that had been under Lostai rule wanted safeguards put in place to ensure the Lostai Empire not be allowed to regain strength again. The United Rebel Front occupied Losta while they continued their search for hostages being held at Lostai military camps across the sector. Skirmishes between United Rebel Front troops and diehard Lostai military squadrons occurred frequently at these outposts.

Prisoner trades had not yet started, so Zorla, like many other Lostai military officers, sat languishing in a cell on Penstarox. Montor and I went to see him. The minute we approached, he stood, trying to appear dignified, but was a pale shadow of the omnipotent military leader he had once portrayed himself to be.

His eyes narrowed in contempt as he snarled at me, "You have won this battle, Mina, but this war is far from over. You will pay for what you did to me."

I walked up close to the force field around his cell and stared down at him. The fear in his eyes brought me satisfaction. He took a step back.

"I suggest you improve your attitude, or we may forget to distribute supplies to your family's neighborhood. Take the message I left on your body to heart because next time we will not be so merciful with you or your loved ones...if you even know that sentiment."

Montor chimed in.

"I would love to take my time to kill you, painfully, joint by joint, bone by bone, organ by organ. I could do it without putting a finger on you. Instead, you and I will engage in some long chats in the next few days. I will happily extract from you every last bit of Lostai military intelligence you house in that warped mind of yours."

Zorla practically shrank before our eyes.

With Montor's approval, Amber and I traveled to Earth three times before the wedding. Thankfully, all were safe trips with no complications. I discreetly met with my close family. Everyone, including the kids, seemed to understand the importance of keeping my and Amber's whereabouts a secret. I prayed my situation would not cause trouble for them down the line.

We held the wedding ceremony at Penstarox and set up a holographic simulation of a temple as we did before. Similarly, we set up another room for the banquet and a third for our wedding night. We set up special lodging at the military base for the guests that needed to travel to Aranda for the event. The wedding was attended by soldiers, family, and close friends, basically the same people who were there for our first wedding. We also invited Taraxi, Lanext, Bexin, and the other three Jomoloxti who had accompanied us on Amber's rescue mission. They were also celebrating their community's successful relocation to a Namson province, thus returning them to their ancestral roots.

This time, after everything that had happened with Kindor, there was no way Noroma would allow us to assign him to deliver me to Montor during the wedding procession. She still eyed him with suspicion. There was no need to search for another surrogate family member. I was accompanied by the person who rightfully deserved that role. `

"Dad, how are you feeling?"

"Never better. I always regretted not being able to walk you down the aisle. Now, that wish has come true. Although, I'm still not sure that all this is not really Lydia slipping me some funny mushrooms."

We laughed as he led me to the front of the queue. Behind me stood Chris and Bobby, and behind them were Damari and Amber. I smiled at Kindor and Lorret, who were holding Josher's hands in the other line, facing me, followed by Lasarta and Foxor. Montor stepped in front of them, handsome as ever, his eyes glistening. I heard his voice in my mind.

"Mina, today you look even more stunning than you did at our first wedding. I cannot recall a day when I felt luckier."

Each queue promenaded around the room toward the center table where Noroma awaited us. She made a proclamation, after which Dad nodded to Montor, who offered his arm to me, and we stood before her together. There were some parts of a typical Arandan wedding that were skipped since we had performed them during our first wedding. We already had each other's names tattooed on our arms. The only key that could unlock the bracelet Montor had gifted me when he first proposed had already been destroyed. This time around, Noroma delivered a special speech before concluding the ceremony.

"Ever since I first met Mina, she has forced me to rethink the words I usually use at these types of celebrations and my notions of what is appropriate female behavior. At her first wedding, she offered a warrior's toast that not even Arandan female soldiers would have dared to utter. During her son's *Bendorai*, she requested he be blessed with the virtue of GENEROSITY when most Arandan families request COURAGE and STRENGTH. She has confronted and influenced Arandan male warriors that tower over her, including Montor. Today is no exception. Montor and Mina's journey to this moment has been an unusual road. They have faced obstacles that would have dissuaded even the most ardent couples. Montor credits his wife's stubbornness for this—"

A smattering of giggles interrupted Noroma's speech. A stern look from her quieted everyone.

"But it is more than that. There are many aspects of Mina's personality and customs I do not understand, but there are two things of which I have no doubt. First, Mina and Montor share a deep love that I have come across only occasionally. They took the parts of their lives that were out of their control and molded them into a connection that transcends circumstance, race, and culture. In more ways than one, I believe they have saved each other's lives. They deserve to be happy together. Secondly, Mina and Montor have shown uncommon courage defending their relationship, their family, and, as part of the United Rebel Front, all of us. We owe them both a debt of gratitude, as we do all our soldiers. Today, I proclaim them husband and wife until one of them breathes no more. As High Priestess, my blessing for them and their family is unconditional."

She purposely looked across the room, as if making sure everyone was paying close attention.

"I wish them long, happy lives together and expect this community to do the same. Montor and Mina, you may show your affection for each other."

We caressed each other's cheeks as is typical for Arandans. Similar to our first wedding, Montor requested permission to kiss me since it was something out of the ordinary. She extended her arms, offering her consent. He cupped my face in his hands, and our lips touched. My heart fluttered with emotion as the room erupted with the sounds of cheering and well wishes.

THE END

I hope you enjoyed reading **The Curse of Sotkari Ta** trilogy as much as I loved writing it. As I wrote the trilogy, I became fascinated by the layers that make up Montor's personality. If you are interested in Montor's backstory, the prequel, **Song of the Caged Warrior**, is now available. It is the story of his childhood and rise in the Lostai military told in his voice. Here we learn how he becomes the person who Mina meets in **The Curse of Sotkari Ta, Book One.**

Find **Song of the Caged Warrior** here:
https://mybook.to/SongoftheCagedWarrior

A NOTE FROM THE AUTHOR

Thank you for reading *Rising From The Curse, The Curse of Sotkari Ta: Book Three*. Please consider taking a moment to write a review on Amazon, BookBub, and Goodreads. This means a lot to self-published authors such as me.

I hope you have enjoyed this trilogy. I'm very excited to be working on a prequel about Montor's childhood and backstory. I've always found Montor's personality fascinating and hope readers will enjoy learning more about how he becomes the person we meet in *The Curse of Sotkari Ta, Book One*.

In the meantime, I would love to connect. Find all my website, book, and social media links at the following site:

https://direct.me/mariaaperezauthor

LEXICON AND PLACES

<u>Lexicon</u>

- **Barinta** – (Arandan) collaboration, Montor assigned this name to his spacecraft
- **Bendorai** – (Arandan) ceremony that celebrates when a child is presented with their first amulet, usually one revolution (year) from their birth date
- **Bomar** – (Arandan) bread
- **Carinbo** – (Arandan) sleepy child, equivalent to "sleepyhead" in English
- **Fa** – (Arandan) shortened version of uncle, mainly used by young children
- **Faristo** – (Arandan) uncle
- **Fastorec** – (Arandan) A holographic martial-arts game Josher likes to play with Montor
- **Golorax** – (Arandan) A holographic space battle game that Josher plays at the recreational holographic rooms near his home at the Arandan enclave on Fronidia

- **Goria** – (Arandan) large purple berry used in sweet pies and desserts
- **Gotumi** – (Arandan) vegetable native to Aranda considered a delicacy
- **Grem** – (Namson) dessert consisting of pockets of dough filled with sweet, macerated fruit
- **Grimah** – (Lostai) literally means "to mate" but used as a curse word equivalent to "damn it" or "fuck" in English
- **Hanstoric** – (Arandan) jumper, slang word that refers to the laptop-like device required to travel through space using the transportal
- **Hemilta** – (Arandan) Icing-coated, crisp wafers used to sweeten the bitter coffee-like beverage called yomoso
- **Himaney** – (Arandan) Good luck.
- **Jomeney** – (Arandan) Literal translation is "widow's syndrome." A vulgar and derogatory term, referring to a female as desperately needing sexual intercourse.
- **Jonjuri** – (Arandan) victory
- **Jouter** – (Fronidian) A dish of vegetables and grains topped with fish, served in an individual crockpot
- **Kantarext** – (Sotkari) curse word equivalent to "damn" in English
- **Lirinium** – (Lostai) the hardest metal known to the Lostai
- **Lizon** – (Arandan) ray gun
- **Lo Ro** – (Arandan) shortened version of grandmother, mainly used by young children
- **Lo Romasta** – (Arandan) grandmother
- **Lo Ta** – (Arandan) shortened version of grandfather, mainly used by young children
- **Lo Taristo** – (Arandan) grandfather

- **Lorin** – (Namson) deep-fried mashed tubers filled with ground shrimp
- **Marz** – (Namson) province
- **Mizora** – (Lostai) phaser rifle
- **Namit** – (Arandan) please
- **Omori** – (Aradan) a special receptacle made of a rare metal used to preserve the cremated remains of only the most honored Arandan soldiers.
- **Pasi** – (Sotkari) Partial light, referring to those Sotkari that are telepathic, but do not possess other enhanced abilities
- **Ro Ma** – (Arandan) shortened version of mother, mainly used by young children
- **Ro Masa** – (Arandan) as part of the Bendorai ceremony, the person designated to take the place of the mother of a child in the event something happens to the parent, equivalent to "godmother" in English
- **Romasta** – (Arandan) mother
- **Sa veranttay** – (Fronidian) term of endearment used by Fronidian females towards males they care about, equivalent to "beloved and handsome male" in English.
- **Santrock** – (Namson) domesticated beast mounted to play the Namson sport of "vernit"
- **Shermont** – (Arandan) curse word equivalent to "damn it" in English
- **So** – (Arandan) shortened version of aunt, mainly used by young children
- **Somasta** – (Arandan) aunt
- **Stampu** – (Arandan) highly intoxicating beverage consumed in small shots
- **Ta** – (Sotkari) Enlightened, referring to those Sotkari known as "Sotkari Ta" who are fully evolved,

possessing the full array of telepathic, blocking, mind-control, and telekinetic abilities

- **Ta Masa** – (Arandan) as part of the Bendorai ceremony, the person designated to take the place of the father of a child in the event something happens to the parent, equivalent to "godfather" in English
- **Tan** – (Arandan) Free or freedom
- **Ta Ri** – (Arandan) shortened version of father, mainly used by young children
- **Taristo** – (Arandan) father
- **Teronix** – (Arandan) dough pockets filled with savory vegetables in a tasty broth
- **Tomdarox** – (Arandan) animal with black fur that looks like a large bear with red eyes.
- **Torixa** – (Arandan) family, Mina assigned this name to a spacecraft used to rescue Montor
- **Vatimex** – (Fronidian) Fronidian martial art
- **Vernit** – (Namson) sport played by the Namson, players mount a domesticated beast and throw balls to their teammates, the object of the game is to get a ball over a goal
- **Vimor** – (Arandan) small, deadly pistol that delivers narrow, radioactive beams with precision
- **Vona** – (Lostai) small craft known for maneuverability and strong plasma beam weaponry capable of destroying larger vessels
- **Vormey** – (Arandan) wine
- **Xarim** – (Arandan) a martial arts defensive move involving tucking the chin, stepping sideways, and elbowing the opponent hard twice in the groin
- **Yomoso** – (Arandan) strong, bitter coffee-like beverage
- **Yomurati** – (Arandan) to help or rescue
- **Zateim** – (Namson) Chieftain

- **Zirem** – (Lostai) long rod used as a weapon to deliver painful electric burns
- **Zorinto** – (Namson) intoxicating beverage made from fermented grain and sour juice

Places

- **Aranda** – planet in the Soma Quadrant plagued by civil war and later invaded by the Lostai. It is characterized by red oceans, pink sand, and a mustard-colored sky. Natives are known as Arandans. Aranda becomes the birthplace of the United Rebel Front, an insurgency against Lostai rule.
- **Coroxt** – Lostai labor camp where Mina's Earth husband, Joshua, was taken
- **Dit Lar** – small planet near Sotkar in the Morex Quadrant with breathable atmosphere. It is the location of a transportal that allows immediate travel across galaxies
- **Frazin** – small Fronidian village that borders an exotic vacation spot called Jamboran
- **Fro Gantar** – Fronidian capital city
- **Fron Onta Space Station** – one of Fronidia's largest space stations, providing docking for several thousand different types of spacecraft, transport pods, and shuttles
- **Fronidia** – technologically advanced planet in the Soma Quadrant focused on economic power and influence. Friendly towards refugees. Prefers to remain neutral as much as possible towards belligerent planets and/or factions within the quadrant. Many Sotkari Ta that fled Sotkar after the

Lostai invasion settled in Fronidia. Natives are known as Fronidians

- **Liberated Sotkar** – The portion of planet Sotkar that had been liberated from Lostai control. This represented the majority of the planet except for a territory in the Southwestern continent named Losarex.
- **Losarex** – territory in the Southwestern continent of Sotkar that remained under Lostai control after the United Rebel Front uprising
- **Losta** – planet in the Morex Quadrant whose government is focused on increasing their empire and military might throughout the galaxy. Natives are known as Lostai.
- **Marimbo Tu** – small island on Sotkar, home to Sotkari insurgency home base
- **Mastazo** – Fronidian province where a large refugee center is located
- **Members Only** – a venue owned by Colora and Jortan that offers dining, dancing, and lodging with guaranteed privacy, one is located in Fronidia, another in Renna One and a third on another planet within the Soma Quadrant
- **Morzaki** – a cold, barren remote region on planet Losta
- **Namson** – planet at the outer edge of the galaxy, taken over by the Lostai, home to a race of frog-like people, many of who have embedded Sotkari Ta genes. Natives are known as The Namson.
- **Nexori** – Lostai military station in the Morex Quadrant
- **Norimar Yu** – Sotkari province bordering the Lostai-controlled southwestern territory on Sotkar known as Losarex

- **Penstarox** – a remote island on Aranda, home base of the Arandan rebellion
- **Renna One** – planet in the Soma Quadrant under Lostai control, famous for resorts and recreation, but also where Lostai employ slave labor at mining camps.
- **Rondarium** – A large Fronidian town near Zuntar where Josher was born
- **Rovera** – small Sotkari village
- **Solaro** – rural mountainous area on Sotkar where Kaya lived
- **Sotkar** – a planet in the Morex Quadrant, home to a people whose evolutionary transition resulted in some being born with telepathic and telekinetic abilities. The Lostai took advantage of the division between the Sotkari people to annex it to their Empire. Sotkari flora and fauna are characterized by their bioluminescence. Natives are known as Sotkari.
- **Sporia** – a region in Norimar Yu that borders the Lostai-controlled Southwestern continent of Sotkar
- **Tan Aranda** – Signifies Free Aranda and is the name of the Arandan rebel home base located on the island of Penstarox
- **Tormix** – planet in the Morex Quadrant that eventually joins the United Rebel Front. Natives are known as Tormixians.
- **Tremoxtar Mor** – a large island on planet Sotkar, home to many vacation and recreational resorts
- **Ventamu** – The name of the Arandan coastal country (and clan) where Montor is from. All people from Ventamu carry that as their surname.
- **Wayont** – remote Fronidian mining town

- **Xixsted** – Lostai science station located on the third moon of Losta (the Lostai home world)
- **Zalbadar** – small Fronidian city with a rest stop
- **Zamandi's Room** – An entertainment and restaurant establishment on Renna One that offers various bars, dancing and dining venues, and caters to the Soma Quadrant's rich and famous
- **Zuntar** – Fronidian village where Kindor and family lived and operated a restaurant

ACKNOWLEDGMENTS

The Curse of Sotkari Ta series represents a milestone in my life that has been long in the making. First and foremost, I am thankful that God has given me the opportunity to achieve my dream of becoming a published author. Next, I need to recognize the many people who helped me take the stories in my head and share them with readers.

Big hugs of gratitude to my husband, who supported me when I decided to take early retirement, giving me the time and space to devote to my writing. He works hard so I can stay at home and follow my dream. He's always steadfast by my side. I love you, honey!

My sons were patient when I demanded the TV be turned down and understanding of my other quirks during all the days, weeks, months, and, yes, years that I've devoted to this series. They also offered objective opinions on the cover art and back cover blurbs. My love for you is beyond all galaxies and star systems.

My friend, Joanna, is a space opera fan, just like me. In addition to being my very first alpha reader, she has been a great cheerleader and advisor along the way. I am very grateful to my sisters, Sylvia and Wilma, and my best friend, TP, who also alpha read my books. Their different perspectives helped me mold the early versions of my story into something beta readers could work with. I can't thank them enough for the motivation they offered along the way. Thanks also to my Rising From The Curse beta readers, Andi McKenzie, Mary

David-Snow, Sylvia Perez, and Y. Bocquet, for their valuable feedback, helping me flesh out my characters, and inspiring me to make the story better. Thank you to my proofreader, Kelley, who was exceptionally thorough and expeditious. Many thanks to my ARC readers.

I am deeply thankful to my editor, Stephanie Hoogstad, for her beta reading, her excellent editorial guidance, and for taking the time to review other pieces of the puzzle. I couldn't have done this without her.

Thank you to my cover designer, Christian Bentulan. You patiently held my hand each step of the way and brought my characters and theme to life.

I must give a shout-out to my #WritingCommunity and #vss365 tweeps for welcoming me into their Twitter groups and for their advice and encouragement. Stephi Simone's guidance has been extremely helpful in several aspects of my writing projects including the Jamaican patois dialogue used by the character, Damari. I am so grateful for her friendship. A very special thanks to Migs (@OminousHallways), who wrote the beautiful introductory poem. He earned my trust early on, and I consider him a friend.

I am lucky to have been blessed with two sets of parents: my biological parents and my aunt and uncle. I am grateful for their love and for teaching me the meaning of family, hard work, perseverance, and generosity.

Last, but not least, I thank the readers, current and future. I hope you enjoy my stories for many years to come.

AUTHOR'S BIO

Maria A. Perez was born in Yonkers, NY, and grew up in New York City. She also lived in Puerto Rico and now resides in Boca Raton, Florida. She holds a Bachelor's in Business and has spent a successful career in Corporate America working in Accounting and Finance. Early retirement has allowed Maria to focus on her dream of writing and becoming a published author. She is married with two young adult sons and a labradoodle daughter. Maria enjoys reading all genres, although she's partial to dystopian, space opera and romance series such as *The Hunger Games*, *The Expanse* and *Outlander*. A diehard "Trekkie" and *Star Wars* fan, she is fascinated with the possibility of what is out there in unexplored space and the potential of the human race.

www.ingramcontent.com/pod-product-compliance
Lightning Source LLC
Chambersburg PA
CBHW030757210726
48290CB00002B/307